THE CAUTIOU[

As far as Sister Nerys Kent is concerned,
nothing could be less hospitable than
the great red-dust outback of Western
Australia. Nothing, that is, except the
reception given her by Dr Hallam Vale,
senior partner at the tiny hospital in the
mining town of Kolbardi . . .

*Books you will enjoy
in our Doctor Nurse series*

HEARTACHE IN HARLEY STREET by Sonia Deane
DOCTOR ON THE NIGHT TRAIN by Elizabeth Petty
LOVE ME AGAIN by Alexandra Scott
A MODEL NURSE by Sarah Franklin
NURSE ON THE SCENE by Lindsay Hicks
ISLAND DOCTOR by Clare Lavenham
TABITHA IN MOONLIGHT by Betty Neels
MARINA'S SISTER by Barbara Perkins
EXAMINE MY HEART, DOCTOR by Lisa Cooper
INTENSIVE AFFAIR by Ann Jennings
NURSE IN DOUBT by Denise Robertson
ITALIAN NURSE by Lydia Balmain
PRODIGAL DOCTOR by Lynne Collins
THE HEALING PROCESS by Grace Read
DREAMS ARE FOR TOMORROW by Frances Crowne
LIFE LINES by Meg Wisgate
DOCTOR MATTHEW by Hazel Fisher
NURSE FROM THE GLENS by Elisabeth Scott
SISTER STEPHANIE'S WARD by Helen Upshall
SISTER IN HONG KONG by Margaret Barker
THE PROFESSOR'S DAUGHTER by Leonie Craig
NURSE HELENA'S ROMANCE by Rhona Trezise
A SURGEON'S LIFE by Elizabeth Harrison

THE CAUTIOUS HEART

BY
JUDITH WORTHY

MILLS & BOON LIMITED
London · Sydney · Toronto

First published in Great Britain 1984
by Mills & Boon Limited, 15–16 Brook's Mews,
London W1A 1DR

© Judith Worthy 1984

Australian copyright 1984
Philippine copyright 1984

ISBN 0 263 74849 9

All the characters in this book have no existence outside
the imagination of the Author, and have no relation
whatsoever to anyone bearing the same name or names.
They are not even distantly inspired by any individual
known or unknown to the Author, and all the incidents
are pure invention.

The text of this publication or any part thereof may
not be reproduced or transmitted in any form or by any
means, electronic or mechanical, including photo-
copying, recording, storage in an information retrieval
system, or otherwise, without the written permission
of the publisher.

This book is sold subject to the condition that it shall not,
by way of trade or otherwise, be lent, resold, hired out or
otherwise circulated without the prior consent of the
publisher in any form of binding or cover other than that
in which it is published and without a similar condition
including this condition being imposed on the subsequent
purchaser.

Set in 9½ on 10 pt Linotron Times
03–1084–64,000

Photoset by Rowland Phototypesetting Ltd
Bury St Edmunds, Suffolk
Made and printed in Great Britain by
Richard Clay (The Chaucer Press) Ltd
Bungay, Suffolk

CHAPTER ONE

IT WAS almost unbearably hot in the little car, even with the windows open. The breeze was hot and fanned Nerys Kent's face to a glowing moistness. Intermittently she lifted one hand from the steering-wheel to drag a finger across the hollows beneath her eyes where the perspiration kept collecting under her sunglasses.

The breeze tugged at her dark hair, releasing wayward tendrils from the clasp that held it in a high pony-tail for coolness. There was a deep frown above her slightly tense features. The dark prettiness that made most men look twice was, today, lacking its usual vivacity. Sunglasses hid her usually wistfully appealing brown eyes and her sometimes seductively curved lips were compressed in concentration.

Ahead, a mirage shimmered and receded, a mockery of coolness in a hot, dry, dusty landscape. Occasionally a vehicle travelling in the opposite direction passed and the driver waved cheerily, but mostly the road was empty. Like the sky above it, and the almost featureless country slipping endlessly by on either side. Nerys had never felt so hot and uncomfortable, or so alone.

'It's not the best time to be going north,' her friend Carrie had warned when Nerys announced her plan soon after her arrival from England. 'It'll be very hot.'

But Nerys was determined. 'I don't mind,' she said recklessly. 'It'll be an experience, and Daniel says everywhere is air-conditioned.'

Carrie, an old friend from St Margaret's who had married an Australian gynaecologist and emigrated to Western Australia, shrugged. 'Well, I don't suppose you'll be staying all that long.'

Nerys was silent. She was not sure how long she intended to stay with her twin brother Daniel, who was a doctor in a mining town over 1500 kilometres north of Perth. She was

5

not, in fact, very sure of anything lately. What had seemed, a few months ago, an orderly, happy existence, had suddenly collapsed into something akin to nightmare.

She shuddered now as she tried to put the whole thing out of her mind. But it would persist in returning. The vision of the white-walled operating-theatre, herself swathed in green gown, cap, mask, standing ready and waiting. And Chris bending slightly over the patient on the table, then glancing at her, his dark eyes steady, his voice low, perfectly controlled. 'Ready, Sister?' It had only been a routine operation, a perfectly simple tonsillectomy with no expected complications—except that Chris didn't know, or care, how she really felt about him. That was the awful irony, he didn't even know . . .

Her heart began to pound with panic, just as it had then.

'Stop it!' she ordered herself aloud, and stepped down hard on the accelerator. The rather battered Mini surged ahead, rattling alarmingly.

She had bought the car against Carrie and Bruce's advice, because it was cheap and because, as she ruefully admitted later, she had allowed the young man who had parked it in the street near Carrie's house, to talk her into it, even though she was a bit short of money herself, having spent most of her savings on the air-fare to Australia.

Carrie had said that the most sensible thing to do would be to fly to Port Hedland and let Daniel collect her from there. But one morning Nerys got chatting to the car's owner, a university student who wanted to go to Indonesia and couldn't afford it. He'd been trying to sell the car since Christmas and there wasn't much of the long vacation left. He had taken Nerys for a demonstration drive and explained the Mini's various idiosyncrasies, and in the end she hadn't had the heart to refuse to buy it.

'You're too soft-hearted,' Carrie had laughed, but the night before Nerys had left she had sounded anxious when she said, 'It's a long drive. I hope you won't have any trouble.'

Her husband, Bruce, was less diplomatic. 'You'll be lucky if you make it to Geraldton in that heap, Nerys. Still, you can always take a plane from there, if necessary.'

Nerys drew her mouth into a determined line. 'I'm going to make it all the way,' she insisted stubbornly.

When she phoned Daniel to say she was coming, her brother sounded as bemused as he had in the letter which had been waiting for her at Carrie's on her arrival from England. He couldn't imagine why she had suddenly given up her job and crossed half the world to see him.

'It's a pretty God-forsaken hole,' he had written. 'Kolbardi is right in the middle of the desert, and although we're pretty civilised so far as living conditions are concerned, thanks to the mining company that built the town, it *is* the back of beyond, by no means a tourist resort . . .'

There had been more, and a thinly veiled suggestion that she might prefer to stay in Perth for her holiday and he would try to get down for a few days. Daniel had been at Kolbardi for almost a year after hitch-hiking around the world soon after qualifying as a doctor. It was the longest he had stayed anywhere, and Nerys did not expect him to stay much longer. Daniel was a rover, a man with itchy feet who probably would not settle down for a long time yet.

Nerys was the opposite. Flying to Australia to see her brother was not something she would have contemplated in normal circumstances. It had been an impulse, a need to run somewhere, combined with a need to be near someone close to her. There was no one but Daniel, now that their parents were both dead, no other close relatives she could turn to.

The fact that Carrie now lived in Perth had helped her decision. The Brooks' had welcomed her enthusiastically, but with some surprise. Carrie had naturally been curious about Nerys's sudden urge to see her brother, but although she had thought she would tell her friend about Chris, Nerys found herself unable to confess the truth behind her flight from St Margaret's. Now she doubted that she would even tell Daniel. It was too humiliating. All she could hope for was that time would eventually heal the hurt, and the shame.

'Think of something else,' she commanded, and instantly drew back into her mind an incident that had happened earlier in the day. 'That man!' she exclaimed aloud.

It had happened when she had pulled into a service station at a place whose name she never discovered, and which consisted of little more than the service station and a restaurant-cum-store. She had been watching the fuel gauge anxiously for the past few kilometres, for it had flickered on empty rather sooner than she had expected. She heaved a sigh of relief when habitation loomed up ahead, especially when she saw the services sign. She had immediately realised she was hungry as it was past lunch-time, so she parked and went into the building.

In the small, rather dingy restaurant there were only three tables. One was occupied by a family with young children, one by a couple of truckies, presumably from the big semi-trailer she had seen outside. The only available seat had been at the third table, which already had one occupant. Mentally matching the family to the dusty station-wagon she had noticed on the forecourt, and the lone man to the Range Rover that was parked alongside it, she approached his table.

'Do you mind if I sit here?' she asked politely.

He glanced up, a swift appraising look, which took in her figure-hugging terry shorts and skimpy top, and then rested momentarily on her face. His dark green, laser eyes seemed to pulverise her on the spot, and there wasn't even a ghost of a friendly smile on the wide, full-lipped and rather sensuous mouth. His face was deeply sun-tanned and as rugged as a rocky cliff, set above broad, strong shoulders that were emphasised, like the muscularity of his chest, by the short-sleeved white T-shirt he was wearing. His eyes stated very clearly that he did not welcome her intrusion. An odd little sensation ran down Nerys's spine, and cramped her stomach, a feeling of intense dislike combined with a startling awareness of his potent masculinity.

'It's a free country,' he offered in a gravelly tone, and returned his attention to his food.

Rather uncertainly Nerys sat down. He was off-putting, to say the least. She wasn't sure whether to attempt conversation or not. His manner was brusque and she suspected he would snub any friendly overture from her. She felt irritated. So far, everyone she had met in Australia had been friendly and helpful, and this encounter with surliness injected a sour note.

A waitress came to take her order and to bring a sweet for her companion. Nerys could not help noticing the way the young girl looked at him, lashes lowered, her red mouth in a slight pout. She stood in what Nerys felt sure was a deliberately provocative pose, and when she said, 'Will that be all?' there was a flirtatious intonation in her voice. It was obvious that she found this customer attractive.

'I'll have another beer, thanks,' he said, barely glancing at the girl.

She turned to Nerys and scribbled her order on a pad. Before she moved away she cast another glance at Nerys's companion and then looked back at Nerys with an expression that invited her confirmation that he was indeed attractive. Nerys kept her own expression non-committal.

While she waited for her meal, she sat uncomfortably dividing her attention between looking out of the dusty window into the uninteresting forecourt of the service station, and stealing sidelong glances at her companion. His face drew her irresistibly. He had strong features, ruggedly sculpted with stern lines that seemed to deny any humour, although there were faint creases at the corners of his eyes and a perceptible softness at the corners of his mouth which belied the outward austerity of his appearance. She wondered what he was really like, this man with the smooth, dark brown hair, streaked with grey at the temples, and swept smoothly back from the suggestion of a widow's peak above his broad, deeply-furrowed brow.

At last, unable to contain herself any longer, she blurted out, 'Is that your Range Rover outside?'

For the first time he condescended to look at her. Except that he seemed to have been jerked out of a deep reverie, his expression revealed nothing of his reaction to her question, although it must have startled him. Nerys, however, felt she had made not only the most inane but the most impertinent comment of the year.

'Yes,' he informed her shortly, and the hard green eyes discomposed her utterly before focussing again on his plate. There were light brown flecks in them, she noticed during the brief moment of encounter with her own, and his lashes were extraordinarily long and luxuriant.

His compelling looks fascinated her in spite of herself, but his taciturnity goaded her. After a moment she heard herself trying again. 'Travelling far?'

He paused, the last spoonful of his apple pie and cream poised on its way to his mouth.

'Far enough,' he replied, and swallowed the mouthful of food, took a draught of the beer beside his plate, and did not look at her again. He showed no interest in where she was going.

Nerys was forced to acknowledge that she wanted him to. It was idiotic, but she wanted to tell someone that she was going to Kolbardi to see her brother. No, it was even simpler than that. She just wanted someone to talk to. It had been a long, lonely drive and the absence of companionship had betrayed her into thinking of things she did not want to think about. But she could have picked someone more amenable to try to talk to, she thought ruefully. The two truckies, for instance, who were sliding her admiring glances from time to time, would at least have been friendly. This man was a boor.

Contrary to her expectation, he did not hurry to leave because she was there. He called for yet another beer and she was sure, now that he had finished his meal, he was watching her eat hers. But when she glanced up to catch him at it, he seemed to have anticipated her and was looking elsewhere. Only once did they speak again, and that was when she inadvertently kicked him under the table. His legs were long and, stretched out, reached to her side of the table, emphasising his resentment of her intrusion.

'Sorry . . .' She knew she was blushing.

He merely treated her to another annihilating glance, but behind it she sensed the involuntary appraisal of a man for a woman. It was disturbing to be looked at in this way, total indifference on the surface, a sultry awareness underneath.

He left first, with a barely audible, 'Excuse me!' Nerys watched him cross to the counter where he paid his bill and purchased one or two items. She noticed how cheery he was with the middle-aged woman behind the counter and she noticed, too, the coquettish look the waitress, who was standing nearby, gave him as she said brightly, 'Cheerio, come again!'

As Nerys was paying her bill, one of the truckies re-entered and came across to her.

'Are you the Mini's owner?' he asked. There was a hint of irritation in his tone, despite the fact that his eyes roved appreciatively over her long, slender legs and shapely thighs before returning to her face.

'Yes, I am,' Nerys acknowledged, putting the change she had received in her purse.

'Would you mind moving it, miss? It's in the way. We can't get out,' he said, with a trace of impatience.

Nerys blushed scarlet, all the more so because she suddenly realised that the man who had sat at the table with her was watching from a paperback stand near the door, which he had paused to inspect. She hadn't realised he was still there.

'I . . . I'm sorry,' she muttered. 'Yes, of course. I'll shift it right away.' She felt a fool for not noticing that she had blocked the semi's exit when she parked.

What happened next was unexpected and twice as humiliating. The Mini refused to start. Only after a couple of minutes of agitated and self-conscious ramming of the starter did Nerys remember she had been almost out of petrol. She had evidently only just made it to the service station and now, with an empty tank, the engine naturally would not start. She was aware that the semi-trailer driver and his mate were regarding her in a long-suffering way, hats pushed back on their heads, expressions of 'Just like a woman!' on their weather-beaten faces.

'I must be out of petrol,' Nerys explained and looked towards the bowser, which was several metres away. She pursed her lips.

The Range Rover's driver strolled nonchalantly over. 'What seems to be the trouble?' he inquired laconically.

The truckie who had come into the café explained. And while Nerys watched in a kind of helpless fury that was directed more at herself than them, the driver of the Range

Rover reached in and grabbed the steering-wheel, his arm brushing hers as he did so.

'Release the handbrake,' he ordered curtly.

Nerys obeyed, and the two men manhandled the Mini out of the way, guiding it alongside the petrol bowser with her still inside it, cringing with humiliation and reluctantly aware of the brown, muscular arm across the steering-wheel, and the long, smooth hand with tiny tufts of dark hair on the knuckles that gripped it. Suddenly the arm and the man disappeared.

'Thanks, mate,' said the semi-trailer driver as he leapt into his cab and his mate joined him. The huge transport slowly glided out onto the road. Nerys got out and, biting her lip, watched the big, green canvas-covered load disappear in the distance. She was aware that her lunch companion was still standing near the car, but on the other side of it, and he was regarding her over the bonnet.

He tapped the bonnet. 'I hope you're not planning to go far in this.'

Nerys bristled. 'What if I am?'

His straight dark eyebrows quivered slightly. 'You won't get far.'

'I've already come from Perth,' she retorted, disliking his tone.

'And it was practically clapped out before you started, I'd say,' he observed with a contemptuous look along the bonnet, which seemed to Nerys to display rather more rust patches than she had noticed before.

She felt irrationally incensed by his criticism and instantly flew to the defence of her bargain buy. 'It's been going very well so far. Just because you can afford to zoom around in a Range Rover doesn't mean everyone can. It'll do me, thank you. I'll get where I'm going, don't worry!'

There was a faint twitching at the corners of his mouth but it wasn't a smile. He wasn't the kind of man who would ever smile much, Nerys thought grumpily.

'You're English, aren't you?' He spoke as though that fact explained all foolishness.

'Yes,' she admitted.

His eyes bored into hers, examining her face in minute

detail for a long time, which she found more disconcerting than ever. The next moment he was as dismissive as before.

'Good luck!' he said, and turned abruptly away. Quite clearly he had no time for foolish females.

Feeling more aggravated by the exchange than was warranted, Nerys filled her tank and then went back into the café to buy a packet of sweets she did not really want, simply to give the Range Rover time to drive off ahead of her. She did not want to take off with that man watching her. He was too unnerving! She was bound to do something stupid. She was annoyed with herself for feeling that way, and when she returned to her car and found the Range Rover gone, although she was relieved, she still felt edgy.

She sank into the well-worn driver's seat, adjusting the towel she had previously spread over it. The car had no seat-covers and the plastic was sticky in the heat, especially against her bare legs. She pressed the starter and was dismayed when the engine did not immediately tick over. She pressed it again, and still nothing happened.

'Damn!' she exclaimed. The warnings of her friends in Perth echoed in her mind, but even worse was the more recent taunt of the man in the Range Rover. She rammed hard on the starter, again and again, until finally the engine leapt into life. A feeling like exultation ran through her as she gently eased the choke back, then released the brake and drove out onto the highway.

'So there!' she mouthed with grim satisfaction, almost wishing the Range Rover man was there to see her triumph. How he would have gloated if she had broken down!

Despite herself she was intrigued by him. In retrospect he assumed an even more satanic aspect, and yet there was, she had to admit, a challenging aspect to his surly manner and his disdain for her. She wondered who he was. A local sheep station owner perhaps. He was deeply tanned and looked as though he spent a good deal of his time out of doors. Then she recalled his hands. They were large, long-fingered hands, strong and capable looking but with a delicacy about them that suggested something other than an outdoor occupation. The way he had held his knife and fork, she recalled now, had been with almost a surgeon's precision. Or was it just that his hands had reminded her of Chris . . .

'Out! Out!' she whispered urgently. 'I will not think of Chris, or St Margaret's or . . . anything. I mustn't. I must forget everything!' She screwed up her face as though the physical effort would help the mental rejection.

The afternoon wore on and the scenery slipped by with a hypnotic sameness. Nerys succeeded in her effort to wipe thoughts of Chris from her mind, but it was at the expense of letting her reluctant musings about the man in the Range Rover circulate in her head. The car was behaving well, and she felt quite smug about it. Men didn't know everything, even about cars. Once or twice she glanced at the fuel gauge. It disappointed her that she seemed to be burning up more fuel than she had thought a car this size would need on a trip such as this.

It was nearly dusk, and she was driving in the lurid glow of a magnificent sunset, when she saw a vehicle ahead of her, slewed in at an angle on the gravel shoulder. She was beginning to feel weary and at first thought it was a trick of the fading light. Then, as she approached, a man stepped into the road and flagged her down.

'If he's broken down,' she thought, 'I shan't be much help.' She braked and pulled into the verge. At the same moment she recognised the vehicle and the man. It was the Range Rover and its driver.

He strode to the driving window and leaned down to look in.

'You!' he exclaimed in a tone that suggested it was little short of disaster.

A wave of elation suffused Nerys. So he had broken down. Well, serve him right!

'I'm sorry,' she said, without giving any indication that she was. 'I'm afraid my little car would never be able to tow a big vehicle like yours. You'll have to wait until someone else comes along.' She met his eyes head-on and added with a self-satisfied little smile, 'Looks like I'll be getting further than you after all!'

He wrenched open the car door. 'Not yet, you won't,' he grated, and all at once she saw the urgency in his face. 'I haven't broken down,' he rapped out succinctly. 'There's been an accident. Young fellow on a motor bike must have hit a 'roo. Killed the 'roo and nearly killed himself . . .'

Nerys leapt out of the car, practically pushing him to one side. 'Why didn't you say so? Where is he?'

Her peremptory tone brought a startled, hostile expression to his face. He was about to speak when she forestalled him with the curt explanation, 'I'm a nurse!'

He looked even more startled, but Nerys wasted no time looking at him. She could see the inert form of the accident victim lying on the ground just in front of the Range Rover. Further away was the dead kangaroo.

Nerys raced over and knelt beside the injured man, aware that all her actions were being closely observed as she felt his pulse, pulled his eyelids back, checked that nothing was obstructing his breathing and took note of his colour and the position he was lying in.

There was no blood except a slow seepage from a graze on his thigh, which was visible through the tear in his trousers and was not serious. But it was obvious that one leg was broken and Nerys feared there might be other, more serious, internal injuries. The motor-cyclist's helmet was lying near him and she guessed the Range Rover's driver had removed it before he slipped the folded blanket under the man's head.

'I hope you haven't moved him?' she said, glancing up.

She received a hostile stare. 'I am aware that it is possible to aggravate a person's injuries,' he said, 'as a matter of fact I . . .'

'Good, I'm glad you know something about first aid.' Nerys cut across his words crisply and delivered a brief lecture on the dangers of moving a patient with possible spinal injuries. His face assumed a blank expression and she was certain he resented her taking charge. It gave her considerable satisfaction, although she felt a bit guilty about that.

'He's in shock and probably badly concussed,' she said, 'in spite of the helmet.'

'He'd probably be dead if he hadn't been wearing it,' commented her companion.

Nerys stood up and said briskly, 'He must be got to hospital quickly. How far are we from Port Hedland?'

'About three-quarters of an hour,' the driver of the Range Rover estimated.

Nerys frowned. 'One of us could go for an ambulance,' she said thoughtfully. Then, glancing down at the injured man, she went on decisively, 'No, that might waste too much time. It would be quicker to take him there ourselves. Is there room in the back of your vehicle?'

His eyes raked her coldly. 'Yes. The rear seat folds down.' He added rather acidly, 'I had every intention of taking the boy to hospital. I was hoping for someone a bit brawnier than a pint-sized Pom to come along and help me lift him in.'

It was unworthy, sparring over a badly injured man, Nerys thought shamefacedly, but she could not help retorting, 'Nurses are pretty strong, you know, even when they are pint-sized—and I'm not all *that* small!' Against his large frame she did, however, feel rather diminutive. Without waiting for a rejoinder, she went on, 'Look, I'll show you the best way to lift him. You take the weight under his shoulders. Like this . . .' She demonstrated without actually touching the injured man.

With a slightly laconic look at her, but without further comment, the Range Rover's driver obeyed her instructions to the letter, and together they carefully transferred the motor cycle rider into the back of the vehicle, where Nerys made him as comfortable as possible. There was little she could do for him, she thought helplessly, even if she'd had a first aid kit with her, which she didn't.

'Don't drive too fast,' she instructed her companion, 'and try not to jolt him around too much.' She added, 'I'll come with you, of course. I suppose I'll be able to find someone to give me a lift back to fetch my car?' She glanced at him, wondering if he would offer, but not at all sure she wanted him to.

'The police will have to fetch the bike, so they can bring your car in too.' He paused briefly, looking at her with an unfathomable expression. 'I suggest you take your luggage. You might not get it until tomorrow, otherwise. You *are* intending to stay tonight in Port Hedland?' he added.

'Yes.'

Hastily Nerys scrambled out of the Range Rover and transferred her luggage. Then she positioned herself next to the patient, glad that at least she was not sitting beside the driver. Almost immediately, darkness descended swiftly like a soft cloak, extinguishing the fiery glow in the western sky and bringing with it a web of stars to ornament the blue-black velvet of the night.

But Nerys caught only glimpses of the sunset and the stars. Her attention was wholly directed at the patient, whose breathing suddenly began to alarm her by taking on a rasping sound.

'Can you hurry up a bit?' she urged in a tight voice to the driver.

He glanced briefly over his shoulder. 'What's wrong?' There was an authoritarian note in his voice.

'I don't like the way this boy's breathing. I'm afraid there might be internal haemorrhaging.'

She caught a muffled, 'Hell!' from the front seat and felt an immediate increase in speed as the driver put his foot down. Nerys bit her bottom lip hard. It was imperative not to jolt the young man about too much, but just as imperative to get him to hospital quickly, where he could be given oxygen and a saline drip, have his condition assessed quickly and his injuries operated on. She crouched over him anxiously, her hand over his, her fingers keeping a check on his pulse and her own heart beating faster than normal as they sped through the darkness.

'Don't let him die,' she breathed more than once, as though it would be her fault if he did. But there was nothing she could do. The only hope for him was to get to the hospital with all possible speed. She glanced ahead through the long beams of the headlamps, with a tight feeling in her throat. The driver's craggy head was silhouetted against the lights and she could feel a tension emanating from him that matched her own. When he spoke she was startled.

'Nearly there,' was all he said, but his voice showed no relief, only a heightened anxiety now that they were close to their destination.

Nerys looked ahead and saw the lights of the town. They were approaching the causeway leading into Port Hedland. Carrie had told her a little about the town, that it was actually situated on an island, that it had once been a pearling town but was now a major port for the export of iron ore mined in the Pilbara. She recalled none of this, however, as they drove into the town. Her sole concern was for the patient.

'Hurry, hurry!' she begged silently, her eyes fixed on the still, young face as though he were someone she knew and cared for deeply. He was about twenty, fair-haired and good-looking, but his features were marred by smeared oil and dust and his hair was tousled and dirty. No doubt his parents were worried sick about him if they had been expecting him. Where was his home? Nerys wondered.

She was so engrossed in her own fiction that she scarcely noticed when they swerved smoothly into the hospital parking area. The Range Rover came to a slow, jolt-less halt and she switched quickly back to reality.

'You'd better tell them it's an emergency,' she ordered briskly. 'They'll bring a stretcher.'

He turned briefly and his eyes met hers with that hostile look again. But he went without question. She saw him running, and then only a moment or two later—although it seemed an age to her—two white-coated orderlies were racing towards the car with a stretcher. Nerys followed in their wake as they carried the injured man into Casualty. She felt drained, her natural relief at having arrived, tempered by the knowledge that the young man's life might well be in grave danger.

The driver of the Range Rover was talking to a nurse as Nerys approached. She heard him say, 'I'll hang on until the police arrive. They'll want details of exactly where it happened.'

The nurse, in a deferential tone, said, 'Very well, Dr Vale.'

Nerys stopped in her tracks, and he chose that moment to turn and meet her astonished gaze. She wished the floor would open and swallow her up. A doctor. He was a doctor! Why hadn't he said so? She recalled with burning shame how she had spoken to him, how gleeful she had been, proving that she wasn't as witless a female as he thought, and all the time . . .

The blood drained from her face. Her knees threatened to crumple under her, and would have but for a super-human effort on her part. She detected a hint of mockery in his eyes, and there was no way she was going to let him see her weakness or her chagrin. She lifted her chin defiantly. She would have a few words to say to him when that nurse left them!

But the opportunity was snatched away from her. Another nurse came hurrying across to them. 'Oh, Dr Vale,' she said urgently, 'Dr Parsons says could you spare a minute?'

He turned an agreeable smile on her. 'Certainly, Sister.' He glanced back at Nerys, the smile fading. 'Excuse me.'

CHAPTER TWO

IT WAS late when Nerys finally walked into the motel on the outskirts of town, where she had been driven by an obliging police constable after she had given them details of the accident.

The police had come to the hospital a few minutes after Dr Vale had disappeared. Nerys had been left standing in embarrassed silence in the Casualty entrance, with an obviously curious nurse, to whom she briefly explained how she came to be involved. The nurse showed Nerys to the waiting-room.

'The police will be along shortly,' she said. 'I expect they'll want to talk to you as well as Dr Vale. When you've seen them, I'll find someone to take you along to your motel.' She smiled in a friendly way. 'Would you like a cup of tea?'

'I wouldn't mind,' Nerys said, 'but if you're busy . . .'

'Not often too busy for a cup of tea,' rejoined the nurse gaily. 'But I'll just check I'm not needed in theatre or elsewhere first.'

Nerys frowned anxiously. 'I do hope he's going to be all right. I'm afraid moving him . . .' She sighed regretfully. 'But there was no other way. It would have taken so long to get the ambulance.'

'He was lucky to be found by a doctor and a nurse,' said the girl.

'Yes, I suppose so.' Nerys was squirming inwardly as she recalled her nervous examination of the boy, with the stranger watching, saying nothing, and then her decision to transport him immediately rather than go for an ambulance. Dr Vale must have thought her unbearably arrogant. There was some satisfaction, but not much, in knowing that he must have agreed with her, otherwise he would have objected.

There wasn't much she could tell the police. They came

while she was sipping her tea, looked her over with appreciative eyes and sat down on either side of her. She explained briefly why she was in Port Hedland and that she was travelling on to Kolbardi.

'The trouble is, I had to leave my car at the scene of the accident,' she said, 'so if you wouldn't mind giving me a lift back there . . .' Her voice rose on a hopeful query.

'No need.' The fair-headed one smiled. 'You leave it to us, Miss Kent. We'll pick up the bike and bring your car in at the same time.' He glanced at his younger, dark-haired companion. 'We'll just have a word with Dr Vale and then run this young lady along to her motel. She's probably dying for a shower and some shut-eye, eh, Miss Kent?'

'Indeed I am!' agreed Nerys fervently. There were patches of red dust on her knees, and her shorts and top were grimy. She felt sticky all over, despite the cool air-conditioning, and she knew she looked a perfect fright with her hair falling out of its clasp and not a touch of make-up left on her face. She didn't know that in this rather dishevelled state she had an even more wistful appeal than when she was spick and span.

'It'll be something to write home about, I guess,' suggested the fair-haired constable. 'There's always some drama in the outback!' He was teasing her, but Nerys didn't mind.

The two policemen left her to ask if they could see Dr Vale but it turned out that he was in the operating-theatre, so the two young constables came back to Nerys saying they would see him later.

Nerys wanted to ask someone how the young motorcyclist was, but she knew it was too early for any solid information. As they were leaving, a middle-aged couple came in, deep anxiety etched in their tanned faces. Nerys glanced at them, sensing that they were the boy's parents. She was tempted to rush over and try to reassure them, but resisted when a nurse came forward to attend to them. The policemen were in a hurry, anyway; and she did not want to delay them.

As they left her a few minutes later at the motel entrance, the dark-haired one said cheerfully, 'Sleep tight, and don't worry about a thing. Your car will be here in the morning.'

'Thanks for the lift. I'm very grateful,' Nerys said.

'I reckon that boy has more reason to be grateful to you,' replied the fair-haired constable soberly. He waved a hand, 'So long. Be seeing you.'

Nerys went into the motel to check in. She was pleasantly surprised when the receptionist said, 'I'm afraid it's too late for dinner, but I could have a tray sent across to your unit if you like.'

Nerys considered briefly and realised she did feel quite hungry. 'Well, if it isn't too much trouble,' she agreed hesitantly.

'No trouble at all.' The tall blonde girl behind the desk smiled, and handed Nerys her key. 'You're in Number 10, just across the courtyard.' She indicated with a wave of her hand the direction Nerys was to take. 'Goodnight, Miss Kent.'

'Goodnight.' Nerys picked up her suitcase and holdall and staggered across the forecourt towards the long row of motel units. She glanced at the swimming-pool, which looked very inviting, and was tempted to take a quick dip, but once inside her unit she decided it was rather late and a shower would suffice.

By the time she had showered and slipped on her nightdress, her tray had arrived and, at the sight of the food, she found that she was even hungrier than she had supposed. Desperate to talk to someone, she was tempted to phone Daniel and tell him what had happened, but she changed her mind about that, too. It was late and he might be in bed, or on duty, or out somewhere. There was really no need to disturb him. She would still be arriving in Kolbardi tomorrow as planned, and it would be a story to relate on her arrival. She wondered if Daniel knew Dr Vale. It was more than likely he did know the doctors at the Port Hedland hospital.

In the morning she was awake early, having spent a somewhat restless night. The unfamiliar rumble of the air-conditioner in her room disturbed her, and from somewhere distant the clanking of what sounded very like a train, followed later by the crashing of metal as though something was being dropped from a great height, had punctuated her dreams.

It was quieter in the early hours, but as the sun came up there were birds calling her awake, so she got up and pulled back the curtains. Outside her window, on a strip of lawn between the unit and a windbreak of hibiscus and oleander bushes, a small flock of orange and brown finches searched noisily for seeds and insects. Overhead, gulls wheeled and, as she watched, a pelican soared gracefully towards the ocean.

Nerys could tell just by looking at the hard blue sky and the dry red dust beyond the motel lawns that it was already hot outside. She dressed in a cool, green cotton tube top and fawn shorts which flattered her slender but generously curved figure and shapely legs.

She fastened her hair back with two combs for coolness and comfort, and applied only a suggestion of make-up over a generous application of moisturiser. At seven forty-five she strolled over to the dining-room for breakfast.

She was disappointed to see no sign of her car yet, but she stopped in her tracks when she saw, parked outside the motel entrance, a Range Rover.

Surely it was *his!* No, why should it be? There were probably plenty of similar vehicles around. He wasn't likely to be staying here. She gulped in air, annoyed at the peculiar tremor that had rocked her heart at the thought that it might be Dr Vale's car.

She was about to continue walking towards the entrance when a man emerged and she saw to her amazement the tall, broad-shouldered frame of Dr Vale getting into the vehicle. It *was* his after all. Momentarily transfixed, she hesitated, then on an impulse ran forward, anxious to ask him about the injured motor-cyclist. But he moved too swiftly for her and was driving away before she had opened her mouth to call his name. She stopped, watching the Range Rover turn into the road alongside the motel. She was puzzled. If he was a doctor at the hospital, presumably he lived in the town. So why would he be staying here?

She shrugged the thought off. There was doubtless a logical explanation, and it was none of her business anyway. He might not even have stayed, she mused. He could simply have been calling for some reason, somebody in the motel taken ill, perhaps. In any case she was not really the slightest bit curious about Dr Vale.

And yet, while she was eating her breakfast, she found herself continually thinking about him and experiencing all over again, with growing chagrin, last night's humiliating experience. His behaviour, on reflection, made her increasingly incensed. Eventually, though, she realised how silly she was being and reminded herself that since she was unlikely to encounter the man again, it was pointless getting all worked up about it.

As she came out of the dining-room the receptionist called her over. 'Miss Kent! I just had a call from Phil's Garage. Your car is there.'

'Oh, is it? Thanks.' Nerys was a bit surprised, since the police had said they would bring it to the motel. 'Where is Phil's Garage?' she enquired.

The receptionist explained that it was not far. 'You can leave your luggage here,' she offered, 'and pick it up on your way through. You'll have to come back past here on your way to Kolbardi.'

Nerys hurried back to her unit, finished packing, and then checked out, doing as the receptionist had suggested and stowing her suitcase and holdall behind the desk. She thanked the girl and then set off to walk to the garage.

There was a light breeze blowing in from the ocean now, and Nerys was thankful for its coolness. As she walked back towards town she could not help but be aware of the all-pervading redness caused by the dust—dust from the earth, dust from the iron ore plants. Every surface was ingrained with it, trees and shrubs were filmed with it, and she knew that by the end of the day her clothes and her skin would bear traces of it, too.

As she entered the forecourt of the garage, Nerys looked around anxiously for her Mini. When she saw it she was immediately filled with dismay. It was ignominiously hitched up behind a tow-truck and looked very forlorn. A man in greasy overalls came out of the repair shop, and she walked over to him.

'Excuse me . . .'

He turned, looked her trim figure over with a distinct flicker of male appreciation, smiled and said cheerfully, 'Yes, miss, what can I do for you?'

'That's my car,' Nerys explained, unable to keep the squeak out of her voice. 'What is it doing up there like that?'

A look of enlightenment came over his face and he approached a step closer and peered at her. 'Ah, you must be Miss Kent.' He extended a large, square hand. 'Phil Darnley's the name. Pleased to meet you.'

Nerys's fingers were crushed in a strong handshake and at the same moment realisation dawned. 'You're English!' she exclaimed.

He grinned. 'Romford, Essex. And you?'

'Oh, well, it used to be Surrey but I've been living in the Midlands for a few years, nursing.'

He nodded. 'And your brother is at the hospital in Kolbardi?'

'Yes, I'm on my way to visit him,' Nerys said eagerly. 'But I had to leave my car down the road last night. The police said . . .'

Phil interrupted. 'We towed it in.' He knew the whole story of course.

Nerys was aghast. 'Towed it in? But it wasn't broken down or anything.' A thought occurred to her. 'I suppose it was because you didn't have anyone to drive it.'

Phil shook his head. 'That wasn't a problem. No, the problem is your car!' He looked at her curiously. 'How long have you had it?'

'Only a few days,' she answered. 'I bought it in Perth.'

He shook his head. 'And somebody sold you a pup, I'm afraid. I'm amazed you got so far with faulty steering, a patched-up petrol tank, worn radiator hose and a wonky starter! There could be more wrong than that, and at a glance the bodywork's practically paint on rust. It's a wonder you didn't have a nasty accident yourself.' He added gently, 'It would never have got you to Kolbardi. It's a dirt road most of the way.'

Nerys felt terrible. She was remembering Carrie and

Bruce's misgivings and her own stubbornness. She should have had it checked over, or looked around for a vehicle more suited to the outback.

Phil Darnley glanced in the direction of the hitched up little car. 'All your gas had leaked out by the time we got there. Hole as big as my fist in the tank. Corroded. And patched up with tin foil and sticking-plaster.'

No wonder she'd kept running out of fuel before she expected to, Nerys thought ruefully.

'Can you fix it?' she asked, reading doubt in his face before he even answered. 'I'm supposed to be in Kolbardi today.'

Phil said flatly, 'I could patch it up in a couple of days, but it wouldn't be safe, not on dirt roads. To fix it properly, I'd have to send for a couple of parts from Perth.' He considered her lengthily. 'To be perfectly frank, it'd cost more to fix than the car is worth. You'd be better off flogging it for scrap.'

'Scrap!' Nerys was horrified. 'But I can't!' She bit her lip. He was right of course. It would be foolish to lash out more money on having the car fixed if it wasn't worth it. But how was she to get to Kolbardi without it?

Phil read her thoughts. 'Don't worry, you can go out to Kolbardi on the bus.'

'Is there a bus?' Nerys was astonished.

'Yes. Twice a week. Unfortunately it went yesterday. You'll have to wait until Friday now.'

Nerys was crestfallen. 'I was so looking forward to getting there today. My brother's expecting me.' She heaved a sigh. 'Oh, well, it can't be helped. I'll just have to phone him and tell him I've been delayed. I hope I'll be able to check back in at the motel.'

She was talking more to herself than to him, disappointment welling up in her at the disarray of her plans. Suddenly she felt bleak, as though everything was conspiring to make her regret her impulsive decision to visit Daniel. While things had gone smoothly, she had maintained her equilibrium. But all at once she felt very alone and directionless, just as she had two months ago after she had walked out of St Margarets forever . . .

Suddenly becoming aware of Phil Darnley's speculative gaze on her, she jerked back to reality. It was silly to drop her bundle just like that, simply because her bargain car had proved to be a foolish mistake. She swallowed hard and asked, 'Where do I catch the bus?'

As Phil started to explain, a vehicle swung into the forecourt and a man got out and strode across to them. Nerys had her back to him and did not notice his approach. So when Dr Vale, looking aggressively handsome in an open-neck fawn shirt and light brown shorts appeared at her side, she was startled and blushed furiously as she glanced up into his incisive green eyes. A spark of hostility flashed between them, but at the same time a spark of something else. He was compellingly attractive, Nerys thought, despite his glowering look and abrupt manner.

'What's up?' he demanded, slanting a look from her to Phil and back again, sizing up the situation and knowing at once that she was agitated about something.

'Phil was just telling me where to catch the bus for Kolbardi,' Nerys explained.

'Kolbardi? Is that where you're going?' He showed surprise as well as curiosity.

'Yes, but my car's had it.' Nerys gritted her teeth on the last words, hating having to admit that fact. His face, if not his words, said plainly, 'I told you so!'

There was a twist of smile lifting the corners of his mouth, and Nerys flinched. He had told her the car wasn't much good, too. One glance and he had known better than she that it wouldn't last the distance. Silently he had deplored her reckless ignorance, and she had hated him for it. Now she had to admit he'd been right. She'd had her moment of triumph, taking charge at the scene of the accident, but he had caught her out on that, too. The triumph was all his now, and he was enjoying it. Putting people down was obviously his forte.

Phil explained what was wrong with the car. 'And as the repairs will cost more than the car's worth, I've suggested she take the bus.' He stopped, a flash of inspiration lighting up his eyes. 'But of course you'll be . . .'

Dr Vale forestalled what he had obviously intended to

say. Looking rather disdainfully at Nerys, he said, 'I've one or two things to attend to today, but I'll be going back myself tomorrow. I'll give you a lift.'

Nerys was astonished. 'But don't you . . . I mean, what do you mean you're going *back* to Kolbardi?'

Her gaze was enmeshed by his and, caught in the trap of those unfathomable green eyes, she was scarcely aware of Phil excusing himself to attend to another customer. There was something hypnotic about the brown-flecked, green irises that locked with hers in a half-challenging, half-contemptuous way, for the long moment before he spoke.

At last he said, in a tone that suggested he was surprised she didn't already know, 'I'm at the hospital there.'

'Oh!' Nerys was completely stunned. 'Oh, I see.' Her heartbeat was suddenly a trifle rapid, and the breathlessness that went with it caused her to fumble for words. The implication of his revelation began to sink in. She murmured lamely, 'I thought you must be at the hospital *here*.'

His gaze left her face and travelled slowly down over her bare shoulders, the shapely outline of her breasts under the cotton tube top, the modest expanse of midriff that separated her top from her shorts, right down to her slender ankles and feet in their green sandals. When his gaze returned to her face it gave no indication of his assessment, but she felt as quivery as though he had stroked her.

He asked casually, 'I presume you're visiting someone in Kolbardi?' He folded his arms unhurriedly across his broad chest and relaxed his stance a little, while still impaling her with his eyes.

'Yes,' Nerys faltered. 'I'm going to stay with my brother.' The pressure of the green eyes was almost too much for her, and her voice quavered as she went on, 'He—he's a doctor at the Kolbardi hospital, too.'

There was some satisfaction in seeing the amazement in his eyes. 'Good God!' he exclaimed. 'You mean you're Dan Kent's sister?'

Whether he was mortified or just incredulous, Nerys could not be sure, but his eyes became more penetrating than ever. She nodded, feeling almost as though she had confessed to a crime.

'Well, for heaven's sake, why didn't you say so in the first place?' he blasted at her.

Nerys was a bit taken aback. 'I don't go round telling everyone who I am!' she retorted, adding with emphasis, 'Any more than you do!' She packed as much meaning into the last words as she could, still smarting from his failure to tell her he was a doctor last night.

He ignored her outburst and said in a milder, thoughtful tone, 'So you're Nerys Kent. You know, I had quite a different picture in my mind. You're not a bit like Dan. I thought he said you were twins.'

'We are, but we're not identical.'

There was a slight lift of the dark brows. 'No, I can see you're not.' A quizzical look and a faint smile tempered the hardness in his eyes and lent a certain suggestiveness to his remark. Then he glanced at the Mini. 'Pity about your car. You'd better phone Dan and tell him you're coming back with me. Where are you staying?' Nerys told him.

'So am I. It's a wonder I didn't see you there.'

'I saw you this morning,' Nerys said quickly. 'I was going to ask you how the motor-cyclist is, but you drove off before I could attract your attention.'

'He's not as bad as he might have been,' Dr Vale told her, his words more reassuring than his face. 'Compound fracture of the left tibia, torn ligaments in the neck and shoulders. There was some internal haemorrhaging, but the spinal damage is minimal.' He paused and made a wry face. 'He'll be roaring around on that infernal machine again in a couple of months, I don't doubt.'

'I'm so glad he's not as bad as I feared,' Nerys said with genuine relief.

'It's always better to fear the worst.'

Nerys felt very uncomfortable with last night still hovering between them. 'I'm sorry if I—I sort of took charge last night. I was a bit bossy. Why didn't you say you were a doctor?' she blurted out.

He was laughing silently at her. 'It seemed so churlish to spoil your big scene, when you were coping so efficiently. I couldn't fault a thing you did.'

Nerys flinched at his mocking tone. She couldn't very well tell him that she wasn't usually like that, but that her attitude last night had been coloured by the way he had treated her at the service station. She said, stiffly, 'You couldn't expect me to know. You didn't even have a medical bag.'

His face became grave. 'No. Not that there was a great deal I could have done, even so. As a matter of fact my bag had been stolen the day before when I stopped to use the facilities at a service station. Foolishly I didn't lock the car.'

Nerys was a little surprised that he should admit this lapse to her, but it did make him seem a little more human, perhaps even partially explained his bad mood yesterday. 'Any chance of getting it back?' she asked.

He shook his head. 'There was a mob of teenagers there in an overcrowded estate wagon and I have my suspicions. Not that they'll have found any drugs worth having. I don't carry much around with me when I'm on holiday.'

They were almost having a conversation, Nerys thought, in some wonder. Since discovering that she was Dan's sister he had thawed quite a bit and seemed bent on being more diplomatic. She felt a warm glow of pleasure seeping through her. If only he stayed like this he could be a pleasant companion for the long drive out to Kolbardi. She was almost glad she now wouldn't have to negotiate the dirt road alone.

'Well, I mustn't detain you,' she said lightly. 'Thank you again for the offer of a lift. What time do we leave in the morning?'

'Early,' he said. 'Be ready at six-thirty. We'll miss the heat if we set off then.'

'How long does it take?' Nerys inquired.

'About two and a half hours.' His eyes held hers in an embarrassingly long encounter which, now that he had adopted a softer approach, set her nerve-ends tingling more than ever.

As a way of breaking the spell she said the first thing that came into her head. 'By the way, what was that awful racket during the night?'

'Racket?' Evidently he had slept through it all. 'Was there a party?'

'No, not that sort of noise. It was a fair way off and sounded at first like a train. Then there was this awful crashing sound, as though something was being demolished.'

A gleam of understanding crossed his eyes, and the brown-flecked irises danced with amusement. 'Oh that! That was an iron ore train coming into the crushing plant. What you heard was the ore trucks tipping their load into the crushers. I grant you, even at this distance it makes quite a din.' He eyed her speculatively. 'You don't know much about the Pilbara, do you?'

'Well . . . no, not much,' Nerys confessed. She added earnestly, 'I do know that Port Hedland is an iron ore port, and as I've got all day to spare I'll be able to have a look around. By tomorrow I might be quite a bit better informed!' She added diplomatically, 'Perhaps you could suggest what I ought to see.'

He did not answer at once, but continued to absorb her face as though it offered some unique clinical interest. Finally, he said in an off-hand tone, 'I'll do better than that. I'll show you.'

Nerys was taken aback. 'But I thought you had things to do?'

A glimmer of a smile cracked his mouth. 'This evening I am going to a party. Today I am a free agent after I've picked up some things from the hospital. That won't take more than a few minutes.'

Nerys nevertheless protested. 'But I don't want to encroach on your time.'

He angled a mocking glance at her. 'But what would Dan say if I left his sister to her own devices in a strange town? What a boor he would think me.' He did not wait for her to register any further protest, but went on in a tone that suggested he was accustomed to giving orders and having them obeyed. 'Come on, I'll run you back to the motel. You can phone your brother and explain the delay while I do what I have to do. I'll meet you in the bar in half an hour or so. OK?'

Nerys nodded meekly. 'Yes, all right. Thanks.' She wondered whether she really liked the idea of sight-seeing with Dr Vale, or not.

CHAPTER THREE

BACK IN her motel room, which she had been able to re-book easily for one more night, Nerys considered Dr Vale's proposal again, and not without some fresh qualms. Did she really want him to take her sight-seeing around Port Hedland? One half of her said definitely not, the other half suggested it would be much more pleasant than wandering aimlessly alone.

She toyed with the idea of pleading a sudden headache and nausea because of the heat, but she rejected that. In spite of herself she was curious about this aloof but powerfully attractive man and, as she told herself in the end, Dan might be a bit puzzled, even put out, if she turned down the invitation on a flimsy excuse. Dan had never mentioned the man by name, but then she hadn't had all that many communications from her brother over the last year, so it was hardly surprising.

She picked up the telephone and asked the switchboard to put in a call to Dan. When the connection was made, she spoke eagerly into the receiver. 'Daniel!'

He knew at once who it was. 'Nerys! Where are you? I thought you'd be almost here by now. What did you do, sleep in?' Without waiting for her answer, he plunged on anxiously, 'There's nothing wrong is there?'

Daniel's welcome tones flooded into her ear and for a moment she was almost too choked to reply. Her longing to see him almost overwhelmed her.

'No, nothing's wrong,' she assured him quickly on a catch in her breath. 'Just a slight change of plan.' Briefly, she explained the situation, skipping fairly lightly over last night's drama and not, of course, mentioning her contretemps with Dr Vale.

Daniel's reaction was a trifle unexpected. He laughed loudly. 'So you've run into Hallam. How was he?'

'Fine.' She realised that she had not known his first name

33

until now. Hallam. Unusual, but it seemed to suit him.

'No, I mean to you?'

Nerys hesitated, wary. 'Oh, friendly.'

'How friendly?' Daniel asked in a sly tone.

'He's offered to show me around Port Hedland, though I can't imagine there is much to see. It looks a rather dreary place to me.'

Daniel chuckled. 'You might find it quite interesting. With Hallam!' A pause and another chuckle. 'He has a bit of a reputation, so watch your step.'

'Daniel, really! I can take care of myself!' Nerys protested.

'I'm sure you can,' replied her brother, 'but Hallam Vale has quite a way with him. Wish I knew what it was!' he added darkly. 'Most of the girls I know have fallen for him.'

Nerys laughed. 'Do I detect a hint of jealousy?'

'You certainly do,' said Daniel. 'Hallam is a bit of a hard act to follow, I guess. And the fact that he's a lone wolf type and never lets himself be tied down only makes him all the more fascinating, apparently.'

'I should say you're two of a kind,' said Nerys pointedly. 'Since when have you been the settling down type? I bet there's a string of broken hearts scattered wherever you've been!'

Daniel laughed. 'Well, I'm glad you've met up with him, anyway. It'll be a good chance for you to get to know each other.'

A few minutes later, observing Hallam Vale from the entrance to the motel bar, unnoticed by him for the moment, Nerys wondered if in fact it would be. She wondered, too, what special chemistry made some men more attractive than others. There was no doubt that Dr Vale was dangerously so—her own instincts had told her that, before Daniel had warned her of his apparently fatal charm.

His rugged face with its slightly uneven features was not conventionally good-looking, but there was something about the hard line of his jaw, the broad sweep of his forehead and the smooth contours of his hair that intrigued in an inexplicable way. He was perched astride a bar stool. His shirt was casually open half-way to his waist, revealing a cluster of dark hairs on a firm, muscular chest. The wide-belted shorts fitted snugly over his slim waist and flat stomach and emphasised his athletic legs. He was alone in the small bar and staring moodily into a glass of beer, which was why Nerys was able to pause unseen before entering.

When she moved he looked up, and then surveyed her lazily as she approached. 'Drink?' he enquired.

'Thanks. A lemon squash, please.'

She hoisted herself onto a stool next to him. This brought her closer than she had anticipated and, since it swivelled as she mounted it, she accidentally brushed her knees against his thigh. The contact sent an unexpected shock wave through her so that she shrank back, clamped her knees together and stared at a poster on the wall with feigned interest.

After a moment, embarrassed by the silence between them, she said, 'You've been on holiday?'

'Just a few days away.'

'Did you have a nice time?'

'Not bad. I visited some friends on a sheep station just south of Carnarvon. Near the coast. Did some scuba diving.'

Nerys glanced at him. 'Fishing?'

He shook his head, and although he did not quite smile the hard contours of his face eased slightly. 'Photography.' He eyed her speculatively for a moment, as though suddenly thinking of something else entirely, then went on, 'There were a couple of dugongs that come in to the beach, quite close. Fascinating creatures. I hope I got some good pictures.'

'Dugongs?' queried Nerys, wishing she did not have to sound so ignorant. 'What are they?'

'Aquatic mammals. Not fish. It is believed that ancient mariners may have mistaken them for mermaids.' He laughed softly. 'They must have had too much rum because the dugong is not a particularly pretty animal to the average onlooker.'

'But you find them beautiful,' ventured Nerys, detecting something in his tone to suggest it.

His look was sharp, as though he suspected she might be mocking him. Then he said slowly, 'All living things are beautiful, each in its own way.' His eyes rested on her face, still enigmatic, but pulsing with the kind of look she would have expected from the kind of man Daniel had described. Before, he had disguised his masculine interest in her. Momentarily now it was fully exposed. She wondered if he realised it. She was disturbed by the look and half wished she had pleaded a headache after all.

He stood up abruptly. 'If you've finished your drink we might as well go.'

Nerys slid off her stool and found, to her surprise, a steadying hand under her elbow. 'You're sure you want to do this—show me round? You don't have to be polite just because of Daniel, you know,' she said.

His eyes narrowed. 'Hardly,' he said abruptly.

He took her first on a tour of the town, pointing out places of interest. Of special appeal to her was the Royal Flying Doctor Service base, an unusual building, designed as a geodesic dome and reputedly cyclone-proof, so Hallam told her.

They went in and the operator on duty showed them over. Nerys was intrigued by the vastness of the area covered by the service, and the efficiency of the network that could bring medical assistance to almost any isolated spot. A call came through while they were there. A man had broken a leg on an outlying sheep station. Instantly the procedure was put into motion and an aircraft was speedily despatched to pick him up and bring him in to the hospital. Hallam and Nerys slipped away while the operator was busy organising it.

'Would you like to see over an iron ore crushing and loading plant?' Hallam asked as they made their way back to the Range Rover. 'Or doesn't that sort of technical stuff appeal?'

'I'm sure it would be very interesting,' Nerys said, with conviction, 'especially if it explains those noises in the night!'

'It'll do that all right,' Hallam rejoined, slipping behind the wheel and glancing at her with an odd kind of smile as she settled herself in the passenger seat. He added, 'There are guided tours every day, but I think I can get us in for a private look around.'

'So you're a man of influence,' remarked Nerys, and caught another sharp look from him.

He shifted his sunglasses slightly up his straight, bony nose. 'Not really. But one automatically becomes well known after a spell in the north.'

'You've been here long?' she asked.

'A few years.'

'And before that?' she ventured, curious about his background.

'I used to live in Sydney,' he replied shortly, and started the engine. His tone suggested that he did not intend to enlighten her further.

Nerys, however, could not contain her curiosity. 'Don't you ever hanker for civilisation?' she asked as they pulled out and headed for the port area.

He slid a brief, dismissive glance in her direction. So brief, she decided she must have imagined the slightly bitter twist to his mouth, as he said, 'Civilisation is merely a matter of opinion.'

Nerys fell silent. She had a strong feeling that she had violated taboo territory. He did not welcome intrusion into his private life, and to persist might make what was at best a somewhat uncomfortable situation, even more so.

At the gate leading to the Kolbardi Mining Company's crushing and loading plant, Hallam got out and spoke to the security guards on duty. After a few moments he returned.

'We can drive round,' he informed her, 'but we're not permitted to get out of the vehicle.'

'Open sesame!' murmured Nerys, greatly impressed, as the gates were automatically opened to allow them through.

The tour of the whole plant was more interesting than she had expected, and that was partly due to Hallam's concise, well-informed commentary on everything they saw. She could not have failed to be impressed, besides, with the complexity of the operation. She was not a little awed by the stark red dust-encrusted machinery, particularly that which was involved in loading ore onto the immense bulk carriers that were berthed at the wharf.

'It's like a science fiction monster,' she said, watching in amazement as the giant bucket-wheel reclaimer scooped up the crushed rock from the stockpiles and transferred it to the massive loaders, which moved it by conveyor-belt into the holds of the enormous ships. There seemed to be few people about, which added to the robot-like impression.

'It's all too mind-boggling for me,' Nerys confessed, finding it difficult to contain most of the statistics about iron production in the Pilbara that Hallam was rattling off. It would be enough to remember that it was very impressive.

He revved the engine. 'Let's go and look around the port. You'll be able to see the carriers a bit closer up there.'

They left the car in a car park near the entrance to the port area and proceeded on foot. As they were passing the tall, mushroom-topped control tower, a helicopter came in to land nearby.

'The pilot flies out to the carriers,' Hallam explained, adding, 'Port Hedland is a pretty busy port these days.'

'I can see that,' Nerys commented. She had just noticed an immense, black-hulled ore carrier nosing slowly in across the harbour. They stood and watched it being skilfully guided by the tugs which nudged it closely, and then walked along the wharf to take a closer look at one of the carriers already berthed.

'It's odd, isn't it,' Nerys remarked, 'how much you take for granted? I've never once thought about where the raw materials come from to make things like cars and food-blenders and all that.' She stopped, feeling she must sound very naive.

But Hallam didn't scoff. His hand fell gently onto her shoulder. 'Wait until you see the mine,' he said. 'That's the real start of it all.' He turned her round with a light pressure of his fingers and she felt herself quiver at his touch. She also caught an unfathomable look in his eyes that was all the more disturbing because she wasn't quite sure what it meant. 'What about some lunch? We can go to a restaurant, or we can pick up some sandwiches and take a walk down by the old jetty if you prefer.' He added with a touch of concern, 'But maybe you've had enough sight-seeing. It's fairly hot today.'

'I'm fine,' she said, 'and I'm loving it. It's much more interesting here than I expected. Let's get sandwiches and come back.' She smiled up at him, her enthusiasm real. 'Unless, of course, you'd rather . . .' she began, suddenly feeling that perhaps he was angling for a let-out.

'Nothing else I'd rather do,' he replied with unexpected gallantry and a quirky little smile for her. 'Come on!'

Disconcertingly, he grabbed her hand as they headed back into the town, but after a moment he let go, perhaps regretting the gesture, she thought.

Nerys was surprised to find that there was a well-stocked and air-conditioned supermarket, where they bought bread rolls, cheese, cartons of iced coffee and apples. Then they walked back to the port and down to the old wooden jetty, where they sat in the shade under the rotting piles to eat their lunch.

Hallam entertained her with snippets of history, telling her about the early Dutch explorers who had charted the coastline, the privations of the pioneer sheep farmers, and how the port had once been a centre for the pearling luggers around the turn of the century.

'There's a graveyard of Japanese seamen and pearlers,' he said. 'Very old and very overgrown. It's near the ocean and when the wind whistles through the long grass you can almost hear the creaking of the luggers' rigging and see those inscrutable oriental faces with their rich prizes of pearls. I expect a lot of them died of the bends.'

Nerys was watching his face as he spoke. He was a man capable of intense and diverse feeling, she thought, and at that moment Daniel's picture of a rather frivolous charmer did not quite fit. Neither did her own of a moody, disdainful and somewhat aggressive man. There was no doubt that Hallam Vale was a complex personality.

It wasn't long before the sea-birds discovered them and their food, and they were soon surrounded by eager gulls and terns and the rather more reserved pelicans. The pelicans floated across the oily water in a small flotilla, gliding diffidently in to the shore and then waddling with ungainly steps across the sand towards them. Unlike the gulls, however, they were somewhat disdainful of bread and cheese.

'They probably thought we were fishing, and they're disappointed,' laughed Hallam, as one came nearer and regarded them with a baleful eye.

'They're magnificent,' breathed Nerys, who had never seen pelicans quite so close to before. 'I used to love watching them on the island in the lake in St James's Park whenever I was taken to London as a child. They were always so still they seemed to me like statues, and it used to surprise me when one of them took off into the air or the water. Look at that one—he looks so intelligent!'

'They aren't intelligent enough, unfortunately,' said Hallam, his face growing grim as he leaned forward, looking intently into the group. 'Look at that one over to the left, hanging back a bit. It's got a fishing-line hooked up in its bill.' His voice had deepened with concern.

'How could that have happened?' Nerys was horrified.

'They hang around fishermen and pinch their catch if they can. Sometimes thoughtless fishermen discard tangled lines and it's not only the pelicans which get entangled in them. Other birds do too, and usually around the feet. Often it proves fatal.'

Nerys looked at him, dismayed. 'How awful.' She glanced back at the pelican. A length of nylon fishing-line trailed behind it towards the water's edge. 'Do you think there's a hook in its bill?' she asked, troubled.

'Most probably.'

Nerys turned to him urgently. 'Surely we can do something?'

He looked at her for a moment. 'We could try.'

She was eager to. 'Well, let's do it! we can't just leave it like that. It might not be able to fish properly. It could die of starvation.'

Hallam rose slowly so as not to scare the birds too far away. 'Try and keep them interested,' he said.

Nerys wanted to ask what he intended to do but he was already striding back up the beach, so she returned her attention to the injured pelican, trying to tempt it closer with the remaining scraps from their lunch and wishing she had a fish to offer instead. It did not appear very interested in the food, but was obviously curious about her, perhaps hoping she would eventually produce a fish if it was patient enough.

'Come on,' she called softly, 'we won't hurt you. Come on. You must let us help you.'

She was still murmuring the same kind of encouragement when Hallam reappeared, returning so quietly she did not hear him until he dropped down on the sand beside her. Most of the pelicans had returned to the water and were paddling back and forth gracefully, still hopeful of a feed, but the injured one had remained on the beach.

'I think he knows we're trying to help,' said Nerys.

'He's hungry,' Hallam said, and held out a fish.

'Where did you get that?' Nerys was astonished.

He smiled smugly, then explained. 'Saw a bloke fishing and begged it off him. Old Charlie Murdoch, one of the local characters. He doesn't leave lines around for the birds to tangle in, thank goodness. He's got sense.'

'But what are we going to do?' Nerys had noticed he had brought a blanket and asked what it was for.

'First you must catch your patient,' Hallam said with a grim expression, 'before you can operate on him. Now, first we tempt him with the fish.' He held out the silvery fish and immediately the pelican's interest was heightened. So was that of the others who had retreated, and they all began to come ashore again. Hallam said to Nerys, 'You hold the fish out and try to keep his attention on it, while I see if I can grab him.'

'Do be careful,' Nerys warned as the large beak of the bird loomed closer.

Hallam moved slowly around the bird until he was right behind it. The pelican was so interested in the fish it became unwary and, seizing his opportunity, Hallam threw the blanket over the bird and pinioned its huge, powerful wings. Briefly, the bird thrashed about—then all at once it was calm. Hallam wrapped the blanket more securely around it and carried it into the shade of the jetty.

'Now let's take a look at you, old man,' he murmured in a

gentle voice as he laid the bird on its side, still keeping a firm grasp on its body. To Nerys he said, 'Take my belt off, will you?'

She looked startled.

'I'll have to strap the patient up,' he explained. 'Do it from behind so you don't scare the bird.'

'Oh, yes . . .' Rather self-consciously she reached her arms around his waist and fumbled with the buckle, then slid the wide leather belt through the tabs.

'Thanks.' The look he gave her was a trifle wry, and she knew that her embarrassment showed. She didn't know why she should feel that way, but there was something about the close personal contact that unnerved her.

Deftly, with her assistance, he fastened the belt around the bird. It was only just long enough. The pelican did not struggle, but intermittently opened and closed its bill in a breathless kind of way. Its yellow-rimmed brown eye was glazed and wary, but it made no attempt to attack them.

'It's all right,' Nerys soothed, 'we're not going to hurt you.' To Hallam she said, 'Oh, why can't they understand we only mean to help?'

He did not reply. He was drawing a pair of forceps out of his pocket. He gave Nerys a fleeting smile. 'I managed to replace most of my medical kit at the hospital this morning. Now, I think I'd better hold the bill open while you remove the hook, which I suspect is firmly embedded in the flesh behind the bill. Do you think you can manage it?'

'I can try,' she said, meeting his gaze unflinchingly.

'You don't have to if you'd rather not,' he said. 'I know it's a rather frightening beak.'

Nerys shot him a scornful look. 'You don't imagine I'm going to funk it, do you?'

'We could take it to a vet,' Hallam said, 'but that would mean more trauma for the poor thing. If we can get the hook out here, we can set it free straight away.'

'Well, let's try,' said Nerys impatiently. 'Open wide!'

Although she would never have admitted it to Hallam, she was a bit nervous as his strong fingers prised the bird's bill open. But she saw the hook exactly where he had said it probably would be. At least the bird hadn't swallowed it!

She could see that it was going to be fairly tricky removing it, and she would tear the skin in doing so, but there was no other way. She gripped the forceps tightly and reached it, taking hold of the shank of the hook firmly. To her amazement, the pelican did not struggle. In fact, it didn't appear to feel a thing as she tore the vicious-looking hook through its flesh. As it came out, a thin trickle of blood appeared.

'Good girl!' praised Hallam triumphantly, letting the pelican's bill close gently. 'There you are, old man, you'll be OK now. Just don't go meddling with baited fish-hooks again if you know what's good for you!'

The pelican eyed him with an uncertain expression.

'Will it be all right?' Nerys asked. 'I couldn't help tearing the flesh and it was bleeding a bit.'

'Salt water will kill any infection,' Hallam assured her. He unstrapped the belt and removed the blanket. The pelican just lay there for a moment, apparently unaware that it was now free again. Hallam offered it the fish and it stood up and snapped at it.

'Off you go, mate,' urged Hallam, 'and don't forget to say thank you to the nurse!'

The pelican gave an odd, strangled sort of cry and then, spreading its great wings, half flew, half ran towards the water's edge. In a few moments it had rejoined the rest of the group who were cruising along at a distance. Nerys saw it suddenly gulp down the fish which it had retained until then in its pouch.

'It'll be able to fish for its supper more efficiently now, I hope,' Hallam said.

Nerys was feeling a curious kind of emotion. She had never assisted at an operation on a bird before. She felt a wave of pleasure wash over her as she saw the proud creature sailing erect on the swelling ocean. It was the same kind of feeling she always had when a human patient had recovered and was going home.

'Wasn't too difficult, was it?' Hallam asked with satisfaction.

She said teasingly, 'I thought you were a doctor, not a vet!'

He laughed. 'I'm not aware that the Hippocratic oath was exclusive to humans!'

'Well, I think it was very compassionate of you,' said Nerys with genuine admiration. 'Not everybody would have bothered.'

'No,' he said, looking at her with a half-smile. 'You're right, they wouldn't.'

Their eyes met lengthily and again Nerys was aware of a very disturbing aspect of him. And again she heard the echo of Daniel's warning in her ears.

They strolled around the port for a little while longer, watching reef herons and gulls, a kestrel hovering over the mangroves, launches and fishing-boats coming and going, and all the other perpetual activity of the busy port.

At length Nerys said, 'As you're going out tonight, I expect you'd like to get back to the motel soon. I've had a lovely day, Hallam, and I'm very grateful to you for showing me around. I confess I had no idea it would be so interesting.'

He considered her with a quizzical expression on his handsome features, as though he was weighing her up for some task. 'Life is full of little surprises,' he said, and his eyes narrowed as he added, 'I've had a few myself today.' He withdrew his gaze and said crisply, 'Yes, we'd better be getting back.'

'I'm going to have a shower, then dinner, and then I'm going to relax and watch television,' Nerys announced, with a little sigh of contentment.

His hand dropped firmly on to her shoulder. 'Oh, no, you're not,' Hallam Vale stated in a tone that defied argument. 'Because you're coming to the party with me.'

CHAPTER FOUR

HALLAM VALE was a man you simply didn't say no to, Nerys reflected rather sombrely as she stood under the tepid shower, luxuriating in the invigorating sting of the jets, leisurely sliding the foaming soap over her smooth skin. She had already acquired a slight tan during her few days in Perth, lounging by Carrie and Bruce's swimming-pool.

Fortunately, she had the kind of nearly olive complexion that did not burn too easily, but slowly and evenly tanned to an attractive colour, darkening to an alluring duskiness around her eyes and mouth.

She wished in a way she had said no to the party, but it was too late now. She had accepted Hallam's invitation, just as she had accepted his offer to show her around Port Hedland and to give her a lift to Kolbardi. She had wanted to say no each time, but instead she had said yes. Was it because of a weakness in herself, she wondered, or the natural authority in him?

She smiled ruefully to herself. To be honest, it was probably a bit of both. She was feeling a bit lonely and there was no doubt about the man, he had style and a certain intriguing quality that was hard to resist. And he was used to people saying yes. He was, she felt sure, used to ordering people around, making decisions and expecting them to be carried out.

What puzzled her most was why he had, at the last minute, asked her to go to the party with him. He didn't have to. It meant that he must have had to telephone his host or hostess to ask if he might bring her. Whoever it was would be bound to say yes, Nerys reflected wryly, just as Dr Vale would expect. She doubted that he had already made the request before inviting her. It was pure impulse, she felt certain. She hoped the party-givers would not mind having a stranger thrust upon them.

Nerys had brought one long dress, which she judged

45

would be suitable for the occasion and nice and cool. It had a shirred bodice and narrow shoulder straps, and it showed off her well-shaped shoulders and neck, giving just a little provocative interest to her bosom. The blue and green swirls of the pattern were cool and flattering to her dark colouring.

She hoped it would be casual enough. Hallam had told her that it was to be a very informal party and she could wear anything she wanted. His eyes had strayed flatteringly over her while he spoke, almost caressing her bare arms and legs, until she felt the clothing she wore was superfluous.

Nerys pulled her hair back for comfort, brushing it smoothly off her forehead and lifted it a little at the back with combs, so that is silky waves fell in an attractive cascade to the nape of her neck. Around her throat she fastened a blue-green pendant on a silver chain. It matched exactly the colour of the dress. A dab of powder, careful shaping of her expressive eyebrows and a swift dash of coral lipstick, and she was ready. Hallam knocked on her door as she was putting her make-up and a handkerchief into her silver-mesh purse.

'Ready!' she called out, and ran to open the door.

The open admiration in his eyes was a bit of a shock, and for a long moment they stood and just looked at each other. Nerys felt his eyes taking in every inch of her, and she could not help her own swift, encompassing glance that took in his white safari suit and deep blue shirt. He looked casual but dashing, and the thought crossed her mind that there would be few women who would not feel elated to be escorted by this man. Physically, she had to admit, he made most of the other men she had ever known seem uninspiring.

'Very nice.' His eyes told her that this was a deliberate understatement, and she could not help a swift flutter of gratification that she had stirred his senses so potently.

'Casual enough?' she asked anxiously.

'You'll do,' he murmured, with the same meaningful understatement.

Nerys stepped outside and pulled the door shut behind her. Hallam took her arm as they walked across to where his Range Rover was parked. It was only a few minutes' drive to the house where the party was being held, and on the way he gave her some brief background.

'The host and hostess are mining people. He's an engineer at Kolbardi. They have a house out there as well as here. Klaus more or less commutes. His wife is Barbra. Klaus and Barbra Albrecht.'

'I hope they don't mind you bringing me along,' Nerys ventured.

'Not at all. They are very hospitable people and wouldn't have liked to think you were spending the evening alone in a strange town, any more than I would. We pride ourselves on our hospitality to strangers, you know.'

Which is the only reason he invited me, Nerys thought. It wasn't because he specially wanted my company. He was probably bored stiff being with me all day, but he felt duty-bound to make a gesture so I wouldn't go away and say the locals weren't friendly. She shrank into the seat, a little deflated, then chided herself that his reason was as good as any. She didn't want there to be any other reason, did she?

The sun was going down in a fiery sky over the Indian Ocean, the pall of red dust that hung over the town making the blaze even more of an inferno, the clouds leaping across the sky like giant flames. Like the blast-furnaces that would turn the iron ore into steel, Nerys mused—steel to make massive things like bridges and skyscrapers, and delicate precision instruments like scalpels and scissors and needles, pacemakers and pins . . . She smiled to herself. It was strange how, checking an instrument tray before an operation, she had never once stopped to think where it all came from, how it had started in the ground as solid rock.

The garden where the party was being held was festooned with coloured lights. Hallam led Nerys along a path between sweet-smelling frangipani bushes and around the corner of the low, ranch-style house. Voices came from the rear of the house, and eventually they emerged on to a patio where groups of people were drifting about.

Hallam paused, looking around, and Nerys, feeling suddenly rather self-conscious, hung back a little. A tall blonde woman spotted them and immediately her face lit up with a welcoming smile. She almost ran across the patio towards them. But it was Hallam she greeted, appearing not even to notice Nerys.

'Hallam, darling, so lovely you could come!' Her voice was low and husky and she clasped his hands in hers and pushed her upturned cheek towards his mouth. It was almost a whisper when she added provocatively, 'I can't tell you how I've missed you.'

She was a woman of about thirty, slender but voluptuous. Her natural blonde hair set off a perfect tan, which was further enhanced by the vivid orange dress she was wearing. It was strapless and moulded to her curves. The skirt was split to reveal smooth, shapely thighs. Nerys was a bit taken aback at the blatantly sexual look she gave Hallam, the intimate smile that played about her full, inviting mouth. Her manner implied some kind of special relationship. For some odd reason, Nerys was disappointed.

Shifting her gaze reluctantly to Nerys, whom she affected to notice for the first time, the woman lifted her brows slightly.

'And who is your friend, Hallam?' She seemed surprised that he was accompanied. Nerys suspected that she was not pleased.

Hallam said evenly, 'Barbra, I'd like you to meet Nerys Kent.' They were the first words he had spoken, Nerys realised. 'I rang Klaus and told him I was bringing her. Her car broke down and she's stranded in Hedland tonight. She's Dan Kent's sister, here for a visit. Luckily, I shall be driving back to Kolbardi in the morning. Nerys, this is Barbra Albrecht.'

Nerys caught her breath. This was their hostess! She glanced at the woman's left hand, still clutching Hallam's, and saw the rings, a wide gold band and two very expensive diamonds on the third finger, plus a couple of dress-rings on the middle finger. Barbra obviously liked jewellery.

Their hostess flicked her blonde hair with a gesture of petulance. 'Klaus didn't tell me you'd rung, or that you were bringing anyone. But he is so forgetful!' It was lightly said, but carried a hidden barb, Nerys thought. It was not hard to deduce that all was not well between Barbra Albrecht and her husband.

Then, as though suddenly remembering her manners, Barbra said in a rather off-hand tone, 'But of course you are welcome, Nerys.' She dropped Hallam's hands with a look that was faintly reproachful, and a spark of jealousy gleamed in her blue eyes.

You've no need to worry about me, Nerys could have told her. I'm not likely to be a threat. Obviously, Barbra regarded Hallam as her special property which, Nerys reflected, he gave every indication of being. That he should be interested in a married woman disappointed her and diminished him somewhat in her estimation.

'It was kind of your husband to invite me. Thank you,' she murmured politely.

'Come and have a drink,' Barbra said airily, flouncing away with a beckoning wave of her long, carefully painted fingertips. 'Klaus has made a real knockout of a fruit punch if you're game to try it!' Her rather shrill tones rang out across the garden as she called, 'Klaus! Hallam's here!'

Heads turned as Hallam and Nerys joined the clusters of guests who were scattered about the patio. Several people greeted Hallam, and quite a few eyes looked Nerys over with curiosity, some with unconcealed admiration. From the far side of the patio, a large man with almost white-blond hair approached them. He was wearing a blue and white apron emblazoned with the words *Chief cook and bottle-washer*. He greeted them with a broad smile and his sharp blue eyes appraised Nerys and registered instant approval.

'Klaus, this is Nerys Kent,' Hallam said, with a light touch on Nerys's arm as he ushered her forward. 'Nerys, meet Klaus Albrecht. He is exactly what it says on the apron! Toiling over a hot barbecue, are you, Klaus?' he jokingly added.

'As always!' returned Klaus good-humouredly, and turning to Nerys, 'I am delighted to meet you, my dear.' He shook her hand warmly. 'Delighted, indeed. Welcome to the party. I'm glad Hallam brought you along.' He glanced mischievously at Hallam. 'You were always the connoisseur!'

Nerys blushed, feeling that she was receiving rather too much attention and that Barbra resented it.

'What about this knock-out punch of yours, Klaus? Barbra recommends it,' Hallam said dryly.

Barbra put in smilingly, 'Why don't you organise a drink for Hallam, Klaus? And then he can give you a hand with the barbecue. I'll introduce Nerys to everybody and fix her a drink at the same time.'

Nerys would rather have had Hallam to make the introductions but she had no choice, so was obliged to follow Barbra. She had the feeling that separating her from Hallam had been deliberate. She might have arrived with Dr Vale, but it was clear that Barbra did not intend her to monopolise him. Or was she just being over-sensitive? Perhaps Barbra was simply a good hostess, eager to make a stranger feel at ease.

Barbra stopped at a group of half a dozen people, caught hold of Nerys's hand as though she was a child and dragged her closer. Conversation ceased as they intruded, and all eyes were turned with interest on the newcomer.

Barbra said gaily, 'I want you to meet Nerys Kent. She's Dr Kent's sister. You all know Dan, don't you, out at Kolbardi?' She went on, 'These are all real fair dinkum locals, not fly-by-night mining types. Joyce and Gary Lange run a hairdressing salon, Phil Darnley owns the newest garage in town, and that's his wife, Claire, next to him. And next to her is Sinclair Wilson, sheep station owner and playboy millionaire!'

'Come off it, Babs!' protested the rangy young man in a pale blue shirt and dark blue trousers. There was a definite air of casual affluence about him, Nerys noted instantly, and it was not just the cut of his clothes. Barbra's description was probably accurate. The smile he gave Nerys was welcoming and, like his eyes, expressed clear masculine interest.

Barbra turned to Nerys and winked broadly. 'He pretends to be poor, but he owns one of the biggest sheep runs in the west.' She gave a meaningful smile. 'And amazingly he's still a bachelor!'

Nerys murmured, 'How do you do?' looking around the

group. Much to her relief, she could feel friendly vibrations coming from everyone there. She had always been a little shy of strangers, especially in groups, but these people seemed very easy-going. It was as she glanced around the group that she realised she already knew one of them, but his name had not registered when they were introduced and he looked different out of overalls.

He grinned at her when he saw that she had finally recognised him. 'Nice to see you again, Nerys,' Phil Darnley said.

She felt a shade foolish. 'Oh! Of course, I'm so sorry, I didn't recognise you at first!' she apologised. 'And I'm never very good at names.'

Claire Darnley looked at her husband with raised eyebrows and a teasing smile. 'I don't think I know about this!' she said, but without any archness in her tone.

'Yes, Phil, what have you been up to?' joked one of the others, while Nerys began to go pink.

Phil, unruffled, explained about her car, and Nerys came in ruefully with, 'I'm afraid I didn't have it checked thoroughly before I bought it. It was my own fault.'

'Well, be careful of anything Phil tries to flog you to replace it,' warned Joyce Lange teasingly. 'It might be worse!'

'I wouldn't dare,' said Phil, straight-faced, 'not while Dr Vale has her under his wing!'

Nerys happened to catch Barbra's eye as Phil made the remark and there was a perceptible darkening of her gaze, a slight curl to her vividly painted lips. She said coolly, 'Oh dear, you haven't got a drink yet. I was going to get you one, wasn't I? Perhaps you would oblige, Sinclair?'

Barbra turned a sunny smile on the young station owner, who moved with alacrity to Nerys's side, as their hostess made an excuse and drifted away. Obviously these were the only introductions she intended to make.

'Just tell me what you'd like and I'll get it,' Sinclair offered, absorbing her face with a flattering look.

'I think I'll try Klaus's punch.' Nerys moved back a step. His face was a little too close to hers.

While he was gone the conversation devolved on Nerys,

her visit to her brother and commiserations about the car. All were eager to know her impressions of the country she had not seen before, and she was telling them how she had enjoyed her stay in Perth when Sinclair returned with her drink. She was aware that he took care to brush his fingers against hers as he transferred the glass to her hand, and a moment later she caught a look being exchanged between Joyce Lange and Claire Darnley. It said quite clearly that Sinclair was behaving according to form.

Another couple joined the group and were introduced to Nerys, and after a few minutes there was a drift, with other people stopping to talk, until finally Nerys found herself temporarily alone with Sinclair on the outskirts of the gathering. She looked around for Hallam but could not see him anywhere. She could not see Barbra, either.

Sinclair was saying, 'I do love your accent, Nerys. You have a very musical voice. It conveys a great warmth of feeling.'

She was taken aback. 'Well, thank you . . .'

'I'm sure it must be a pleasure to be in hospital and have you as a nurse,' he continued. 'I'm sure you'd be very kind.'

Nerys swallowed. He was overdoing it a bit, seeing they had only met half an hour ago. She was glad when the Darnleys and the Langes drifted back to them.

'What's this?' said Gary Lange, 'a private tête-á-tête? Bit early in the evening, Sinclair, even for you, isn't it?'

Sinclair looked only faintly annoyed at the interruption.

Claire said, 'Have you ever known Sinclair to let the grass grow under his feet? Watch him, Nerys, he could charm the fairy off the Christmas tree!'

'I hope Klaus isn't going to be much longer with the food,' said Phil prosaically. 'I'm ravenous.' Everyone laughed.

A moment after he had spoken there was a loud shout of, 'Come and get it!' and Nerys found herself hustled along the patio to where the barbecue was gently sizzling. There were long trestle tables set with dishes of salad, bread rolls and a variety of other tasty-looking foods.

It was here that Nerys caught her first glimpse of Hallam. Hardly to her surprise, he was talking to Barbra, who was positively sparkling. By the way he was smiling at what she was saying, one could easily believe that he was very much attracted to her. Nerys felt a prick of resentment because he had brought her here and then dumped her. Then she reminded herself that that was scarcely fair. Barbra had snatched her away, and besides, she was not his responsibility. It wasn't as if he had left her out on a limb. And yet there was an underlying, and unfair, niggle because he had not at least sought her out to ask if she was enjoying herself.

Watching them, Nerys could not help wondering about Hallam and Barbra. They were obviously attracted to each other. But did it go further than that? Were they lovers? And Klaus, was he aware that his wife was flirting with Hallam right under his nose? Nerys looked around for him and saw that he was busy near the barbecue fire. Perhaps he did know, and didn't care. It was none of her business anyway, but still the knowledge that Hallam was playing around with another man's wife rankled with her. She did not want to disapprove of Hallam Vale.

She turned away and made a deliberate effort to erase these confused thoughts from her mind. Sinclair was urging her to fill her plate with food, which she now did. Since he seemed determined to monopolise her, and since she had no real objection to it, Nerys allowed herself to be led back across the patio to sit on a low wall a little removed from the main party.

Sinclair smiled at her admiringly. 'I'm glad you're going to be around for a while.'

'Oh, well, I don't expect it will be very long,' Nerys faltered.

'I shall have to have a word with Dan,' he said in mock seriousness, 'and make sure he keeps you in Kolbardi for a while.' He added meaningfully, 'I often go in to Kolbardi.'

Nerys did not know how to reply. His meaning was quite clear. He hoped to see something of her. She considered him thoughtfully. He was a very pleasant young man, a little over-powering perhaps, and rather flowery, but she decided there was no need to be off-putting. There might not be much to do in Kolbardi. And flattering masculine attention would help to keep her from brooding over Chris. Anything that would help her to get over that disaster was welcome.

After a moment or two Sinclair said, 'So you're a nurse? Medicine must run in the family, seeing your brother is a doctor.'

Nerys laughed as she denied it. 'Not really. Our family had always been farmers, and I don't think there were any other medical offspring until Daniel and me. Our parents were farmers.'

'You said "were"—are your parents not still living?'

Nerys shook her head. 'They both died several years ago. It was rather tragic. Mother had an accident driving to visit a friend, and my father had a fatal heart attack when he was told about it.'

Sinclair laid a sympathetic hand on her knee. 'Poor Nerys, all alone . . .'

'I have Daniel,' she corrected, keeping her voice purposely light. She did not want pity. She and Daniel had come to terms with their loss and she preferred not to have the subject raised if it could be helped. She said pointedly, 'But this is a party, we mustn't be morbid!'

'No,' he agreed, then commented, 'So you come from a farming tradition. How very interesting.' His eyes devoured her avidly. 'I knew we must have something in common.'

'I don't think the kind of farm I grew up on would bear much resemblance to yours!' said Nerys with a grin.

'No, perhaps not. At least not in size. But it's the spirit of the land, isn't it, the challenge of the elements, the satisfaction of conquering nature . . .'

Nerys felt uneasy. 'I . . . I don't think my father saw farming quite like that. He believed in working *with* nature, not against it.' She smiled quickly in case he thought she was rude to disagree with him. 'Of course, farming must be very different in a country like Australia.'

'Very different,' he agreed, then added casually, 'Perhaps you would like to see a sheep station sometime?'

'Oh, I would!' she said eagerly.

'Then I'll have to arrange a trip out to Yeramba Springs

for you,' Sinclair promised at once. His eyes were weighing her up in a thoughtful manner.

'Is Yeramba Springs your property?' Nerys half wished she had not voiced her enthusiasm quite so readily. She did not want Sinclair to jump to the conclusion that she was as eager about him as she was about seeing a sheep station.

'It is. Tell you what, I'll come and fetch you from Kolbardi some time. You can stay over a couple of nights and have a really good look around the place.'

Cautiously, Nerys replied, 'I wouldn't want to put you to any trouble.' She wanted to ask if he lived alone, but did not want to sound too prissy.

'It'll be no trouble,' he said, and as though he had guessed her train of thought, added, 'You'll be well chaperoned, don't worry. There are several women on the station, including my mother, who loves having visitors.' His eyes teased her a little. He laid a persuasive hand on her arm. 'You'll come?'

She was reassured but still reluctant to make a definite arrangement. 'I would like to, Sinclair, and it's very kind of you to invite me, but I'd better not make any definite arrangements until I've seen Daniel.'

'Of course,' he agreed affably. 'No rush. My mother is down in Perth at the moment but she'll be coming back soon.' His eyes roamed her face eagerly, making very clear his admiration for her. His smile was confident. 'You have a very intriguing face, Nerys. One cannot help wondering what thoughts are lurking behind those lovely big brown eyes.'

Nerys had the feeling she was being swept along rather too swiftly into something she had not really had time to consider carefully. Or perhaps she was reading too much into Sinclair's offer of hospitality. She stood up and, more abruptly than was perhaps polite, said, 'I think I'll help myself to some more salad. Shan't be long.'

To her relief he did not go with her, and this gave her the opportunity to avoid him for a while. Several people spoke to her and after a short time, daring to look back to where she had left him, Nerys noticed that Sinclair was no longer there. She swung her gaze around and saw him mingling with some of the other guests. If he had regarded her abrupt departure and non-return as a rebuff, it couldn't be helped.

That it would take more than that to rebuff Sinclair Wilson, Nerys quickly discovered. Not much later, she was looking around for Hallam, who had kept his distance all evening apart from a passing word or glance, when Sinclair reappeared at her side.

'So this is where you are,' he said, and slipped his arm around her waist, briefly squeezing it. 'I've been looking for you everywhere.'

Nerys smiled brightly. 'I've been just about here all the time. You couldn't have been looking very hard!'

'I've been admiring you from a distance,' he said.

'That I do not believe,' she answered, keeping up a light, bantering tone. 'I saw you flirting with any number of glamorous women. It's your stock-in-trade, isn't it?'

He chuckled. 'The secret is never to let any woman think you're serious until you really are!' He added with an ironic smirk, 'Flattery gets you everywhere!'

His line wasn't exactly subtle or polished, Nerys thought with mild distaste, but under the slightly vapid exterior she suspected there lurked a man who knew exactly what he was doing. She was not sure she cared for his cynical attitude to women.

'Not with me it doesn't!' she countered, giving the remark some weight in case he thought she was just being coy.

He was still smiling into her face in a somewhat bemused way when Hallam Vale appeared out of the shadows and joined them. Nerys was surprised by the way her heartbeat quickened at the sight of his tall, handsome figure, and the foolish wish that Sinclair would go away and leave her with him.

'Hello, Hallam.' Sinclair greeted the doctor casually, but there was a tinge of resentment for the interruption in his tone.

'Enjoying yourselves?' Hallam enquired looking at Nerys, the question directed more to her than her companion.

'I'm having a great time,' she said. 'Everyone is so friendly, I haven't felt like a stranger at all.'

He allowed his lips to form a slow smile. 'I'm glad we've been living up to our reputation.'

Nerys was not sure whether she was imagining it or not, but he seemed edgy, a little tense. She wondered why. A silence descended on the trio. None of them seemed able to find anything to say.

Finally it was Barbra who breezed across the patio towards them, not to claim Hallam as Nerys expected, but to persuade Sinclair to play the piano.

'Some of the younger ones want to dance,' she said. 'In the rumpus room.' She glanced at Hallam and they exchanged a look that Nerys felt betrayed their intimacy. 'I'm sure Nerys would like to join them,' she said.

'Sure,' agreed Hallam at once. 'We'll be right over. As soon as we've had a drink.' He glanced at Nerys. 'Klaus's punch hasn't knocked you out yet?'

'Not yet!' she laughed. 'It's very nice.'

Sinclair drifted off rather reluctantly, or so Nerys thought, in the wake of his hostess, and a few moments later strains of his piano-playing wafted out on to the patio. Hallam made no move to get Nerys the promised drink.

'We won't stay too late, as we're making an early start in the morning,' he said.

'I'm not bothered about dancing,' she said. 'We can go now if you want to.'

'Soon.' His eyes observed her slantingly. 'You seemed to be getting along well with Sinclair.'

'He's a very pleasant person.'

'And I suppose he invited you up to Yeramba Springs for a weekend, sometime?'

Nerys was a bit taken aback by his sarcastic tone. 'Well, yes, he did as a matter of fact.' She felt suddenly on the defensive.

Hallam shrugged. 'That's his style.'

Nerys bridled. 'What do you mean by that?'

There was cynicism in his tone as he derided, 'Don't tell me you haven't seen through Sinclair Wilson?'

'I don't know what you mean by that, either.'

'Sinclair Wilson has quite a reputation where women are

concerned,' he said slowly, his eyes glinting. 'But perhaps you don't mind that.'

His tone incensed her. 'Maybe I don't,' she retorted hotly. 'I'm out with you, after all, and from what I've heard *you* have something of a reputation, too!'

His eyes held hers and she felt demolished, as she had yesterday in the roadside café where she had shared his lunch-table. His mood had changed drastically since they arrived at the party, she thought bleakly, and not a little puzzled. He had softened while he was taking her sight-seeing, but tonight he was back to being the scratchy individual she had encountered and fallen foul of yesterday. She wished she knew why he was so moody.

Suddenly he gripped her arm. 'Are you inviting me to prove it?'

Just about everyone else had gone from the patio. Only one or two couples were lingering, and one pair were kissing in the shadows some little distance away. The piano music was soft and dreamy. Sinclair was playing a medley of sensuously romantic numbers.

For a moment there was no more than a swift electrical charge between them, and then Nerys was in his arms, crushed against that broad, hard chest, and he was kissing her with a force that took her breath away. The hand that spread across the small of her back dragged her against him roughly, a roughness matched by his other hand, which clasped her neck and gave her no room to escape his punishing lips.

A wave of anger and indignation swept over her at the ignominy of this assault, but was quickly overridden by an involuntary shiver that told her how practised he was in feminine arousal. And when his lips gradually ceased to batter hers and began to move in a gentler but even more arousing way, she felt her resistance crumbling and the rigidity of her resisting body melting like snow in a desert. The heavily sweet perfume of frangipani mingled with the sharply astringent maleness of him, and was more intoxicating than any punch she had ever tasted.

When he lifted his lips from hers, she gave a little surprised gasp. He said cruelly, 'Well? Are you satisfied?'

'That was a despicable thing to do!' she hissed at him, anger now overriding her other, at once deeply regretted, feelings.

She glanced quickly around to see if anyone had noticed them. The patio was quite deserted now, but suddenly she realised that someone lurked in the shadows near the house, a figure with blonde hair. Barbra turned and walked back into the house. She had come out to look for them, Nerys felt certain, and had surely seen what had happened.

Hallam made no apology. He said, 'If you really don't want to dance, we might as well go.'

Nerys was only too glad to get away from the party, and she couldn't wait to get away from him, too.

'Damn the man!' she thought angrily as they walked across the patio to take leave of their hosts.

Barbra was not difficult to find. She looked them over haughtily and Nerys felt deeply embarrassed. She said in a light tone that Nerys was sure disguised her real feelings, 'And where have you two been hiding?'

Hallam did not attempt a reply. He merely said, 'I think it's time we were off, Barbra. Terrific party. See you in Kolbardi soon. We'll just say goodbye to Klaus.'

Barbra's brief glance in Nerys's direction was little short of venomous. 'Do you really have to rush off?' she said plaintively to Hallam, linking her arm with his. 'The dancing is just warming up.'

Hallam disengaged himself and said firmly, 'It's after midnight, Barbra. Another time, perhaps.' His tone made it quite clear he would not be persuaded.

She did not try, but reached up and kissed his cheek. 'Goodnight, Hallam.' She looked coldly at Nerys. 'Nice to have met you.' From her tone it was clear she meant the opposite.

They said goodbye to Klaus and a few others, and finally managed to extricate themselves. Nerys was glad she did not have to say more than a few brief words to Sinclair, since he was still at the piano.

He squeezed her hand and said, 'I'll be in touch!' But the look he shot Hallam was a trifle suspicious.

On the drive back to the motel Hallam was silent. Nerys

had nothing to say either. She felt ridiculously churned up inside. What sort of man was he really? Was the scratchy, disdainful Hallam Vale the real man, or was the gentle companion of earlier today his true self, or was he the man of violent passion who had so recently held her in his arms?

Stealing sidelong glances at his stern profile as he swung the Range Rover around corners and finally into the motel forecourt, she brooded on the subject and came up with no clear answer. The only thing that was clear was that he had wakened a response in her that not even Chris had ever done, and she deeply deplored it.

His unit was in the same row as her own. It was only a few steps from the parking bay to her door, so she did not expect him to accompany her.

'Well, thanks for the party,' she said, forcing a lightness she did not feel into her voice. 'Goodnight, Hallam.' In spite of her effort to sound nonchalant, the words came out stiffly.

He was looking down at her and in the dim light she could not see his expression. For one moment she thought he was going to drag her into his arms again, but in spite of that she did not move. She stood motionless in the shadows, aware only of the stars glittering above, the tang of seaweed on the air and the powerful magnetism of the man beside her. There was even a treacherous desire that he would kiss her again.

It took Hallam to break the spell. He said abruptly, 'Be ready at six-thirty sharp. Goodnight.'

CHAPTER FIVE

NERYS WAS so disconcerted by all that had happened during the evening that for once she forgot to set her travelling alarm clock. She was also tired. The events of the past two days, and the previous night's fragmented rest, had finally caught up with her. She slept soundly, oblivious of extraneous noises, undisturbed even by dreams. When she finally stirred it was still early—only six-fifteen—but not early enough.

In a panic she leapt out of bed. She had only fifteen minutes to get ready! She was determined not to be late and give Hallam Vale a reason to deride her. Her suitcase was ready except for the items she had needed for last night and this morning, so it would not take long to finish packing it. Automatically, she headed for the shower, then stopped. There simply wasn't time, however quick she was. There wasn't even time to make the cup of coffee she craved.

'Oh, damn!' she wailed, flinging off her nightdress and hastily shoving it into her suitcase. 'What an idiot I am!'

Then she calmed down. It wasn't exactly a catastrophe not being able to shower. She'd had a shower before going to the party last night, after all. A liberal dusting with talcum would have to do this morning. She grimaced fiercely at herself in the dressing-table mirror. It was more important to her pride not to keep Dr Vale waiting.

Like a mad thing she flew around the motel unit, checking she had left nothing behind, and a couple of minutes before six-thirty she sat on her suitcase and jammed it shut, locking it securely. She glanced at her watch with a smirk of satisfaction and carried her suitcase, holdall and handbag outside.

Hallam was standing beside the Range Rover when she emerged, tall and rugged, looming larger than life against the sun. He was clad in khaki trousers and a short-sleeved shirt, unbuttoned to reveal a glimpse of dark chest hair and deeply tanned torso. Ridiculously, she experienced an involuntary lurching inside her, and knew that last night had not just been an aberration. The man still attracted her in a way she would rather he did not. Somewhere deep down an instinct warned that to become emotionally involved with Hallam Vale would be as disastrous as it had been with Chris.

'Good-morning!' she called cheerfully as she lugged her suitcase across to the vehicle and resolutely ignored her racing heart. He did not come forward to assist her, but abruptly took it from her as she came up to him and stowed it in the back of the Range Rover.

'Morning,' he grunted unsmiling, and glanced at his watch as though she was late.

He gave her an all-encompassing look that didn't miss a detail of her attire, from her sandalled feet, her green shorts and green and white striped top on up to her swept-back hair, which she had hurriedly plaited and neatly coiled at the back of her head. Her drawn-back hair emphasised the delicate bones of her face and gave her a somewhat gamin air. He seemed in no hurry to shift his attention.

'All ready?' she asked, quailing a little at his off-putting tone and dissecting look. Suddenly she felt antagonism surfacing as it had in the roadside restaurant when she had first encountered him, and yet at the same time she was uncomfortably aware of him as a man, and the regrettably uncontrollable effect he was having on her senses.

'And waiting,' he said shortly.

'It's only just six-thirty,' she protested, glancing at her watch and meeting his gaze with a smile.

'Get in,' came the clipped reply. 'No point in hanging about here.' As she walked around to the passenger side, he added, 'I presume you paid your bill last night?'

'Before we went to the party,' she told him. 'I didn't think there would be anyone around at this hour of the morning.'

He gave her no credit for this forethought, but slid behind the steering-wheel and started the engine. Nerys heaved a small sigh. He was definitely still in a churlish mood this morning. Secretly she had hoped he might have reverted to his more companionable self of the early part of yesterday, but it seemed she was to be disappointed. It was going to be a tedious couple of hours or so, sitting beside him.

All at once it occurred to her that perhaps he thought she was still mad at him because he had kissed her. She therefore decided to dispel any notion he might have that she was either angry with him, or wary of him.

'I enjoyed the party,' she offered brightly as they swung out of the motel entrance and headed away from town. 'They were all very friendly people.' She had said it before, last night, but it was the only way she could think of now to start the conversation.

'Especially Sinclair Wilson?' he murmured, his lips barely moving.

'Oh, him!' Nerys said dismissively, with a laugh. 'He's quite a character, isn't he? People like him don't really expect to be taken seriously, I'm sure.' She added slyly, taking the opportunity offered, 'And nor do you, I imagine. You don't have to feel foolish about kissing me, you know. I realise it was just a silly impulse and I won't hold it against you.'

'I don't feel foolish,' came the grunted reply.

'Well, that's all right then,' Nerys said lightly, but she still felt that it wasn't. She sensed an underlying hostility towards her, but there didn't seem to be any reason for it. She had only met the man the day before yesterday, after all.

Although it was early there was considerable glare from the sun, so Nerys put on her sunglasses, commenting on the need for them casually. But there was no rejoinder from the man alongside.

As the minutes ticked by and Hallam still offered no conversation, she began to feel edgy. She found herself thinking about last night again, and those moments on the patio when he had held her in his arms and kissed her. In spite of her efforts to view it otherwise, the memory was deliciously sensuous.

Habitation was soon left far behind and on either side of the road stretched a limitless plain of red rock and dust, patchily carpeted in grasses and dotted with grey-green gums. Here and there was a tree that was a brighter green than the rest. After a while Nerys remarked on them.

Hallam said briefly, 'They're kurrajongs,' which left her very little the wiser.

They had long since left the bitumen road and were travelling along a graded dirt road. Red dust swirled up behind them and stones rattled against the mesh guard in front of the windscreen. Nerys could smell the dust in her nose and taste it in her mouth, and when she touched her cheek her finger was stained with it.

The scenery offered little variation. Nerys had heard Australia called a timeless land, and as they sped along the rough, pot-holed road, she felt it to be true. There was a primaeval stillness about the landscape, as though nothing had occurred to change it in millions of years. Here and there were rocky outcrops, sometimes as big as small hills, sometimes a mere scattering of large stones, looking as though they had been tipped there at random by some mad rockery planner who had never come back to finish the job. Occasionally a smudge of reddish-purple hills appeared on the horizon, and once they crossed a dry creek bed, with only the ragged lines of trees to show where the water sometimes ran.

The all-pervading colour was red, with rusts, ochres, browns and derivative shades all merging to a hot, ruddy vista that both repelled and hypnotically attracted. It came as a surprise in this barren, uninhabited landscape that seemed to go on forever, suddenly to see, looming out of the distance, a train. Nerys had forgotten the iron ore trains.

'There's a train!' She exclaimed involuntarily, as sunlight flashed off the metal of the locomotive and she realised what it was. The moment after she felt foolish.

'It's the iron ore train from Kolbardi,' Hallam said, and with unexpected loquaciousness, added, 'One hundred trucks of iron ore heading for the crushers and bulk carriers.' He glanced at her briefly, and she looked eagerly for a softening of his features but did not find it. He added teasingly, no doubt because of what she had said yesterday,

'More power-stations, knives and forks and saucepans!'

'And trolleys, and beds, and theatre equipment,' she said.

The seemingly interminable train eventually passed them, and for a while longer they could see the track glinting in the sunlight, snaking through the scrub not far from the road. Then the road turned and they lost sight of the railway. Because Hallam had opened up a little about the train, Nerys ventured to start another conversation—but was soon silenced by his monosyllabic replies. Looking askance at his profile she could not decide whether his taciturnity was simply indifference to her, or some kind of deep preoccupation. His brow seemed to be permanently creased this morning, but that could have been due to the glare.

Ahead, along a stretch of straight red road, a mirage quivered and danced as the sun rose higher, looking very inviting with its illusion of water rimmed by trees. From time to time a few sheep fled from the roadside, but that was the only sign of life apart from crows. Nerys remarked once that she had not even seen a kangaroo.

'You'd have more chance of seeing them at dawn,' Hallam said, 'or dusk.'

They did not pass another vehicle, and Nerys reflected soberly that it was lucky the Mini's shortcomings had been discovered. If she had broken down on this rough road she could have been waiting for help for hours, days even. It could be very frightening to be stranded in this wild country, in intense heat.

She stared ahead through the windscreen and out of the side-window, and gradually became hypnotised by the scenery flashing past. She was not aware when she dropped off to sleep, only that when she awoke she found her head resting comfortably against Hallam's shoulder. Instantly she sat bolt upright as though jerked away by an electric shock.

'Sorry, I must have dropped off,' she apologised.

'Half an hour ago,' he told her drily, and there seemed to be suppressed amusement in his brief glance. He knew she felt embarrassed.

'Oh, did I? I'm sorry—it must have been uncomfortable for you.'

There was no reply.

'We must be nearly there,' Nerys said, looking at her watch.

'See that range of hills up ahead?' Hallam said. 'That's where we're heading. There's a whole mountain of iron in those hills and they've only whittled away a fraction of it so far.'

Nerys viewed the approaching range with a feeling of excited antipication. In a very short time now, she realised, she would be seeing Daniel again. A few minutes later they entered the town of Kolbardi. It came into view quite dramatically. The Range Rover rounded a bend in the road and there it was, a splash of green on the edge of the rich red foothills of the iron range.

'So this is Kolbardi,' she murmured, as Hallam drove slowly along a wide, tree-lined street. 'It's bigger than I expected.'

'We're the second largest and fastest growing iron town in the Pilbara,' said Hallam, waving to a passing motorist.

The houses on either side were set well back behind leafy screens and patches of lawn. Sprinklers turned lazily on some of them.

'It must take a great deal of water to keep gardens going in this arid country,' Nerys remarked.

'There are several artesian bores that provide the town with water,' Hallam told her. 'We have an adequate supply, but nobody wastes water here.'

A couple more turns and they were in another leafy street, at the end of which Nerys glimpsed a long, low, white-painted building that she rightly guessed was the hospital. It was set well back and shaded by eucalypts and casuarinas, and there were splashes of colour from bougainvillaea and hibiscus amid the verdant greens of other tropical plants. Hallam pulled into a parking area in front of a sign with his name on it. Not far away was another sign with a pointing arrow, indicating the reception area.

Hallam was pointing in the opposite direction. 'That's

where you'll be staying,' he was saying, as he indicated a small bungalow nestling amid the trees to one side of the hospital.

'Where do you live?' Nerys asked.

He looked at her in mild surprise. 'I live there, too. Dan and I share the house. But don't worry, there's plenty of room for you.'

Nerys knew that her face must be a picture of dismay, and she felt that the fact gave him a certain malicious satisfaction.

He added rather caustically, 'I don't suppose you'll be staying all that long, will you?'

She gave him a cool look. 'I have no idea. That will depend on Dan.' It occurred to her that as the senior doctor he doubtless had a right to a say in the matter, too. He did not suggest as much, however.

'I expect you'll find Kolbardi rather boring.' Hallam sounded as though he hoped she would.

She met his gaze with challenge. 'I'm not easily bored!'

'I wouldn't count on Sinclair Wilson to liven things up,' he said laconically. 'He's just as likely to forget his invitation.'

'I never count on anything,' she returned icily. 'Or anyone.'

He opened his door, saying, 'I'll take you over to the house, and if Dan isn't there I'll ferret him out and send him over. He's probably up at the hospital.' He glanced at his watch. 'Or taking surgery.'

Nerys glanced across at the hospital building, glimpsed the figure of a nurse behind one of the windows and wished Daniel would magically appear. She'd had enough of the surly Dr Vale's company for one morning.

But he was already lifting her suitcase and his own large grip out of the Range Rover and striding towards the bungalow, leaving her to follow with the rest of her luggage, dodging the sprinklers which were watering the lawns fronting it.

The house was neat and unpretentious, with a veranda on three sides, and as they walked up the front steps Nerys heard the faint whirr of an air-conditioner.

Hallam dropped his own luggage and held the door open for her. An act of chivalry she had not expected.

'Go through,' he ordered peremptorily. 'Your room will be the one next to the kitchen.'

Nerys, feeling a bit like a just-hired maid, obeyed. The hall was bare and the room that looked like a living-room was sparsely furnished but comfortable-looking. Two closed doors on either side of the short passageway would, she guessed, be Dan's and Hallam's rooms. Seeing the door he had indicated, she pushed it open and went in.

'Oh, this is nice!' she exclaimed in pleased surprise on seeing the cool green bedspread and matching curtains that let in a soft, filtered light and seemed to bring the greenery of the garden right into the room.

'Jean's work,' said Hallam briefly, looking around with an air that verged on disapproval. He glanced at Nerys, one of those annihilating looks that made her tremble.

'Jean?' she queried, dropping her holdall on the floor and tossing her handbag into the cane armchair near the bed.

'Jean Grace. Mrs Grace is our treasure,' Hallam explained. 'She comes in daily to clean up after us and she cooks our evening meal. We manage to scrape together our own lunch and breakfast.'

'She must be a treasure indeed,' remarked Nerys.

'I'll leave you to it,' Hallam said gruffly. 'The bathroom is just opposite.'

He was exerting the bare minimum of polite helpfulness, Nerys felt. If only he sounded more friendly. She was beginning to feel quite apprehensive, almost wishing she hadn't come. Perhaps Dan didn't really want her here either. She would be an unwelcome intruder in their bachelor establishment. Well, if that was so, she certainly wouldn't stay more than a couple of days.

When Hallam had gone, Nerys quickly unlocked her suitcase and shook out a fresh cotton dress to change into. Then, taking the big green bath-towel that was folded over the end of the bed, she went across to the bathroom to enjoy the shower she had missed that morning. It was bliss and she lingered longer than she should have.

As she came out, she heard voices in the passageway near

the front door. One of them was Daniel's. So delighted was she that she paused, eager to see him at last. It had been nearly two years since they had last met. She forgot for a moment that she had not stopped to unpack her dressing-gown and was garbed only in the bath-towel she had wrapped around her.

'Nerys!'

Daniel, bright and breezy as he always was, suntanned as she had never seen him before, and grinning all over his face, strode down the passage and swept her into his arms, lifting her off her feet in a big, brotherly hug as he planted an affectionate kiss on her forehead.

'Daniel! You twit!' Nerys was laughing happily as he set her down again. Everything was all right now.

But unfortunately not quite everything. Suddenly the corner she had tucked in to hold the towel in place around her came adrift and it slipped to the floor, leaving her standing for all the world like a statue unveiled. Scarlet with embarrassment, she hastily picked up the towel and wrapped it around her again. Daniel was, of course, laughing uproariously.

'Hey, no need to blush!' he teased. 'We're both doctors! We see plenty of nubile young women, you know!'

But Nerys had caught Hallam's eye, and the sardonic expression on his face made her flesh tingle. Maybe they did see plenty of naked female bodies in the course of duty, but that was different. There was a certain clinical detachment when people were ill. When Hallam had looked briefly at her unclad body just then, it had been with the eyes of a man, not a doctor.

'I'd better get dressed,' Nerys said, her voice quavering as she tried to laugh.

Daniel teased. 'Why? You look splendid as you are—doesn't she, Hallam?'

His colleague did not reply and Daniel, still shaking with suppressed laughter conceded. 'All right, come into the kitchen when you're ready.' He eyed her questioningly. 'What do you drink? Tea, coffee or beer? It's a bit early for the hard stuff.'

'Whatever you're having,' Nerys said. 'I don't mind.'

She fled from the scrutinising green gaze of Dr Vale, cursing her brother's ebullience and her own stupidity. She wished she had not bothered to have the shower until later. Now, every time he looks at me, she thought with a skin-tingling sensation, I shall be sure he's seeing me as he did a moment ago.

Back in her room she took a firm hold of herself. Don't be silly, she reprimanded her rather distraught reflection. For heaven's sake, what does it matter? He's not going to rape me just because he saw me with no clothes on! He wouldn't dare try anyway, not with Dan around to protect me. She managed finally to laugh at herself, but it was nevertheless slightly nervous laughter. I wish I'd been born more brazen, she thought, pulling on the lemon yellow sundress she had dragged from her suitcase before going to shower. And I wish I didn't blush so easily.

Taking a deep breath, she finally emerged and walked boldly into the kitchen. Daniel and Hallam were sitting at the table, talking and drinking coffee. Daniel broke off what he was saying and spoke to her.

'Ah, Nerys, pull up a chair. We made coffee, OK? Hallam says you didn't have breakfast, so if you'd like some toast?'

Nerys was not hungry. 'No, thanks. Coffee is all I need.' Her eye caught Hallam's and there was a gleam of sardonic amusement in the flecked green irises.

'Didn't you have time for a shower this morning?' he enquired idly.

'No, as a matter of fact I didn't,' she answered, realising now that her impulse to do so on arrival had given her away. 'I'm afraid I forgot to set my alarm and I overslept.' She tilted her chin defiantly. 'I didn't want to keep you waiting!'

'I would have waited for you,' he said mildly, and with an infuriatingly bland expression that made Nerys seethe. He switched his attention back to Daniel. 'I'll take over for the rest of the day, Dan.' He rose, pushing his chair back, leaning his hands on the back of it as he contemplated them both.

Daniel protested. 'You're officially still on leave.'

Hallam shrugged. 'It doesn't matter. I'm back and I've

nothing special to do. I'll call you if you're needed. You entertain your sister.'

Daniel grinned. 'Wouldn't you rather do that for me?' He added to Nerys, 'All the nurses fall head over heels in love with Hallam.'

'How very flattering,' murmured Nerys rather dryly, and met Hallam's gaze with a look that she hoped would convey to him that the generalisation certainly wouldn't include her.

'Dan exaggerates,' Dr Vale replied shortly and, with a blunt farewell, left them.

Daniel watched him go thoughtfully, then said, 'He's a bit moody this morning. What did you do to him?'

'Nothing!'

Daniel's eyes were teasing again. 'Nerys, I wish you could have seen your face when the towel fell off! It was scarlet!'

'I didn't think it was very funny,' she said, a bit ruffled.

'Hallam loved it, I'm sure,' her brother replied. He regarded her narrowly. 'You don't like him much, do you?' He sounded disappointed.

'I don't think he likes me,' she stated.

Daniel stroked his chin. 'Strange. Hallam's quite a wow with the ladies as a rule.'

'Well, maybe he just doesn't take to me.' Nerys lifted her shoulders indifferently. 'It doesn't matter.'

'It will if you go falling in love with him,' said Daniel forthrightly. 'I don't want a case of unrequited love on my hands.'

'Oh, come off it, Daniel,' Nerys said rudely. 'What makes you think I go round falling for every handsome male I trip over?'

He grinned affectionately. 'No, I guess I know you better than that. It was just—just that, well, I was sort of hoping you and Hallam would hit it off.' He gave her a searching look as though he thought she might be deceiving him.

'Now, wait a minute!' broke in Nerys, alarmed. 'If you've some crazy notion of match-making . . .'

Daniel chuckled. 'Not a bit. I prefer to let nature take its course. If the chemistry doesn't work, that's all there is to it.

I confess, however, I had hoped you might provide distraction from Barbra . . .'

'Barbra Albrecht?' Nerys said quickly.

Daniel's eyebrows rose. 'You've met her?'

'Hallam took me to a party at the Albrechts' place last night.'

Daniel's interest flared. 'Indeed! He does seem to have taken you under his wing yesterday. What went wrong?'

'Nothing. He was just being hospitable because I'm your sister. He doesn't have to like me to be that.'

Daniel shrugged, obviously puzzled. 'Well, I'm not going to pry if there's something you'd rather not tell me. You noticed, I'm sure, that Barbra fancies Hallam?'

'It did look a bit that way,' Nerys said cautiously. 'But she's married.'

'Exactly!' Daniel's eyes flashed angrily. 'Hallam is a fool, and so too, if you ask me, is Klaus. He's a great guy, Klaus, but too wrapped up in his work to see what's going on under his nose.' He sighed. 'I like Hallam tremendously, Nerys, and I admire him as a doctor. But I also like Klaus and Barbra, although I think she's a bit of an idiot to carry on the way she does. I don't want to see their marriage crumbling. Maybe it's nothing serious, just a flirtation. I hope so.'

'There's really nothing you can do,' Nerys said, and on a warning note, 'You can't interfere . . .'

'I don't intend to. I wouldn't even mention the subject to Hallam.' He sighed deeply again. 'The trouble is, towns like this aren't very good for marriages. The living is a bit artificial, the locale is remote, the life isolated, despite all the amenities. The climate doesn't suit everyone. Some wives can't stand it and go back to Melbourne or Perth or wherever they come from. Some adapt and love it. It takes a certain kind of person to live up here.' He emptied the dregs of the coffee-pot into his cup. 'But enough of that. What about you, love? You haven't really told me why you're here.'

'To see you, of course, brother, dear!' Nerys replied, smilingly, but unable to keep the evasiveness out of her voice.

'I know I'm irresistible, even to my doting sister,' joked Daniel, 'but there's more to it than that. I know you. We're twins, after all. Something went wrong, didn't it?'

Nerys hung her head, her heart racing. She wanted to tell him everything, but the words wouldn't come. She knew he would understand, but still she couldn't tell him.

'No, not really,' she lied. 'I just got fed up with the daily routine and decided it wasn't fair you having all the adventure. We're both cast in the same mould, after all.'

He shook his head. 'I don't think we are. Not quite. We're not identical twins. I'm the foot-loose and fancy-free type, but you're one to put down roots. As a matter of fact, I'm amazed you're not married to some nice dedicated GP in the country somewhere.'

Nerys laughed. 'Just find me one!'

His gaze was accusing. 'You are running away from something, sister, but if you don't want to tell me about it, I won't probe. Never did a wound any good to muck about with it. But let me guess—broken heart?' He smiled understandingly as Nerys non-committally shrugged. He reached across the table and gave her arm a reassuring pat.

She said at last, 'If you must know, there *was* someone, but it just didn't work out. I felt I had to get away for a bit.'

'Was he married?'

Nerys was startled at his perception. 'Yes,' she admitted in a low voice.

'And you didn't find out until it was too late, and you were already in love with him,' said Daniel. He thumped the table. 'There are some bastards around!' He looked steadily at her. 'No, I'm not asking for details. But any time you want to talk about it, I'm here.'

'Thanks,' Nerys answered, feeling suddenly emotional. 'I'm glad I came, Daniel. I was afraid you might think me rather stupid and a couple of times I've wished I hadn't been so impulsive. Are you sure you don't mind my being here?'

'I'm delighted,' he assured her. 'You can stay as long as you like—or feel you need to.'

'But what about Hallam?' she pressed hesitantly. 'I don't think he's going to like it if I'm around for too long.'

Daniel was firm. 'Don't mind Hallam. He'll change his tune. I don't believe he really dislikes you. He's just a bit cranky over something at the moment.'

Nerys hoped he was right. 'Can I see over the hospital some time?' she said.

'Sure. Any time you like. We could stroll over after lunch, perhaps. That's the best time. There's not a lot to see, really. We're quite a small outfit, but very well equipped. We mostly only handle routine cases. Anything a bit complicated is flown to Hedland or Perth. Most of our cases are minor accidents at the mine, kids with broken arms, burns, confinements and epidemics of flu or enteritis. Some galah shot himself in the foot last week out kangaroo-shooting, and we've got an alcoholic in at the moment, drying out. He's a regular!'

They chatted on about what they had both been doing since they had last met, and Nerys gradually felt herself relaxing. Daniel was a tonic. Somehow, without even trying, her brother always managed to help her see everything in its proper perspective. If only Hallam Vale didn't live in the same house, she reflected ruefully, her stay with Daniel could be a very pleasant one.

Eventually, he said, 'We'd better rustle up some lunch. Hallam will be over shortly, I expect.'

Nerys glanced at her watch. The time had flown while they were talking. 'I'll get it,' she offered. 'Just tell me where everything is.'

Daniel grinned. 'I must say it'll be handy having a woman about the place all the time. We don't like to impose on Jean's good nature too much. I suppose you wouldn't mind sewing on a few buttons, doing a spot of ironing and knocking up a meal for a couple of helpless bachelors on Jean's day off, would you?' He grinned. 'Your cooking's better than the hospital's!'

Nerys said teasingly, 'That's quite a list! As a liberated woman I ought to object, but I won't. I shall feel less guilty about imposing if I earn my keep.' She stood up. 'Right, now where is everything?'

Daniel gave her directions and assisted in the preparation of the simple salad. The table was set and the food ready

when Hallam reappeared. He registered no particular reaction when told that Nerys had prepared the lunch, and
throughout the meal he practically ignored her, spending
most of the time discussing a case with Daniel.

'Well,' said Daniel at last, 'there seems to be only
one solution. Send the woman to Perth for more tests.
That'll show whether her symptoms are psychosomatic or
not.'

'That's the whole point,' said Hallam. 'Her husband
won't let her go. He says he can't afford to have her
joy-riding up and down to Perth unless there's something
really wrong with her.'

Daniel nodded. 'It's what subconsciously she probably
wants to do—get away from Kolbardi for a bit. Can't we tell
him it's her nerves and she needs a spell down south?'

Hallam's lips were pursed. 'I tried that and he laughed in
my face. He said her nerves were perfectly all right.' He
spread his hands helplessly. 'Unless she has a breakdown,
we can't force him to let her go.'

Nerys was listening to their discussion with only half an
ear. Her mind was drifting, as usual, on to dangerous
ground—back to Chris and the happiness that had turned to
misery. She should have been wiser, of course. She should
never have let him charm her. Her only excuse was that
he had charmed everyone the minute he set foot in St
Margaret's.

He was tall, good-looking, very dashing, and he'd been
abroad for several years, working in America. She had
fallen in love with him too easily, letting her heart rule her
head, flattered that he had chosen her from amongst all the
other nurses. She had paid for her simple trust, her head-
strong emotions. He had simply announced one day that his
wife would shortly be joining him. She had stayed behind to
settle their affairs in the States, and to allow their two
children to finish their terms at school.

He had said, quite matter-of-factly, that it would be
better if they didn't see each other any more outside the
hospital. She had been totally stunned. The realisation that
she had merely been a stop-gap came as a cruel blow, but
his lack of feeling, the fact that it had never occurred to him

that she might have fallen in love with him, was even more shattering. She felt cheated and betrayed, and worst of all humiliated.

So, that day in the operating-theatre when his eyes had met hers, cold, unfeeling, unaware, her nerve had snapped and she had run from the room in a blind panic. The intensity of her feelings in that terrible moment washed over her now, as though it was happening all over again, and the wave of emotion forced her back to reality.

Daniel and Hallam were still discussing the same patient, but they seemed not to have reached any definite decision regarding her. Preoccupied, they had not noticed Nerys's reverie. Feeling drained, she quietly began to collect the plates and carry them to the sink, at the same time returning the uneaten food to the refrigerator.

Daniel suddenly said, 'Nerys is quite domesticated, thank goodness. We had a flat together in London once when I was at medical school, and all the fellows used to clamour to be asked home to tea.'

Hallam's eyebrows twitched and a glimmer of a smile hovered on his lips. He was almost amiable when he said, 'Was it just the cooking they fancied?'

Nerys blushed. And Daniel said, 'Well, what do you think? She's not bad to look at, is she?'

'Daniel, you're putting poor Hallam on the spot and embarrassing me,' protested Nerys. She was a little exasperated with her brother. Did he have to make it quite so obvious that he was trying to throw them together?

Hallam rose. His smile was slightly crooked as he said, 'There were quite a few people at the Albrechts' last night, Dan, who would certainly agree with you.'

He excused himself and strode out of the kitchen. Nerys felt a sense of relief when he had gone. She turned on Daniel. 'You're a beast, Daniel. You don't have to be so obvious.' He just laughed and picked up a tea-towel.

When they had finished the washing-up Daniel took Nerys on a short tour of the house and garden, and afterwards they strolled across the intervening lawns to the hospital. In the heat of the afternoon there was a drowsiness over the whole town, and scarcely a breath of air stirred even the thin needles of the pine-like casuarinas which mingled with the eucalypts. The hospital was very quiet except for the whirring of the air-conditioning and the occasional footstep on vinyl-tiled floors.

After some of the older city hospitals she had nursed in, Nerys felt vividly the contrast of lightness and airiness in this small, single-storey hospital where everything was sparklingly modern and new. If there was an indefinable air of temporariness about it, it was offset by the fact that it was easy to see that medical care here was every bit as conscientious and thorough as in any city hospital. Daniel explained that the mining company spared no expense in providing comforts and facilities for its employees, and that included up to date medical care.

Daniel escorted her through the two main wards and proudly introduced her to those patients who were awake. Nerys lingered a little longer to talk to the several children who were in hospital for various reasons, and she got caught up in quite a long conversation with an elderly man who was recuperating after a slight heart attack. He was a widower who had come up to live with his daughter and her family. His son-in-law was a mining engineer and in the space of a few minutes he had told her his life history. Daniel left them together, inviting Nerys to come along to the office when she was ready.

Presently she left the patient and made her way to the office, directed by one of the nurses she had previously been introduced to. She had seen no sign of Hallam and deduced, rightly, that this was where she would find him. He was standing with his back to the window when she entered. Daniel was swivelling back and forth in the chair near the white metal desk. As she pushed open the door after giving a preliminary warning knock, Hallam shifted his gaze to her.

Nerys was struck by how different he looked in a white coat. The whiteness of the material emphasised the ruggedly chiselled features, and she knew by the way her blood was suddenly pounding in her veins that whatever she might wish to the contrary, she could not help finding him attractive. He had the kind of magnetism it was necessary to fight, and she must make sure that her defences were impregnable at all times.

'Come in, Nerys,' he said, in a tone that was pleasant but reserved. 'I hope you've enjoyed your tour of the hospital.'

'Yes, I have, thank you. It's all vastly different to what I've been used to, of course, and yet very familiar in a strange way.' She smiled engagingly, hoping to see a further softening of the granite face, but there was no change in his features.

In any case, both their attentions were suddenly diverted by Daniel thumping the desk and saying triumphantly, 'Why didn't I think of it at once?'

'Think of what?' queried Hallam.

'Nerys! She'll fill in for Sister Wimbourne.'

A startled expression came into Dr Vale's face as he darted a swift glance at Nerys, who was equally startled.

'Daniel, what are you talking about?' she demanded.

'Sit down,' he invited, indicating the other chair near the desk. He went on immediately. 'We're in a bit of a fix. Sister Wimbourne has just had a phone call from Perth to say her mother's been taken ill. Hallam's arranged for her to go down on the next plane—fortunately there's a company plane going direct from here in the morning—and we were just discussing whether we ought to try and arrange for a relief sister to come back on it. But it's short notice, and until Janet sees her mother we won't know how long it will be for.' He paused and smiled confidently at his sister. 'What do you say, Nerys? How would you like to run Kolbardi Hospital for a bit?'

Nerys was completely thrown. It was the last thing she had expected to happen. She looked at Hallam. She felt Daniel was being rather presumptuous asking her, when Hallam was in charge. And, she thought a trifle wryly, she suspected *he* ran the hospital, not Charge Sister Wimbourne.

She said hesitantly, 'I don't know, maybe Hallam doesn't . . .'

Daniel interrupted, speaking directly to his senior. 'My sister is a thoroughly competent, triple certificated nursing sister. She has nursed in several major hospitals in England. I will stake my reputation on her competence.'

'Daniel!' Nerys protested, colouring.

Hallam's eyes were stony. He didn't want her to work at the hospital, she was sure of it. He was desperately looking for a valid reason why she should not. She wished Daniel wasn't so thick he couldn't see it. Hallam did not like her, and Daniel had put him on the spot. It was up to her, she realised, to refuse point-blank and rescue him from his dilemma.

Before she opened her mouth, however, Hallam spoke. 'I'm sure Nerys's experience and qualifications would be more than adequate for the situation, but she is on holiday, after all, and since we don't know yet how long Janet will be away, it would hardly be fair to impose . . .'

Daniel interrupted again. 'I dare say we'll know in a day or two what the prognosis is on Janet's mother, and as Nerys is a free agent I'm sure she won't mind staying on an *ad hoc* basis, will you, Neri?'

Nerys swallowed. Daniel was quite determined. 'Well,' she said, and hesitated. She knew Hallam didn't want her. But she had hoped to stay in Kolbardi for a while with Daniel until she sorted herself out. Hallam's living with her brother had made that awkward. She knew that after a few days she would feel she ought not to continue imposing. However, if she was doing the hospital a favour she would feel justified in staying. Also, strangely enough, the idea of nursing in this somewhat unusual situation had real appeal. It would be different, a new experience.

'There you are, I knew she'd agree,' Daniel said.

Nerys laughingly protested, 'I didn't! But if you'll let me get a word in, yes, I'd be happy to fill the breach.' She glanced across at Hallam, and went on, 'If it doesn't cause any sort of administrative problems, or cut across the usual procedures and, of course, if Hallam's agreeable.' She shot her brother a reproachful look. 'After all, Daniel, I presume he does have the last word around here.'

Daniel did not give Hallam a chance to speak. 'Exactly!' he said with some satisfaction. 'What he says goes.' He looked at his superior. 'I'd appreciate having my sister stick around for more than just a few days,' he said, with a twinkle in his eyes for Nerys. 'We haven't seen much of each other lately. But I know she feels she's imposing and will be scooting off again on the next bus unless she has a good reason for staying.' He added craftily, 'And she'll be very useful for all kinds of domestic chores we don't dare ask Jean to do!'

Hallam's eyes shifted to Nerys, their greenness very penetrating, and shadowed, she thought, with doubt. He didn't want her to stay, but Daniel was twisting his arm.

'Very well,' he said at last, 'if you're quite sure you want to, I'll put you on roster as from tomorrow.' There was a slight pause, and then he added, not without some effort, she felt sure, 'Thank you for being willing to step into the breach at such short notice. Hopefully, Sister Wimbourne will not be away for long.'

Daniel rose. 'Well, that's settled that problem. I suppose you'd like to go back and unpack now, Neri?'

Nerys nodded, and they left together. Daniel said he had to go to the bank and do one or two other things, so he left her at the bungalow. It did not take her long to hang up her clothes and stow the rest of her belongings in a chest of drawers. She was just thinking about making a cup of tea, expecting that Daniel would probably return shortly, when there was a rattle at the front screen door.

'Nerys! Can I come in?' a female voice called out.

Surprised that anyone knew her name, Nerys hurried down the hall, calling, 'Yes, come in!'

A tall, red-haired girl in nurse's uniform entered. She smiled a greeting and held out her hand to Nerys, who saw behind the polite demeanour that the girl was anxious about something.

The anxiety was explained when she said, 'I'm Janet Wimbourne. Hallam told me I'd find you here.' Her accent was unmistakeably Scottish. 'It's marvellous of you to step in at such short notice. I was feeling really bad about having to go off in a rush, especially as we've practically a full house at the moment and everyone is pretty busy. It was a bit of luck your being here at precisely the right moment. A godsend, you might say.'

'I'm so sorry about your mother, Janet, and I'm glad you came over. There's quite a lot I'd like to ask you. I was just going to make a cup of tea. Would you like one?' Nerys invited her in.

'I never say no to a cuppa,' declared Janet.

They were still sitting at the kitchen table discussing the running of the hospital when Jean Grace arrived to prepare the evening meal. She, too, spoke with an English accent, and revealed that she had emigrated from Devon over twenty-five years before.

'But I've never lost my accent,' she admitted with a laugh.

'Just about everyone I meet seems to be a Brit. It looks as though we're taking over the country!' Nerys said.

The other two laughed. 'Not quite!' said Jean. 'But sometimes I do think we are the new pioneers! So many of us seem to come to these out of the way places. I suppose it's all a bit of an adventure.'

Janet added, 'We've got two English girls on the nursing staff, a girl from Wales who manages the catering and three on the cleaning staff who all hail from the UK. Oh, and one of the nurses is a New Zealander. I tend to forget Cathy comes from there because her accent is so similar to Australian.'

They chatted in a friendly way for some time while Jean began preparations for the evening meal, and then Janet said she must dash as she had to pack and be ready for an early start in the morning.

'I'm afraid it'll be early for you too,' she told Nerys apologetically. 'You're on at seven.'

'I'm used to it,' said Nerys.

When Janet had gone Nerys stayed in the kitchen helping Jean, who was eager to tell her more about Kolbardi, the mining people, and her own experiences. Nerys was just setting the table when there was a second caller. Another female voice called out, 'Anyone home?' and the front screen door banged.

'In the kitchen, Gayle,' Jean, who evidently recognised the voice, called out.

Nerys glanced up as a small, dark-haired girl appeared in

the doorway. Her deep blue eyes alighted on Nerys with interest.

'Hello, you must be Dan's sister. You're not much alike, are you?'

'We're twins,' said Nerys, 'but not identical.'

'I'm Gayle Desmond,' the newcomer introduced herself. 'Hi, Jean, how's things?' She dumped a pile of paperbacks on the table. 'A few more for the hospital library.'

'Gayle works in the mine office. She's a book-keeper. All the men love her because she doles out the wages,' Jean said.

Gayle laughed lightly. 'Not when I short-change them!' She returned her attention to Nerys. 'Are you staying long, Nerys?'

Nerys explained the situation and Gayle's eyes widened. 'Well, that's a bit of luck, I must say. Not for poor Janet, though. I bet she's worried sick. It must be serious if she's flying down in such a rush.' She added, 'Do you know what's wrong with Jan's mother?'

'Heart, I think.'

Gayle nodded sympathetically. 'Hmm. It could mean she'll be away for some time. She might even have to get a job back down there. Jan won't like that. She loves it up here. I bet her boyfriend isn't too happy, either.' She smiled at Nerys. 'So we could have you with us for quite a time, unless you get sick of the outback, of course. I suppose Dan's keen to keep you around for a bit. It's nice to have someone from one's family around sometimes.' She sounded a bit wistful and Nerys guessed that perhaps she did not have any family of her own—but it was not really the moment to ask such a personal question.

Gayle picked up the books. 'Well, I'll just drop these in at the hospital.'

'I could do that tomorrow if you're in a hurry,' Nerys offered.

'Oh, no, I'll do it,' said Gayle quickly. 'It's no trouble.'

When she had breezed out, Jean said, 'Nice girl. She'll make someone a good wife.'

'Dan?' suggested Nerys, detecting a certain tone of voice that made her suspect that was what Jean meant.

Jean laughed a little ruefully. 'Unfortunately, at the moment she seems more struck on Hallam. It won't come to anything, of course. It never does with him. He's a real loner. Oh, he takes women out from time to time, but never seriously. I often wonder if something embittered him way back. He'd never tell you, though.'

'Perhaps he just prefers independence,' said Nerys.

'Maybe. He's a close one, anyway, and that seems to intrigue most women. He offers a challenge, I suppose. What do you think of him, Nerys?' Her eyes sparkled with humour.

'I don't know him very well yet,' said Nerys cautiously. 'He's been very considerate, but in a rather off-hand way. To be quite frank, I don't think he's all that keen on me staying here.'

Jean looked around in surprise. 'Really? He seemed very amenable to the idea when Dan said you wanted to come. Told him you could stay as long as you liked.'

'That was before he met me,' said Nerys dryly. 'I think I must have rubbed him up the wrong way somehow.' She hadn't meant to confess that to Jean, but it had slipped out.

'I'm sure you'd never do that,' said Jean. 'You seem a very easy-going sort of girl to me. Maybe he's just got something on his mind. I'm sure you'll all get along fine. They're a great couple of lads, those two—well, Hallam's not exactly a lad, he must be thirty or so— and both fine doctors, too. We're lucky to have them at Kolbardi.' She frowned and gave a little shrug. 'Sometimes I think they're both rather wasted here, to be quite frank.'

'I don't think Daniel will stay much longer,' said Nerys. 'He usually gets itchy feet after a bit, and he's been here longer than anywhere. I don't know about Hallam, of course.'

'He's been here around five years. I've never heard him say a word about wanting to go anywhere else and when I asked him once if he wouldn't rather work in the city, he just said a flat no.' She opened the oven door and looked in. 'There, that's OK. Just let it simmer for another half-hour or so and it'll be ready.' She glanced at Nerys and smiled. 'Doubtless you'll get the job of serving up!'

Nerys laughed. 'Yes, I expect they'll want me to play mother! That's men for you!'

CHAPTER SIX

NERYS MADE doubly sure she did not forget to set her alarm clock for the next morning. She moved quietly about the house so as not to disturb the two men, whom she deduced were still sleeping since their doors were closed and there were no dirty dishes in the sink. She fixed herself a light breakfast, washed her coffee-mug and plate and then strolled across to the hospital.

The gardens were cool and quiet in the early morning, but where the sun slanted through, even at this hour its warmth was noticeable. Sprinklers were lazily turning on the lawns and Nerys had to detour slightly to avoid being soaked. There was no breeze to swirl the red dust around or even to stir the flamboyant bougainvillaea. The bright flowers and deep green foliage contrasted vividly with the white hospital walls and the deep blue sky. A couple of colourful parrots broke the silence as they fled screeching from a low bush at her approach.

One of the night nurses, Ann Martin, was going off duty when Nerys arrived. She greeted Nerys warmly and they spent a little time discussing the routine. After Ann had gone, Nerys visited the wards where breakfast was being served and chatted to some of the patients she had not met yesterday. Everyone was surprised and, it seemed, pleased, that Dr Kent's sister was going to be in charge until Sister Wimbourne got back.

The morning slipped by with a host of tasks presenting themselves, but it did not take long for Nerys to familiarise herself with her new situation, and as the day wore on she felt she was settling in quite well already.

She saw little of Hallam, but quite a lot of Dan, who was naturally eager to help her over the first day's obstacles. And Nerys was glad that it was her brother, not Hallam, who kept a watchful eye on her that first day. Hallam, Daniel told her, was taking surgery that morning, and there

85

was a mother and baby clinic in the afternoon.

It was almost time for Nerys to go off duty when a man appeared in the doorway of her office. Nerys glanced at him questioningly. 'Can I help you?'

He strode in, looking her over in a rather disconcertingly familiar way. He was a tall, well-built man, with a shock of tawny hair and very blue eyes. He was strikingly good-looking in an arrogant kind of way. He swaggered a little and eyed her with keen interest.

'Hello, you must be Dan's sister, Nerys. Janet was telling me about you on the way to Perth.'

'I'm sorry, I'm afraid I don't know who you are,' Nerys answered cautiously.

'Rod Troughton,' the man supplied. 'Had to take a quick trip to Perth to pick up some spare parts, and I brought back some stuff for the hospital. Hallam about?' His eyes flicked over her caressingly.

'I don't think so,' Nerys said. 'You could check his office if you like.'

'Doesn't matter, I'll dump the stuff here,' he replied, and went out. A few moments later he returned carrying a large cardboard box. He placed it on the floor near her desk, then straightened up and gave her his full attention.

'Makes a nice change to see a new face in town. Especially such a pretty one!'

His manner was disarming and Nerys relaxed her earlier reserve to smile at him. 'Thank you.'

'Ever worked in a mining town before?' he enquired.

'No, never. I only arrived from England a few days ago,' she explained.

'Yeah? Well, it'll be a bit of an experience for you, won't it?'

'Most certainly. One I hope to enjoy, as well as learn from.'

He grinned meaningfully. 'You'll learn all right. There's some tough characters around here. You want to look out.'

'Thanks for the warning, but I think I can take care of myself.'

He laughed softly. 'You look pretty vulnerable to me.'

He leaned forward and tilted her chin with a large, rough hand. 'Well, it's great to know you, Nerys. See you around, I expect.'

'Yes, of course,' Nerys faltered, a little unnerved by the unexpected contact.

She was even more unnerved when she realised that they were no longer alone. Out of the corner of her eye she saw Hallam Vale standing in the doorway looking at them, and there was an expression of distaste on his handsome face. He came abruptly into the room.

'G'day, Rod,' he greeted the man peremptorily.

Rod Troughton turned round. 'Oh, g'day, Hallam. Just dropped in that stuff you wanted picked up.'

Hallam's tone was dismissive as he said, 'Thanks, Rod.'

Rod Troughton winked at Nerys and laid a hand on her shoulder. 'See you, Nerys. Maybe I'll give you a call sometime?'

She did not know how to answer, or even whether she wanted him to. 'Oh, all right,' she faltered.

He was gone an instant later and, as the door swung shut behind him, Hallam glanced up from the box of supplies he had been staring at and said in a rather sarcastic tone, 'Looks like yours is going to be a busy line.'

His words did in fact prove to be true to some extent. Rod Troughton did phone her, and during the next week took her to see a film, to play tennis and out for a meal. He also invited her to the regular monthly dance at the community centre hall.

Daniel teased her about Rod in front of Hallam, and although Nerys tried not to be embarrassed, for some reason she was. Hallam did not comment at all, but there was a suggestion in the green depths of his searching gaze that he did not altogether approve of her choice of companion.

In between times Nerys had two phone calls from Sinclair Wilson, much to her surprise. Contrary to Hallam's expectation, he had not forgotten at all. The first time was just for a breezy chat, and the second time was to say he hoped to get over to Kolbardi to see her. Unfortunately he had to fly to Perth for a few days, but she wasn't to forget she had promised to visit Yeramba Springs and he would definitely arrange something when he got back.

Unfortunately, Hallam answered the telephone when Sinclair rang both times, and later he remarked a shade caustically, 'Looks like your social life is beginning to warm up in earnest.'

Why he should disapprove of her going out with Rod Troughton or being phoned up by Sinclair Wilson, Nerys could not fathom. It was not as though he wanted to take her out himself. Such a suggestion had never been made, not that she had expected it would be, even in the name of hospitality. Hallam had done his bit where she was concerned. She was just another nurse at the hospital now, and the fact that she was Daniel's sister gained her no special privileges there. At home he was mostly polite, but always withdrawn.

Hallam's attitude towards her puzzled her. Some days he was very austere, unfriendly almost. Other days he would seem to be unbending a little, and then he would clam up again. Never was there any sign of the other Hallam Vale she had glimpsed that day he had taken her sight-seeing in Port Hedland. It seemed as though that day had been an aberration, one that he did not intend to repeat. And yet, because she knew he could be so different, she could not help being intrigued by him.

Getting ready for the dance which Rod Troughton had invited her to, Nerys wondered if Hallam would be going. Daniel was, she knew, but Hallam had not mentioned it. She had been a little undecided what to wear and had finally chosen her one long dress, the same one she had worn to the Albrechts' party in Port Hedland. She did her hair in the same style, too.

'Ver-ry nice,' approved Daniel when she presented herself, ready to go. He glanced at his watch. 'I expect Rod will be here any minute. If you don't mind I'll skip along and pick up Gayle.'

'You wouldn't be a bit sweet on Gayle Desmond, would you?' Nerys teased.

To her surprise, Daniel looked slightly embarrassed. 'I take her out now and then,' he conceded.

'You don't have to pretend with me,' said Nerys with a smile. 'Good luck! She's a nice girl.'

He shrugged. 'And she has more than one boyfriend!'

'Good for her! You men need to be kept on your toes!'

When he had gone she wondered about the guarded expression in his eyes. Was it possible that her brother was in love? As she was wondering, Hallam came in. He had been out on an emergency call.

'Was it serious?' Nerys enquired as she endured his slow, encompassing gaze.

'No.' He did not elaborate and she did not ask.

'Are you going to the dance?' she questioned.

'I don't know. I might look in later,' he said slowly, his eyes drifting over her. 'Where's Dan?' he added.

'He's gone to pick up Gayle.'

Hallam nodded. 'I suppose you're waiting for Troughton?'

'Yes, I am.' She admitted it reluctantly, and saw the distaste forming in his eyes. Why he did not like Rod, she could not imagine. From her experience of Rod Troughton she thought that he was very pleasant and she had enjoyed his company. At least he was friendlier than Hallam Vale, she thought defiantly.

As she spoke, Rod arrived, so with a swift, 'See you later, perhaps,' she escaped.

The community hall was quite a large one, and for the evening tables had been arranged around a central dance floor. On the stage at one end a five-piece band was playing, calling themselves, Nerys noted with amusement, the Kolbardi Minors. The hall's normally harsh lighting had been softened with coloured shades suspended below the fluorescent fittings, and the sides of the stage had been decorated with tubs of tropical plants, brought in, no doubt, from people's front porches and verandas, specially for the occasion. The night-clubbish atmosphere that had been created helped to disguise the starkness of the venue.

As they entered, Daniel spotted them and waved them over to a table where he was sitting with Gayle and another couple. The music started as they were about to sit down and Rod insisted on dancing, so Nerys allowed him to whisk her straightaway onto the dance floor. He danced with flair and pressed her close against him so that she could feel the hard muscles of his thighs through the thin material of her dress.

'You're very light on your feet,' he said, smiling down into her face. 'All that dashing about the wards keeps you supple.'

'Perhaps,' she agreed, smiling back at him. It was easy, she had found, to forget Chris when she was with Rod.

He was the kind of man who revelled in his masculinity. And tonight there was no doubt that he looked dashing in the pearl grey suit he was wearing, with a red shirt flaring under the jacket. He might be the kind of man who thrust his maleness at women, but so far he had not tried to take any liberties with her and she found him very likeable. He had a bold sense of humour, if a little *risqué*, and he knew all the town gossip. By the end of the dance he had pointed out who was running which racket, who was gambling the housekeeping, having an affair with whom, in debt, or whose marriage was on the rocks.

On the last subject, Rod mentioned the Albrechts. 'I mean, look at Barbra,' he whispered close to Nerys's ear. 'She's any man's who wants her, and Klaus isn't even aware of it, poor sucker.'

'I don't think you're being quite fair,' Nerys protested.

His eyebrows rose. 'No? Well, just you keep an eye on her and Hallam Vale, and if they don't disappear shortly for half an hour or so, then I'm a Dutchman.'

Nerys had not noticed Hallam arrive, but now she saw him dancing with Barbra Albrecht, and she had to admit there was a rather blatant intimacy in the way Barbra's head rested against his chest. It seemed she didn't care who saw them. And neither, presumably, did Hallam.

Nerys firmly told herself she had no intention of keeping her eye on either of them, but as the evening wore on she found herself looking for Hallam every time he was absent from their table, to see if he was with Barbra. He and the Albrechts had joined their party and Nerys danced a couple of times with Klaus, but it was Rod who claimed her for most of the time. Daniel, she saw with fond amusement, was totally enraptured by Gayle and it did not occur to him to dance with his sister. The other couple at their table were equally absorbed in each other, and on the only occasion an opportunity occurred, Hallam seemed to prefer to sit out a dance rather than ask Nerys.

Towards the end of the evening, Rod began to hold Nerys even closer as they danced and once, during a particularly slow and dreamy sequence, with the lights dimmed and the floor too crowded to move much, he rocked her to and fro in a rather sensuous manner. Looking into her face, he murmured, 'You're the most beautiful girl who's ever come to Kolbardi.'

'And I bet you've told every one of them the same thing!' she said.

He laughed softly and pressed her head close against his chest. 'I like you, Nerys,' he whispered, 'very much.'

Nerys caught her breath. He had never been so ardent before. He had had a few drinks tonight, of course, and that had probably made him more daring. She did not admit that she liked him too, feeling that it might be encouraging him too much.

Suddenly he lifted her chin and looked steadily into her eyes, a searching gaze that was a little disturbing. 'Let's go outside and I'll show you the stars,' he said. 'They're brighter here than anywhere else.'

Before she could protest, he was dragging her towards the nearest exit and through it into the open air. After the cool air-conditioning inside, the atmosphere outside was thick and warm. That Rod had not hurried her out just to look at the stars was instantly apparent. He pulled her hard against him and crushed her mouth with his in a demanding way. Caught unawares, she was forced into his embrace, and it was a moment or two before she began to push him away. He was strong and did not seem to notice her efforts to disengage herself. He insisted on the full measure of the kiss.

When he let her go he was smiling confidently. Then his lips reached for hers again.

'No, Rod,' she protested.

'No?' His head came up. He was genuinely puzzled.

'No, please . . .' She wasn't sure why she didn't want him to kiss her now. He had kissed her goodnight on previous dates and she hadn't objected.

'Nerys! Nerys,' he chided, 'you can't do that to a man.' There was a glint in his eyes she had not seen before and it made her feel uneasy. She was aware that he was edging her craftily into the deeper shadows, further from the hall.

'Rod, I want to go back inside!' she said in a clear, authoritative tone. It halted him and he looked at her quizzically.

'What's this? You like me, don't you? You've been coming out with me as though you did, and I've been very well behaved.'

Nerys couldn't help laughing. 'Oh, Rod, yes, you have—and really, I'd prefer to keep it that way. Let's go back inside.'

Her words made him frown. He was not a man who liked to be crossed, she realised, and wondered if she had made a mistake in being friendly with him. But to her relief the frown quickly vanished and a smile opened his face.

'All right! But if you will look so deliciously kissable, what do you expect a man to do?' He flung an arm across her shoulders. 'I'm not going to promise not to try and thaw out your cold little heart!'

Nerys was relieved. She wasn't quite sure why she had rejected his kiss. She liked him well enough. It was just that momentarily she had been reminded of the night Hallam had kissed her, and it had evoked a feeling of revulsion towards Rod. As they re-entered the hall, the first person Nerys saw was Hallam, and there was a look on his face that said he guessed what they had been up to.

Well, I guess you ought to know! Nerys said fiercely to herself, and looked around for Barbra, who was nowhere about at that moment.

Daniel said, when they returned to the table, 'Ah, there you are. Rod's been looking after you all right, I hope?' There was no suggestion in his tone that he was being snide.

Feeling that her lipstick must surely be a mess, Nerys

excused herself and went to the Ladies. Gayle Desmond was already there.

'Having a good time?' Gayle enquired, fiddling with the shoulder straps of her pale blue, alluringly revealing dress.

'Yes, lovely, thanks,' Nerys said, hastily repairing her mouth.

'Rod Troughton's quite smitten with you.'

Nerys turned a mildly questioning look on her and Gayle laughed. 'Saw you coming back in! How were the stars?'

Nerys blushed and Gayle went on merrily, 'He's a bit of a wolf, but I expect you know how to keep a man at arm's length if you want to. Rod's a bit brash, but good fun.'

Nerys managed a smile but could think of nothing to say. Gayle was a bit too astute. She wondered how many others had noticed their absence.

Rod was not at the table when the two girls returned and, looking around, Nerys spotted him eventually, standing at the bar talking to someone, a glass in his hand. Perhaps he felt in need of a drink, she thought wryly. She was still staring idly in his direction when a hand suddenly rested on her shoulder, making her jump. She turned her head and, to her surprise, saw Hallam.

'Would you care to dance this one with me?' he invited, his green eyes holding hers steadily.

Her first inclination was to refuse, but the refusal was never spoken. Instead, she heard herself saying, 'Of course, thank you, Hallam.'

She stood up and they moved to the edge of the floor. She gave herself into the circle of his arms, rather rigidly at first, and found them strong and no less imprisoning than Rod Troughton's.

'Enjoying yourself?' he asked.

'Yes.' It was ridiculous, but her heart was racing in a way it had not done when she was dancing with Rod.

'I should watch your step with Rod Troughton,' Hallam warned softly. 'That is, unless you enjoy getting into a tight spot.'

Nerys bridled. 'I really don't know what you mean.'

'Don't you?' His half-smile was laconic.

She said evenly, 'I really don't need your caution, Hallam, well meant though it may have been. I am twenty-six years old and quite capable of taking care of myself.'

'I wonder if you are,' he rejoined with a slow smile. 'I wonder . . .'

'Well, I'm sure it's no concern of yours, in any case,' she shot back, feeling distinctly irritated.

'No, you're perfectly right, it isn't,' he agreed, 'but don't say I didn't warn you.'

She laughed scornfully. 'I must say, it's really good coming from you, that sort of warning!'

His grip tightened and his expression hardened. 'I am not Rod Troughton, whatever you might have deduced from gossip, and you would do well to reserve your judgment whilst you have no evidence against me.'

'A kiss doesn't count?' she reminded him a trifle acidly, somewhat surprised at the vehemence of his denial.

His eyes glittered with a strange intensity. 'If you're the kind of girl who believes she can toss kisses around with impunity in a place like this, then you may be in for a shock. I don't think I need to spell it out. Just take care, Nerys, in case what you get isn't what you want.'

Nerys felt inwardly agitated. 'I really don't know why we're bothering to have this conversation,' she said edgily. 'It's quite pointless. What I do is nothing to do with you. Shall we talk about something else?'

His bottom lip curled in faint disdain. 'Whatever you wish.'

'I suppose Barbra and Klaus are back for quite a while?' she remarked idly. She wanted to needle him if she could. He had needled her about Rod.

'Yes, I gather they are.'

'Barbra is very attractive,' Nerys said.

'Yes,' he answered without a quaver.

'I'm sure most men think so,' Nerys insisted as they passed the subject of their conversation, who was talking vivaciously to three men.

Hallam, too, stared at Barbra, an inscrutable look on his face. Was he jealous? Nerys wondered.

'Doesn't Klaus ever get jealous?' she asked innocently. 'I

mean, every time I've noticed Barbra this evening she's been with a different man.'

He ignored the pointed look she gave him and said, 'I wouldn't think Klaus was the jealous kind. He's much too absorbed in his work to worry about whether his wife is flirting with other men. I presume he trusts her.'

'I hope he's justified,' Nerys commented in a low voice, but nothing she said seemed able to provoke any real reaction from him.

A few minutes later they rejoined Daniel and Gayle at the table. Nerys was aware that the moment they appeared, Gayle's attention wandered from Daniel, to whom she had been listening attentively, and drifted to Hallam. It was not the first time Nerys had noticed it. There was no doubt that Gayle was smitten by the man. He spoke to her in a friendly way and Nerys wondered if he found her attractive, too.

Gayle was not a conventionally pretty girl but she had good features, shining dark hair and a bright, breezy manner. She seemed to Nerys a very easy-going, good-natured girl who would, as Jean Grace had remarked, make someone a very good wife.

She would be the faithful kind, Nerys felt certain. She glanced at her brother and caught an unguarded look. It was a look of resignation with an underlying hint of resentment, and she knew it was because Hallam had so effortlessly been able to divert Gayle's attention to himself. Daniel was, understandably, jealous. Nerys pondered for a moment or two. It was a pity Gayle was starry-eyed about Hallam. She would, she felt, be just right for her brother.

The dance broke up at about one a.m. and Nerys fell asleep almost as soon as her head hit the pillow. She dreamed briefly of Rod Troughton, with whom she was engaged in an unseemly struggle, and then the dream faded into a vivid picture of Hallam standing, feet astride, arms folded, laughing at her. She woke in the morning with the feeling that last night had not been as enjoyable as she had at first believed. Her head ached and there seemed to be a terrible drumming inside it. This, she rapidly realised as she surfaced, was rain on the roof.

Nerys drew back the curtains and looked out. It was teeming down, so heavily she could scarcely see more than a few yards across the lawn. The droplets were bouncing off the grass like pebbles and clattering against the windows. Beneath her window, the pathway was a rivulet of red mud.

The bathroom door was locked, so she went into the kitchen and was disappointed to find Hallam there, not Dan.

'Good-morning,' she said, feigning brightness.

'It isn't very,' he rejoined.

'No,' she agreed. 'Does it always rain as heavily as this?'

'In the wet season it often does. It sometimes means a good deal of local flooding.'

'In the town, you mean?' Nerys busied herself making toast. The coffee-pot was already percolating.

'And around about. Some of the station tracks may be impassable for a few days if the river floods. The road to Hedland might become impassable, too.'

'You mean we're probably marooned here?'

'You weren't planning to go, were you?' he asked, showing by his look that it would not surprise him if she were.

'No, of course not!' She resented the insinuation.

'The town can exist for weeks on its supplies,' he said, 'so there's no need to panic.'

Nerys sat down at the table and buttered toast, spreading it with marmalade and wishing Hallam did not have such a knack of making her feel uncomfortable. She was glad when Daniel breezed in.

'Looks like you'll need your wellies to walk across to the hospital this morning,' he said laughingly.

'I didn't bring any!' rejoined Nerys, feeling cheered immediately.

Half an hour later she was running across the lawn in her bare feet, holding an old black umbrella with two broken spokes over her head. She was shaking the umbrella on the porch, and about to stand it in a corner, when Daniel appeared, having come across ahead of her.

'Emergency,' he said, tight-lipped.

Nerys was startled. 'What sort of emergency?'

'Mrs Fortescue of Ambleside is in labour.'

'Is that an emergency?' Nerys queried, thinking the woman must have been admitted.

'It is. Ambleside is two hundred kilometres from here, and completely cut off! Their landing-strip is under water and there's nowhere suitable for the flying doctor to land. She's a caesarian. She was due to go to hospital in Hedland in a couple of days, but something's triggered things early—two weeks too early.'

'What can we do?' There was a note of desperation in Nerys's voice. She was imagining the poor woman's panic.

As she spoke Hallam appeared, shaking the rain off a waterproof jacket he had held over his head as he ran from the house. He took in their faces with a glance. 'What's up?'

Daniel explained. 'Can't they sent the port helicopter from Hedland? That could land anywhere,' Hallam said.

Daniel shook his head. 'It's out of action, and it could be days before it's repaired. There doesn't seem to be another available anywhere in the vicinity. They're hoping we might get through with a four-wheel drive.'

'Then we'll have to try and do that,' said Hallam without hesitation.

'The roads are all under water. Jim Fortescue tried to get out early this morning when the crisis began, but he didn't dare risk it in case they got stuck, so he went back.' Daniel looked anxious. 'She's in pretty bad shape by the sound of it. The Flying Doctor base has advised what medication to give her, but there isn't much else he can do to alleviate the situation.'

Hallam's expression was one of calm determination. He said briskly, 'Nerys, you know what's needed for a caesarian, I presume?'

'Yes, of course.'

'Well, make sure the medical kit we're taking with us includes everything.'

Nerys's mouth dropped open, she was so astonished. 'B—but aren't you going to bring her back to the hospital?'

His gaze was steady. 'If possible. But there may not be

time. We must be prepared for all eventualities, Sister Kent.'

When she did not move instantly, his lips twisted in a sneer and he added roughly, 'Don't just stand there! If you don't want to risk your neck in flood-waters, or you're squeamish about the possibility of an emergency operation, I'll take someone else.'

Nerys swallowed hard. She had not even thought of any risk to herself and was taken aback at his assumption that she might have done so. She shot him as crushing a look as she could muster and raced off to prepare for the mercy dash.

Daniel came to help her. 'Don't worry,' he said cheeringly. 'Ten to one, none of this will be necessary, and even if it is, Hallam's perfectly competent.'

'I don't doubt that,' Nerys hesitated, looking anxiously at him. 'But just the two of us? Shouldn't we be taking another nurse at least?'

Daniel shrugged. 'Hallam obviously thinks you're efficient enough on your own. And Jim will lend a hand if necessary. Don't worry, Nerys.'

It was only a matter of minutes before they set off. It was still raining but not as heavily as earlier. As she slid into the passenger seat beside Hallam, Nerys glanced at him. His expression was still grim as he looked briefly at her.

'Keep your fingers crossed,' he murmured, his tone milder than previously. 'We might make it, we might not.'

Nerys said with feeling, 'Poor Mrs Fortescue must be frantic right now.'

'Not to mention her husband,' said Hallam dryly. 'Daniel's letting him know that we're attempting to get through.'

At first it seemed there was going to be no problem. The road, although muddy and rough after the night's rain, was negotiable and the four-wheel drive vehicle made good progress. Hallam drove fast and Nerys clung to the door grip to avoid being flung against him from time to time. Neither spoke much. The situation was too tense.

Nerys was rehearsing in her mind the procedures for a caesarian section, an operation she had not assisted at for some time, having spent the last eighteen months as a general theatre sister. She had intended moving to obstetrical nursing but had put it off when Chris came along . . . As the thought of him intruded, she realised suddenly that it hurt less. In fact it was practically gone now. There was just a void inside her.

They had been driving for some time when abruptly the scene changed. At first she thought it was a mirage, but as they approached and it did not recede, she realised it was real water. The road ahead was flooded, and suddenly the water was swirling all around them, a vast lake from horizon to horizon. Huge muddy splashes half obscured their vision. Hallam brought the Range Rover to an abrupt halt and, leaning on the steering-wheel, looked around them to assess the situation.

'We must be about thirty or so kilometres from Ambleside,' he said thoughtfully, 'and Jim said the last ten are dry. So, unless we come across dry spots in between, we've got around twenty kilometres of water to negotiate. We don't know how deep it is in places.' He glanced at her, a quirky twist to his mouth. 'Game to go on?'

'What a question! I didn't come with you to chicken out at the last minute,' Nerys replied hotly, adding, 'it doesn't look very deep. You can see the grass above the water in places.'

'Very observant,' he remarked. 'OK, here we go. We'll have to take it slowly and hope for the best. Keep your eyes peeled and shout if you see any snags ahead, branches sticking up, or anything to suggest a deeper washaway.'

Nerys took a deep breath. 'I'll do my best.'

They moved slowly across the muddy lake, sometimes suddenly dipping heart-stoppingly into a pot-hole, sometimes the wheels seeming to slip and spin and lose their grip, only to regain it a moment later.

When Nerys glanced anxiously at Hallam the first time this happened, he gave her a twisted grin. 'Don't panic! She can handle it. She's built for this sort of performance.'

Once Nerys, looking ahead at the vast shoreless lake of reddish brown, dotted with ghost gums, saw a group of sheep standing forlornly on a patch where only their hooves were covered. 'How do you know we're still on the road?' she said.

'Good question!' said Hallam, tight-lipped. 'I don't! I'm just trusting my sense of direction, that's all.' He sounded testy.

Nerys was silent. She had not meant to criticise. She just couldn't help thinking of the poor woman waiting to have her baby, fearful for its life and her own as well. And her husband must be frantic knowing there was nothing he could do except wait and offer her what comfort he was able.

Another few minutes passed and then Hallam suddenly let out a long breath. 'Ah!'

'What's wrong?' Nerys's anxiety was making her feel edgy.

'Nothing. See that rocky outcrop ahead? That means we're still on the road.'

'Thank goodness for that,' breathed Nerys, who had been more afraid that they were lost than she had been willing to admit. She added with a smile, 'You must have an accurate sense of direction.'

He grinned, but it did not dispel the strain in his face. 'Fairly. But once you get into the wheel-ruts on outback tracks it's difficult to get out!'

'Have we much further to go?' She had been looking at her watch and worrying about the time it was taking to reach the homestead.

'No, but the next bit could be the trickiest. We haven't reached the creek yet, and the road may well have been completely washed away there.'

'Do you know exactly where that is?'

'I expect we'll see,' said Hallam grimly.

And he was right. Where the creek crossed the road, the water was running fast, carrying some debris along with it. It looked frightening to Nerys, who immediately had visions of them becoming bogged in the middle of the torrent. Hallam stopped just before they reached it.

'Why are we stopping?' Nerys asked.

'I'm going to get out and see what's what,' Hallam said. 'We don't want to get stranded and have to walk the rest of the way with the gear, do we?' His glance was only faintly ironic.

'Do be careful,' Nerys urged involuntarily, as he threw open the door.

'Don't worry, I will!' Their eyes met for a brief moment, and for once there was no animosity in his, not even a teasing glint.

Nerys watched anxiously as his tall frame climbed out of the vehicle and strode forward through the flood-waters. She held her breath as he stumbled once or twice, then suddenly stepped into a hole that brought the water almost up to his thighs. It seemed an agonisingly long time while he zig-zagged back and forth, looking for the most solid place for the Range Rover to attempt the crossing. He returned slowly and finally climbed back in.

'Well?' she asked, 'Will we make it across?'

Their eyes met again. His were suddenly warm, encouraging. 'We have to, don't we?' he answered with quiet resolve.

He revved the engine and slowly they set off. It was a breathless few seconds as the Range Rover roared through the water and Nerys, peering out on the off-side, held her breath as it rose higher and higher up the wheels until they were completely covered. And then, just as she thought perhaps they were not going to make it after all and her heart was in her mouth, the vehicle surged out of the deeper trough to bring them onto firmer ground, and they were travelling forward again purposefully, although still with great caution.

The minutes dragged by and Nerys felt a new atmosphere of urgency. A glance at Hallam's face told her that, although he was relieved at getting through, he too was worried about taking so long.

'Not much further,' he muttered once. His eyes were narrow and concentrating, as he stared ahead intently.

The clouds had mostly drifted away and the sun was now hot, the atmosphere uncomfortably humid. Nerys's eyes began to ache from staring through the windscreen at what seemed like an endless inland sea. Then all at once there was a change, which at first did not register. A moment before Hallam exclaimed, she realised that they were coming to the edge of the brown flood-waters. Ahead was dry land.

'We've made it!' she cried. 'Hallam, we've made it! We're through!'

He turned briefly to grin at her, to share her relief, and for a moment there was a rapport between them such as she had sensed that day they had rescued the pelican.

'Now we can step on it a bit,' Hallam said grimly as they left the flood-waters behind, and he put his foot down.

It was only moments until the homestead came into view. Nerys caught her breath. It looked so isolated, a stark cluster of buildings with a few trees surrounding them and the vast, empty sky above, the limitless empty country all around. How unbearably lonely it must be, she thought, living out here, having a baby out in this wilderness. She shuddered. It was even more so when you were cut off by flood-waters.

'I don't know how people can bear to live in such isolated places,' she said spontaneously. 'It must be terrible when you're ill, or going to have a baby like Mrs Fortescue.'

'It used to be worse,' Hallam said, 'before the flying doctor. The Reverend John Flynn who started the service used to describe what he wanted to do as bringing a "mantle of safety" to the outback. And that's exactly what the service does. So long as you have a radio transmitter you can get help, no matter where you are. There's a problem, though, when airstrips are flooded as the Fortescues' is now.'

'What makes people want to live in the outback?' Nerys mused, more to herself than Hallam.

'Many reasons. With the Fortescues it's simply tradition, I suppose. They're both station born and bred. Jim's great grandfather came here from Queensland. He'd emigrated from Scotland in the 1860s. Jim's father took over Ambleside when his father died, and now Jim runs the place, carrying on the same tradition.'

It was the most he had said during the journey, and indicated to some extent the relief he felt that at least they had arrived. A young man was running from the homestead to meet them. It was Jim Fortescue. Worry and strain showed on his tanned face as he greeted them.

'Thank God you made it!' he exclaimed. The man was almost in tears, and Nerys instinctively put her arm around his shoulders.

'Don't worry now,' she said soothingly. 'I'm sure they're both going to be all right.'

Hallam was already striding head of them into the house. Mrs Fortescue was lying in the main bedroom, pale and strained, the heat and humidity not helping to ease her pain and discomfort. An electric fan stirred the air not very effectively.

Hallam's examination of the patient was swift and thorough. He asked a number of questions in a low, soothing voice, and Nerys noticed at once that some of the fear drained out of the woman's face.

Hallam eventually turned to Jim Fortescue. 'Any news from the flying doctor?'

'No.' Jim shook his head, and added anxiously, 'What's the verdict, Doctor?'

Hallam took him a little to one side. 'It's serious, Jim. I don't think we can risk to take her back to Kolbardi. We got through, but there's no guarantee we'd get back as easily. I admit I was hoping they'd have located a helicopter by now. If she was in hospital now, we'd operate immediately.'

'I wanted her to stay in Hedland for the last couple of months,' Jim said, 'but she wouldn't leave me. And she was so well up until . . .' His voice broke, and he looked appealingly at Hallam 'Have—have we lost the baby?'

Hallam shook his head. 'I don't think so.'

'Is there anything you can do?' Jim Fortescue's expression was desperate.

'Yes,' Hallam said, with a straight look. 'We can operate here.' Nerys saw the man flinch slightly, as Hallam went on, 'Naturally there's some risk, but if we do there's a good chance we'll save the child.' He paused again. 'It's up to you, Jim.'

Jim Fortescue moved to the bed and held his wife's hand tightly. 'Glenys?'

She looked at him wearily. 'Yes, Jim, yes, anything . . .'

Her face contorted with sudden pain.

Her husband drew in a deep breath. 'I guess if that's the only way, that's the way it's got to be.'

Hallam dropped a reassuring hand on the man's shoulder. 'Jim, if I knew a helicopter would be here in a couple of hours, I wouldn't do it, but help might not come until tomorrow at the earliest.' He smiled. 'Don't worry, Glenys is in good health and it's quite a simple operation, really.'

Nerys noted with admiration how he managed to convey the maximum reassurance, disguising any apprehensions he might be feeling himself. And she noted, too, the complete trust she saw in Jim Fortescue's face.

'Just tell me what I can do to help,' Jim said matter-of-factly.

'You can help me get the gear in,' Hallam said, 'and you can help Nurse Kent to turn your kitchen into an operating-theatre.' He glanced at Nerys. 'Come on, there's no time to waste.'

One would think, Nerys mused once during the next little while, that Hallam was accustomed to performing operations on kitchen tables. He ordered them both about with clear, precise instructions about everything—from the need for plenty of hot water for scrubbing up, to collecting cushions and pillows to provide support for the patient.

There was a certain amount of improvisation necessary and once, seeing a slightly doubtful expression on Nerys's face, he remarked, 'Pioneer doctors worked under much worse conditions. They didn't have oxygen, or IVDs, or antibiotics, and yet they did many a successful operation on kitchen tables by the light of oil lamps, and often single-handed, without any expert nursing assistance.'

Nerys wondered how true this really was. Hallam's reassurance did not stop her from feeling extremely nervous. She had never dreamed of taking part in anything so unorthodox. A caesarian on a kitchen table! And only the two of them!

Hallam finally looked across at her and murmured beneath his mask, 'Here we go.' Nerys took a deep breath as she caught his eye, and suddenly a wave of panic swept over her.

She wanted to cut and run, just as she had before when she had fled from Chris in a blind panic, her nerve gone. The trembling began as it had then. Someone had stepped into her place then, but now there was no one. She had to go through with it. She must not lose her nerve this time. She could not put any personal weakness before what was required of her, before the lives of a woman and a baby.

Hallam's eyes were holding hers, as though he divined what she was feeling. He said in a clear, calm voice, 'Ready?'

Nerys took a deep breath. 'Ready.' And she was. Her nerve was like steel. There was no danger now of her running away. She knew that this was her chance to expiate the shame and humiliation she had suffered, to prove to herself that she was not a coward.

Automatically she responded to his every command and request. It did not take long. As Daniel had reassuringly said, it was quite a simple procedure, really. The moment Nerys knew that the baby was alive, relief rushed like a warm tide through her, releasing the last bit of tension. Holding the tiny, red, slippery morsel of flesh in her gloved hands, she felt a wonderful sense of triumph. And, looking briefly into Hallam's eyes, she knew he was experiencing the same kind of elation. For an instant they were close, but only for an instant.

Nerys turned to the baby's father. 'You've got a son, Mr Fortescue. Look!'

There was a kind of disbelieving wonder in his eyes above the sterile mask as he looked into the tiny crinkled face. He murmured something which was muffled by the muslin, but his tone conveyed his heartfelt thankfulness.

It was much later, with the sun dipping low to the horizon, that the hoped-for rescue came. Hallam had said it would be too dangerous to attempt to take Mrs Fortescue and the baby back to Kolbardi in the Range Rover that night, as the risk of becoming bogged and stranded was too great, but if no rescue was forthcoming the next day they might take the chance. And so Nerys prepared to spend the night at Ambleside. She and Hallam were with their patient when Jim came into the room to tell them, smiling all over his face, that the Flying Doctor Service had called and there was a helicopter coming out to take them to Port Hedland.

'Where did they locate it?' Hallam asked, relief showing behind his query. Neither patient was in any immediate danger, but he was nevertheless anxious for Mrs Fortescue and the baby to be admitted to hospital as quickly as possible.

'On a fishing trawler, would you believe?' said Jim. 'Sounds as though it's one of those real sophisticated tuna boats I've seen around. They have everything that opens and shuts, including helicopters for spotting shoals of fish. I only hope it's got the range to reach us, and room for Glenys and the baby!'

'They wouldn't be sending it otherwise,' Hallam said with a confident smile.

'How long before it gets here?' Nerys asked.

'Any minute now, I reckon,' said Jim.

'You'd better go along with them, Jim,' Hallam said, 'if there's room.'

'Just try and stop me!' the young man answered, giving his wife's hand a reassuring squeeze.

Nerys quickly set about preparing the patient for transfer to the helicopter, and by the time they heard the clatter of the machine's engine and the whirring of rotor blades, everything was ready. The helicopter was able to land quite near the homestead, and as the engine cut out and the blades stopped whirling, the pilot and a nurse jumped down with a stretcher.

'I wish we'd known about the emergency earlier,' the pilot, an American, said. 'We'd have zapped out here straight away. How's the patient?'

'Both of them are fine,' said Hallam, not without a little justifiable pride, Nerys thought. 'But naturally I'll be happier when I know they're in hospital. A kitchen is not the ideal place to operate in.'

Nerys exchanged a few explanatory words with the nurse, and within a few minutes Mrs Fortescue and the baby were aboard the helicopter. There was just room for Jim, the pilot said, with a grin.

Jim clasped first Nerys's, then Hallam's hand in a strong

handshake. 'Thanks a million,' he said warmly.

It was a great moment when the helicopter lifted slowly off the ground, turned and, gaining height, began to disappear quickly into the distance. Nerys and Hallam watched until it was a speck in the sky, then walked back to the homestead both feeling drained but deeply satisfied. Hallam walked with his hand resting companionably on Nerys's shoulder, and as they entered the house together she knew she was going to have to be very strong with herself.

There was more to the way she felt about Hallam Vale than mere physical attraction. It was something she dare not let develop or it would bring her the same heartache all over again. Chris might be fading slowly from her thoughts and feelings—and in fact she now realised there was more anger left than love—but she must be careful not to replace him with Hallam. There could be no more future in that than with Chris. Hallam was a loner. He liked women, but had avoided permanent relationships. He was hardly likely to change.

His hand dropped to his side as they went up the veranda steps.

'I'd better start packing up,' Nerys said. 'It's getting late.' She assumed that they would be driving back to Kolbardi tonight.

Hallam startled her by saying, 'We're not going to chance driving back tonight. Not in the dark.'

'But we got through!' protested Nerys.

'Sure, but anything could have happened in the meantime. Rains elsewhere might have swelled the flood-waters. It would not be responsible of me to expose you to more risk.'

'But I . . .'

He cut her short. 'Don't argue! The sensible thing is to stay the night here. Jim said we can help ourselves to food and he even said there's a couple of bottles of wine left from Christmas and he'll be offended if we don't celebrate with one of them, at least!'

'He didn't mention any of that to me,' said Nerys suspiciously.

Hallam slanted her a mocking look. 'You're nervous, aren't you? What with my reputation and all. Well, I give you my word, Nerys, I have no ulterior motive in electing to stay the night here. As a matter of fact, I'm whacked, and so are you. I'm sure I'd fall asleep at the wheel if I tried to drive. We both need some sleep. We'll call through to Kolbardi and let them know the situation. In the morning, with luck, the flood-waters will be down and we'll get back in half the time.'

Nerys could only say resignedly, 'I suppose I'd better see about getting us a meal. I'm beginning to feel a bit hungry, aren't you? We didn't have any lunch, remember.'

His hand dropped on to her shoulder again, and he squeezed it firmly. 'Good girl! You always rise to the occasion, don't you?'

For some foolish reason, her eyes filled with tears.

'Hey,' he said gently, 'what's this? Reaction?' His arms drew her against him and cradled her head on his chest, his fingers soothingly caressing her cheek and neck. 'It's all over now, Nerys, and you did a fine job.'

She was so ashamed of her emotion that she broke away from him and fled like a mad thing back into the homestead, to stand clenching her fists in the kitchen doorway, biting her lip and trying to bring back her composure. What a long night this was going to be!

CHAPTER SEVEN

'CONGRATULATIONS, Nerys.' Hallam smiled at her. 'That was a very good meal.' He raised his almost empty wine glass to her. 'You have excelled yourself in every way today.'

Effusive compliments were not his usual style. 'The wine has gone to your head,' she accused.

'Perhaps it has a little,' he admitted, with a slightly wry look that swiftly changed to something else which disturbed her greatly. 'You look quite beautiful sitting there in the dim light, with your hair about your face.' Whether the huskiness of his voice was caused by the wine, or an emotion he was having some difficulty controlling, she could not be sure.

She looked across the table at him in alarm.

He laughed and went on in a more normal tone, 'Don't look so uneasy! I'm not leading up to anything. I don't break promises.'

'I wasn't.' Nerys wished she had not let him see her anxiety. Even in spite of what he had said earlier and repeated now, she could not help feeling a little apprehensive. They were, after all, a long way from anywhere, cut off by flood-waters, totally alone together. But was she only afraid of him—or of herself as well?

He rose, saying, 'Shall we have coffee on the veranda? It's cooler out there. I'll make it.'

Nerys jumped up. 'No, I'll do it. You go and sit down. Put your feet up. You must be very tired.'

He straightened up and took a step or two to bring himself close to her. His fingers slid soothingly around her neck, sending warm, relaxing shivers through her body. 'So must you,' he said softly, then abruptly took his hand away. 'All right, you make the coffee and I'll stack the dishes.'

She would have preferred to do it all alone in order to gain a few minutes to herself to quieten her helter-skelter heart and the rush of emotion that had surged through her at his touch. It was ridiculous to feel so strongly. But he insisted on clearing the table and piling the dishes on the drainer next to the kitchen sink while she filled the percolator and set the coffee on the stove.

'There isn't much to wash up. Let's do it now, and then we can relax for as long as we like over coffee. I noticed that Jim's got a bottle of very good brandy and I don't think he'd begrudge us a nip to celebrate the birth of his son, do you?'

Nerys agreed. She was not entirely happy about making free with someone else's property when they were absent, but she knew Hallam was right. Jim would surely insist on it if he and Glenys were there.

So they washed up while the coffee was percolating. Bending over the sink, with Hallam close beside her, gave Nerys such an unexpected feeling of domesticity that for one blissful moment she had the illusion of being in her own kitchen, with her husband drying the dishes. It was like a glimpse of the future. Only it wouldn't be Hallam—at least that was something she could be sure of.

Hallam was surprisingly talkative. Mellowed by the wine, she supposed. He talked about the problems of medical care in the outback, the peculiarities of new towns like Kolbardi, the unusual emergencies that sometimes arose, like today's, the vital part the flying doctor played . . .

'I love that phrase "mantle of safety",' Nerys said reflectively. 'It sounds so comforting and secure. John Flynn must have been a remarkable man to have envisaged such a scheme and then fought so hard to establish it.'

'He was a visionary,' said Hallam, 'and a very compassionate man. And a damned hard worker. Most city people have forgotten him now, but outback people still remember and are grateful.'

Sitting on the veranda drinking coffee, they were silent for a time. Nerys was preoccupied with her thoughts and the need to put her feelings into order, and Hallam seemed contemplative too. She wondered what he was thinking about. Barbra perhaps. Had there ever been a real love in his life, she wondered, someone he truly cared for? Or had he always been the lone wolf, attracted to women but never wanting a lasting relationship?

She longed to ask but did not dare. Hallam Vale's private life was something she knew he would not want to talk about, and if she pried she would spoil the tranquillity they had achieved this evening.

Staring out into the darkness, Nerys tried to imagine how it would feel to live in a place like this all the time, with the emptiness all around. You would either love it or hate it, she felt; there would be no half-measures. To be alone was something she often craved, especially amid the hustle and bustle of a big general hospital. But to be lonely was something else.

Experienced briefly, the isolation of a place like Ambleside had a peculiar fascination which she could not explain. She felt as though she was on another planet. But whether she would enjoy its remoteness permanently, she could not decide.

Suddenly she yawned involuntarily. Hallam glanced across at her. His face was in shadow, his features barely discernible in the dim light that came from the room behind them. 'Time you went to bed,' he said quietly.

Obediently Nerys stood up. 'Yes,' she agreed. 'I suppose it is.'

Before dinner, after they had packed up the medical equipment and while she was preparing the meal, Hallam had made up two beds. One for her in the spare room, one for himself on the veranda.

'I'll be turning in myself, shortly,' he said.

Nerys said goodnight and went inside, closing the screen door quietly behind her. It was warmer indoors and by the time she had discarded her uniform and stretched out in her petticoat, drawing only the sheet over her, the weariness seemed to have gone and she did not immediately fall asleep as she had supposed she would.

Presently she heard Hallam's footsteps in the passage as he went along to the bathroom. Every sound was distinct in that quiet house. She heard the door open and close, then his footsteps returning along the lineoleum-covered passage.

She caught her breath when suddenly they paused, seemingly right outside her door, but instead of alarm she felt something worse—a sudden, desperate, longing for him. She knew she would not be able to deny him if he came into her room. But he did not. The footsteps passed her door and continued on down the passage, until she heard the screen door opening onto the veranda click shut. A sense of acute disappointment swept over her and she felt cheated.

She lay for a time thinking about it, unable to let sleep claim her, a prey to all kinds of delicious fantasies that she knew were foolish but nevertheless was unable to dismiss. What if he had come in? She knew he had been tempted to, but he was a man of honour and he had promised. But supposing he *had* come in . . . What would she have said to him? Go? She knew she would not. Would she have spent the night in his arms?

She was never quite sure when she made up her mind, but some little time later, restless and too warm, she slid out of bed and, pulling her uniform around her, tiptoed to the door leading onto the veranda. It was as though she was propelled by some force beyond her control. There was a moon somewhere, shedding a pale light so that she could just make out Hallam's bed in the corner furthest from her. She stood holding the screen door half open, staring into the darkness of that corner where he lay, wanting to rush into his arms, yet resisting the desire at the same time.

Suddenly the door creaked in her unsteady grasp. Instantly the figure on the bed sat bold upright.

'Nerys?' he murmured, almost as though he had been expecting her.

'Yes.' She was transfixed now, not sure whether she was terrified or excited.

He came across the veranda towards her and looked down into her face, but there were too many shadows for her to see clearly the expression in his eyes. His hands moved to her shoulders and he said huskily, 'What's the matter?' He was bare-chested and barefoot.

'I—I was too warm. I couldn't sleep.' It sounded just like the feeble excuse it was.

'I couldn't sleep myself,' he said, his voice almost a whisper, his hands gently massaging her shoulders.

And then something seemed to snap. He wrenched her away from the door, which clicked shut. But Nerys did not hear it because she was in his arms and his mouth was almost angrily punishing hers and finding an acceptance she could not help. Slowly his lips became gentler and his hands moved sensuously across her back. Soon they became impatient with the barrier of material and pulled the unbuttoned uniform open to allow his warm fingers to tantalise the bare flesh between her shoulder blades, the rounded firmness of her breasts, until the tremors that shook her whole acquiescing body were almost too much to bear.

'Nerys,' he whispered, 'you shouldn't have come. How am I supposed to resist you now?'

'You don't have to,' she murmured in a small, breathless voice. 'Hallam . . .'

His face was close to hers, his hands caressing her and drawing her closer in against his warm, vibrant body, moulding her to him, arousing her need with the demonstration of his own. For a long minute they clung together, caught up in an emotional vortex that had to be brought to a conclusion somehow. To Nerys there seemed only one way and, although a part of her that was still rational knew she would regret it, that her love would only be returned in physical passion, she could not turn back.

It was Hallam who suddenly pushed her away from him, in as rough a gesture as he had gathered her into his arms moments before. He retained a grip on her upper arms for a moment, then with jerky movements pulled the two edges of her uniform together and overlapped them to hide her partial nakedness.

'Don't ever tempt me like that again,' he said in a voice so low she could scarcely discern what he was saying. To her utter amazement he fumbled with the front of her uniform and did up one button. Then he turned her round abruptly and gave her a push. 'Back to bed. And please stay there. You almost made me forget myself.'

She turned her head. 'Hallam . . .'

'Go, before I change my mind,' he said hoarsely.

She went. She had no alternative. He opened the screen door and pushed her inside. She felt cheated again, but worse than that, humiliated. She had thrown herself at him and he had rejected her. But why? He had shown he was drawn to her, so why hadn't he taken advantage of her weakness? It was a puzzle she could not answer and fortunately sleep eventually spared her the agony of continuing to wonder.

She woke to the touch of a hand on her shoulder, shaking her gently. She opened her eyes to a room flooded with light and saw Hallam standing beside the bed with a cup of tea in his hand. Nothing in his expression betrayed that he was recalling last night.

'Sorry to disturb you,' he said. 'I let you sleep as long as I could, but we must be making tracks soon.'

Nerys sat up, clasping the sheet around her, feeling warm waves of embarrassment as last night flooded back into her mind. 'What time is it,' she asked, yawning widely.

'Eight o'clock,' Hallam said. 'We ought to get away by nine.'

'I'll get up straight away.' She was about to add something inconsequential when she was stayed by a look in his eye that said very clearly now that he was exercising the same self-control as he had last night.

'Drink your tea first,' he said abruptly, and handed it to her. Her fingers brushed his and her hand shook.

'Thank you,' she said, and refused to look at him. She felt so ashamed of last night, and yet she still did not understand why he had behaved as he had, especially when he could look at her this morning as he had a moment ago.

He went out and she drank the hot, sweet tea gratefully. After she had showered and dressed, she went into the kitchen where he was making toast.

'I still feel a bit guilty making so free with the Fortescues' food and drink and linen,' she said.

His gaze was more matter of fact now. There was no sign of any recent emotion, either in the way he looked at her or the way he spoke.

'There's no need,' he assured her. 'Jim and Glenys would expect us to use whatever we wanted. That's the kind of hospitality everyone gives and receives in the bush. When Jim told us to make ourselves at home, he really meant it.'

Nerys sat at the table and poured herself a cup of tea. 'That was quite an experience for me, yesterday. It all seems a bit unreal now.'

Their eyes met and a glimmer of a smile tilted his mouth. 'I'm sure it does. It was quite an experience for me, too.'

Nerys considered him briefly, and said from some intuitive feeling, 'Is surgery your first love?'

His look clouded slightly. 'It used to be,' he said slowly.

'Kolbardi hospital doesn't offer a surgeon a lot of scope,' she suggested.

He shrugged and did not reply.

'I can't think why you stay in a placc likc Kolbardi,' Nerys said boldly. 'Wouldn't you be able to use your talents better in a big city hospital?'

He shrugged again. 'Maybe.'

Why she persisted, Nerys did not know. Perhaps it was just because she was nervous this morning and needed something to say as a cover-up for her real feelings. 'Why did you choose Kolbardi in the first place?' she asked.

His eyes narrowed and there was a trace of annoyance in his reply. 'That's too long a story to waste time telling now.'

Nerys teased lightly, 'You're a bit of a dark horse, aren't you? Do you do it on purpose, or is it because it makes you more intriguing to women?'

His mouth took on an ironic twist. 'Do you think I'm intriguing?'

Nerys blushed. 'Well, a bit, I suppose. I'm always curious about people.'

He tapped his spoon on the saucer, considered for a moment, then said, 'We have a saying up here, not an original one, but a good one. Ask no questions and you'll be told no lies.'

It was abrupt and final. It told her to mind her own business. And it told her, too, that Hallam Vale had something to hide.

They left the homestead just after nine. The day was cloudy again and there was little wind. It was very hot. The flood-waters had receded during the night as Hallam had hoped, and there were no new places where the water even came up to the hub-cups. They reached Kolbardi by lunchtime.

There had been little awkwardness between them. Hallam had not once referred to the emotional moment last night, and in fact had been more talkative than usual on a number of subjects, mainly medical ones, although in the course of their conversations she made the discoveries that they both shared an interest in jazz and reading. His favourite reading was apparently natural history.

'I'll lend you a delightful story about dingoes,' he promised, after they had seen one loping away out of sight amid the rocky outcrops. 'It'll change all your preconceived ideas about them.'

'They're a menace to sheep aren't they?' she said, 'And they savage.'

He smiled at her. 'They are much maligned. Often blamed for what they do not do,' he added. 'They are beautiful, intelligent creatures.'

'How did the dugong pictures turn out?' Nerys asked, suddenly remembering.

'Not bad,' he said. 'Remind me to show you.'

Kolbardi was all agog over their excursion to Ambleside and the following week there was a colourful piece in the local paper about it, greatly exaggerating the whole thing, as both Nerys and Hallam assured Daniel. They were also written up in the Port Hedland paper, with photographs of the arrival by helicopter of the patients.

'I've been here nearly a year and nothing exciting has happened to me,' complained Daniel to Nerys. 'You've been here five minutes and you're in all the papers. I bet it'll get a mention in the *West Australian*, and I gather a few radio stations have picked up the news item.'

Nerys was astonished and rather embarrassed by the whole business. It had never occurred to her that any publicity would attach to the event.

'You are an innocent! It was a human interest story of the best kind. High drama with a happy ending.' Daniel shot his sister a sly look. 'And you two being marooned at the homestead overnight added a touch of romance, naturally.'

Nerys tried not to blush. 'Well, any speculation on that aspect is quite wrong, so don't look at me like that, Daniel.'

He shrugged, disappointed. 'I can't understand why you two don't seem to hit it off.'

'Be sensible, Daniel,' begged Nerys. 'We get along very well, professionally and socially. It's not compulsory to have romance as well, is it?'

He grinned. 'You mean Hallam's never made a pass at you?' There was incredulity in the remark.

'No! Now shut up about it, will you? You're embarrassing me.'

Daniel treated her to a searching look, then, remembering something, said, 'Oh, by the way, Rod Troughton was on the blower yesterday. To talk to you. Something about showing you over the mine.'

'He did promise to arrange a visit for me sometime,' Nerys said.

'I said you'd call him when you are free. Sorry, I forgot about it.'

'I'm sure there's no rush,' said Nerys.

Daniel hesitated, then said, 'I'm not trying to big-brother you, but watch your step with Rod Troughton, Neri.'

'Why?' Her brown eyes were alert.

He shrugged. 'Just watch your step, that's all.' He added with a laugh, 'Call it gut feeling if you like. I don't think I'd trust that guy.'

'I think you *are* big-brothering me,' laughed Nerys, 'but don't worry, Daniel, I can take care of myself.'

She was thinking idly of how both Daniel and Hallam had revealed strong reservations about Rod Troughton when she telephoned him later. But when she heard his bright and breezy tones she put any vague uneasiness to one side. She wasn't likely to become involved with Rod, so there was no need to worry.

Rod arranged a time to show her over the mine. Because of Nerys's shifts it was not possible for nearly a week. It was a long week, not because she was looking forward to seeing Rod, but because it was gradually becoming clear to her that pushing Hallam out of her mind was increasingly difficult.

Sometimes, stealing a glance at him, either at home, or in the hospital, she would long for moments like those she had enjoyed with him that day in Port Hedland, that evening at Ambleside. Yet all the time she knew that such wishing was foolish. The more stand-offish and brusque he was with her, the better it was for her.

Since their return from Ambleside he had reverted to his rather distant attitude towards her, only occasionally showing glimpses of another side to his nature, and always quickly withdrawing, as though he had caught himself out in some failing. Outwardly there was friendliness, but it masked his true feelings, she knew. Underneath there was still that inexplicable hostility towards her.

When Rod Troughton called for her on her day off, Nerys was ready, clad in jeans, sensible shoes and tartan shirt. She had tied a scarf around her hair. Rod looked her over with undisguised admiration as he caught her shoulders in his two hands and surveyed her face.

'I shall have to keep my eye on you,' he said with a smile. 'Every man at the mine will be wanting to date you, especially now you're a heroine!'

'You,' accused Nerys good-naturedly, 'are the most blatant flatterer I've ever met. Come on, let's go, shall we?'

'And you,' he murmured as he opened the car door for her, 'are the most captivating tease I've ever met.'

Nerys caught his eye and tensed a little. She wasn't sure how much was flippancy, how much seriousness. Although she was reluctant to admit it, he always made her feel a little wary, and it wasn't just because of what Daniel had said.

It was only a short drive from the town to the mine, along a winding road through the hills. Red dust billowed up behind the car and the sun blazed down from a clear blue sky. The jagged red rocks that formed the hillsides threw up sharp cutting edges against the azure, and there was an awesome beauty about their barrenness.

Never having seen an iron ore mine before, Nerys was not sure what to expect. When Rod took her onto a viewing platform she gasped in amazement. Before them stretched a vast amphitheatre of benches cut out of the hillsides, beautiful in its symmetry, disfiguring in the way it had gashed mercilessly through the natural beauty of the hills, changing the millions of years old landscape almost overnight.

'So this is where steel begins,' Nerys murmured, awed by the immensity of the operation.

Rod smiled at her indulgently. 'That's right. This is where it all begins. Right here at Mount Kolbardi. See those big trucks? They're hauling the iron ore to the crushers as it's shovelled off the face. It has a preliminary crushing here and then is shipped by train to Port Hedland for further crushing and then loading onto the bulk carriers.'

'Yes, I saw that,' said Nerys. 'Hallam showed me around the port complex when I was in Port Hedland.'

'Oh, did he?' murmured Rod, in a dismissive tone. 'Seems I'm wasting my time.'

'Oh, no, Rod. This is all very fascinating,' Nerys said quickly. To make sure he knew she was interested, she asked a dozen questions and listened intently as he bombarded her with facts and figures about production. He gave her a thorough tour of inspection and she was careful not to mention anything that Hallam had previously told her.

As they walked around she collected plenty of wolf-whistles and admiring looks, and there was an embarrassing chorus of remarks when Rod took her into the canteen for lunch.

'You've probably raised the temperature in here quite a few degrees,' he teased, obviously proud of being the one to show her around.

Later, driving back to town, he asked her to have dinner with him that evening. Since she had done so before, Nerys saw no reason to refuse this time, even though she felt rather less enthusiasm than on previous occasions. The thought slipped into her mind that it would be nice if Hallam would invite her out to dinner, just once. Still, why should he? They dined together at home most nights, anyway.

When Rod called for her, Hallam was the one to let him in. He tapped on Nerys's door and she called out, 'Come in!' She was just pulling up the zip on her dress and was almost ready to go. Hurrying, she pulled too hard and the zip stuck.

'Rod Troughton's here,' Hallam said in heavily disapproving tones. His eyes drifted over her as she continued to struggle with the zip. He moved forward. 'Here, let me.'

She glanced at him, then turned her back towards him.

'Would you mind? There must be a thread caught up in it. I can't quite reach it myself.'

'Keep still,' he said abruptly, and as her hands dropped to her sides, his fingers sought to free the zip.

An involuntary shiver ran through her as his fingers brushed her bare back and she felt momentarily the warmth of his breath on her neck. She closed her eyes, unable not to enjoy the sensation his nearness produced. It was almost as much as she could do not to turn around and throw herself into his arms. But he would push her away if she did, she knew that. This knowledge was an expanding emptiness inside her.

'There, that's it!'

Nerys felt the zip sliding easily the rest of the way up the dress and, turning around, she took a step back, still hardly trusting herself.

'Thanks,' she said.

His eyes held hers enquiringly, but he asked no questions. He merely said, 'That's a nice dress.'

Nerys was surprised. Compliments were not usually forthcoming from Hallam Vale. She picked up her purse. 'Thank you.' The dress was in a deep blue material with a finely pleated, flared skirt and a bodice with a rather revealing V neckline. 'Well, I'd better go,' she added. He was standing in front of the door.

He continued to bar her way as he said, tersely, 'I wouldn't get too friendly with him.'

Nerys lifted her chin. 'Why not?'

'He isn't your sort of person,' Hallam stated emphatically.

'Oh? And how would you know who my sort of person is?' she replied.

'Just warning you,' he rejoined mildly.

'You're worse than Daniel!' she exclaimed.

He was interested. 'Did Daniel warn you, too?'

Nerys was not prepared to admit that her brother had. She wondered if Daniel had said anything to Hallam, though. 'Daniel doesn't interfere in my life,' she said tartly, 'and I'd be grateful if you didn't either.'

'A word of advice scarcely counts as interference,' he complained gruffly.

'I appreciate your concern,' Nerys said, 'but I am capable of making my own judgments. I happen to like Rod Troughton!' She sailed past him. 'Goodnight, Hallam. See you later.' She treated him haughtily so that he would not guess how much she would rather have been going out to dinner with him.

Looking at Rod Troughton across the restaurant table she wondered what Hallam and Daniel had against him. He seemed a perfectly ordinary person. He talked more openly about himself than Hallam, for one thing. He had told her quite a lot about his life before he had come to Kolbardi from Sydney. Tonight he recounted some of the amusing and dramatic adventures he'd had when working in South Africa, Canada and the Middle East. He had told her before that he wasn't married and, laughingly, that he had no children. Tonight, he touched her hand and said that lately he was often tempted to change his mind about being a bachelor.

They were both in a mellow mood when they left the restaurant. Rod suggested a drink at the Kolbardi Club and, although Nerys felt she had already had enough to drink, it was still quite early, so she agreed to the suggestion.

The first person they saw when they walked into the club was Barbra Albrecht. She seemed to be alone. Barbra greeted Nerys in a friendly if slightly distant way, and looked Rod over with an amused smile that made Nerys wonder if there had ever been any intimacy between them.

'Where's Klaus?' Rod enquired.

Barbra lifted her shapely shoulders in an expression of resigned dislike. 'Working. What do you expect? When isn't he working? Some damn thing went wrong today. I don't know what, and I don't care.'

Suddenly her eyes flicked over Nerys's shoulder in the direction of the entrance and an expression of relief crossed her face. Nerys glanced around and saw Hallam Vale approaching them.

'Why, hello, Hallam,' Barbra said in a surprised tone, except that it sounded false to Nerys, who suspected that the rendezvous had probably been previously arranged.

Hallam looked briefly at Barbra, his expression showing nothing, not even surprise. Then he turned to Nerys, treating her to lengthy consideration with his penetrating green eyes. It was enough to cause her heart to leap about in a most disconcerting manner. She felt uncomfortable being there with Rod, whom she knew Hallam did not like. Rod, however, seemed unaware of it.

A few minutes after their arrival a man came over to the table and spoke in a low voice to Hallam, who immediately shook his head. The man turned to Rod and again spoke in hushed tones. Nerys could not hear what was said and wondered what it was all about. She discovered when Rod turned to her and said, 'Feel like a small flutter?'

'Pardon?'

'Gambling. Dice, roulette, two-up . . .'

Nerys was taken aback. She had never gambled on anything other than Premium Bonds in her life. She looked around the club, then queryingly at Rod. 'Is there a casino here?' she asked, surprised.

He laughed. 'Not here! It's not legal. But the boys like a bit of entertainment. Come on, it's only a bit of fun.'

Nerys caught Hallam's eyes. They were hard and disapproving. For some reason this made her feel perverse. She knew he did not approve, so she made up her mind to agree to Rod's suggestion. In any case, she felt uncomfortable with Hallam so near and welcomed the chance to escape that disconcerting green gaze.

'All right,' she said. 'I can afford to lose a few dollars, I suppose.'

Rod was pleased and showed it by squeezing her arm. He stood up and they excused themselves. Barbra looked delighted that they were going. Hallam just looked at them speculatively.

They did not have to go far. It was to a house only two streets away, where the door was opened by a woman who seemed to know Rod and welcomed him warmly. She led them into a large room at the rear of the house, whispered something to Rod which Nerys did not catch, and left them.

Nerys looked around her in amazement. There were at least fifty people crammed into the room, mainly men, but also a few women, apart from the croupiers who were attractive girls in low-cut dresses. The room appeared to be windowless and the walls were draped in thick curtains on two sides.

There was surprisingly little noise, only a low hubbub of talk, the whirring of an air-conditioner, and the precise tones of the croupiers. The atmosphere was one of intense concentration. There were several tables, each one, Nerys noticed, devoted to a different gambling game. One girl moved amongst the gamblers serving drinks.

Rod drifted from table to table, leading Nerys by the hand, speaking to people here and there, watching each game intently. A few of the men looked Nerys over with interest, but most were too engrossed to bother about the new arrivals. At last Rod joined a roulette table.

Nerys was staggered to see the amounts of money that some people were wagering. There was an air of muted excitement that at first communicated itself to her and gave her a sense of great daring. She watched, fascinated, as the chips were raked this way and that across the table, as players looked now elated, now dismal. A drink was thrust into her hand and someone offered her a cigarette, which she declined.

Guided by Rod she played once or twice, and lost each time. Then she risked a third sum and won. This exhilarated her, but next time she lost. 'That's it, Rod! I'm not betting any more,' she said. 'You've lost a fair bit. Let's go now, shall we?'

There was a curious light in his eyes, as though he was infected with some feverish disease, and he said huskily, 'Not yet, sweetheart. I've got to get back what I've lost. It won't take long, you'll see.' His tone was light but there was an underlying tension in it.

He went to another table and Nerys followed reluctantly. During the next half-hour she saw him lose and win a dozen times, but even when he had won back what they had both lost, he would not stop. Nerys began to feel edgy and longed to be out of the place. The atmosphere no longer excited her. All at once it was frightening. The tense faces, the desperate looks, unnerved her. But every time she urged Rod to stop, he refused sharply.

'Rod, you're ahead now,' she said once. 'You've won it all back. Why don't you quit while you're in front?'

He smiled glassily at her. 'Not yet,' he said. 'Just one more go. I've got a feeling this'll be a big killing.'

But it never was, and eventually Nerys became aware that he was losing more than winning. His face had taken on the same desperate expression as some of the others. Tired of watching, she retired to a couch against the wall and waited wearily for Rod to have had enough.

Finally, at two in the morning, when she could barely keep her eyes open a moment longer, a man in a dark suit announced that the tables were closing. There was a murmur of protest but the gamblers were smilingly assured that tomorrow was another day. Nerys got up and made her way through the departing customers towards Rod, whom she could see looking around for her.

'Well,' she enquired, 'did you break even?' She felt irritated with him, both for neglecting her and for being so obsessed with winning.

He was surly. 'Nope.' He took her arm roughly. 'Come on.' The smiling, amiable man had disappeared under a disgruntled, hard facade.

Nerys said, as they walked around the corner of the street to the car, 'Do you gamble often?'

He shrugged. 'Everybody does here.'

'Do the police know about it?'

'Of course they do. They raid now and then, but the venue is constantly changing so there isn't much point.'

He was morose and taciturn on the drive back to the bungalow, and Nerys was glad it took no more than a couple of minutes. She half wished she had left the illegal casino earlier and walked home, as once she had been tempted to do. What had started out as a pleasant enough evening, seemed to have turned sour. She had seen a side of Rod Troughton she did not like very much.

He parked the car in the shadows beneath a spreading tree near the house, and cut the engine.

'Thank you for a pleasant evening,' Nerys said, feeling she did not sound as sincere as she might. 'And for showing me over the mine today. I enjoyed that very much, Rod.'

He reached across and drew her into his arms. 'You can thank me more nicely than that, can't you?' His voice was not as gentle as usual. She had known he would expect to kiss her so she complied, but her response was cool, her instinct to get it over with. There was something about him that made her feel uneasy.

As he lifted his mouth from hers she drew away, saying, 'It's terribly late, I'd better be going in. Thanks again, Rod, it was great.'

'Now wait a minute,' he said, his voice suddenly harsh. 'That's not good enough. I think I deserve a little compensation for my losses. I thought you were going to bring me luck, but you didn't.'

His mouth was hard and demanding on hers, taking her breath away as he bruised her lips with a frightening passion, leaving her in no doubt of his ultimate intentions. As his hands fumbled with the zip of her dress, she struggled wildly, pushing him away, but futilely. He was strong and very determined. To her immense relief the zip stuck again, just as it had when she was dressing. But this only made Rod doubly frustrated.

He pleaded with her now. 'Come on, Nerys, don't be a tease,' he breathed persuasively. 'You know how I feel about you.'

'No, Rod! Don't, please . . .' she begged, really alarmed now as she pushed his hand from her thigh desperately, his fingers pushing her skirt higher.

Instantly he became nasty. 'So you're a fake!' he rasped. 'The goods are not for sale, only to tantalise. Come off it, Nerys, you know what it's all about. You knew what to expect. I haven't been taking you around for nothing, you know!'

'You brute!' she flung at him. And with a supreme effort she managed to wrench the car door open. She almost fell out onto the dusty verge in front of the house, stumbled and began to run towards the front veranda. Crossing the lawn she tripped on a garden hose, and as she fell Rod caught her. He pinioned her arms roughly at her sides and thrust his body against her, his mouth on her lips, forcing her head back as she struggled to be free of his nauseating assault.

She wrenched her mouth away. 'Let me go!' she sobbed. 'Let me go!'

'I bet you weren't so frosty with Dr Hallam Vale that night at Ambleside,' he rasped.

Nerys drew in a sharp breath. 'How dare you!'

He was half drunk she realised, and he was taking out on her his resentment at losing at gambling. He was intent on making her pay for not bringing him luck. She saw his hand raised, was sure he meant to beat her into submission, and she opened her mouth to scream. No sound came out. But the next moment he released her, so abruptly that she didn't know what had happened. Then she saw Hallam Vale with one hand gripping Rod's shoulder and the other fist raised in a threatening gesture.

'When the lady says no she means no,' Hallam rapped out in a dangerous tone. 'So get moving, Troughton, if you know what's good for you. And don't bother her again. Right?'

'Who the hell do you think you are?' There was a truculent jut to Rod Troughton's lip but his resistance was only token. Hallam was bigger and stronger than he was, and when Hallam made another threatening gesture Rod did not pursue the argument but sloped off towards his car. When he was at a safe distance, he turned and said nastily, 'I guess you'll have better luck than me, mate, since you've already been there!'

Nerys shuddered. She stood rigidly, watching him drive away, smarting under the insult, unable to look at Hallam, yet deeply thankful he had been there to rescue her. Why had he been there? Had he just been returning himself?

'Thank you. I don't know what lucky coincidence managed to bring you here at the right moment, but thanks,' she said shakily.

He made no explanation. He took a step towards her and looked down into her face. The moonlight showed contempt in his expression and it hurt to see it. She plucked at the shoulders of her dress, pulling them up over her bare skin, painfully aware of Hallam's scornful gaze. Her hair was in disarray, she knew she must look terrible, and she felt ashamed.

She whispered, 'He was a bit drunk . . .'

'You are a fool,' Hallam said coldly, with harsh, underlying anger. 'If you go around throwing yourself at people, you'll get what you deserve! It's no use fighting when it's too late.'

His eyes held hers and for one appalling moment she felt sure he was going to begin where Rod had left off. She backed away from him. She was remembering the night at Ambleside. She had thrown herself at him then. But she hadn't thrown herself at Rod. It was unfair . . .

He read her thoughts and said in a tone of utter contempt, 'Don't worry, you're quite safe now.' And with that he walked off, leaving her trembling with fury because he had been right about Rod, and suffering a strange kind of frustration because he had walked off and left her without a word of sympathy. He despised her.

'Oh, I hate you!' she breathed irrationally, as she stumbled across the lawn in his wake.

CHAPTER EIGHT

'DID YOU have a good time last night?' Daniel asked next morning at breakfast. His tone did not suggest that he had heard anything of what had happened in the early hours outside the bungalow.

'It was all right,' Nerys said guardedly. She was tempted to tell him all about it in case Hallam did. But the memory of it made her feel such a fool all over again, she could not bring herself to confess. It had been a nightmare, with the crowning indignity her having to rip her dress, in which the zip had stuck, in order to get out of it. She could hardly have roused Hallam and asked him to help her!

'That doesn't sound very enthusiastic,' said Daniel.

Nerys poured herself another cup of coffee, glancing at the clock on the wall to make sure she had time for it. She was on duty in half an hour and she had scarcely slept a wink. She would be dozing off half-way through her shift if she wasn't careful.

For a moment she wavered between deciding to tell Daniel the whole story or only part of it, then made up her mind to take a chance on Hallam keeping his own counsel. One thing she was certain about, she would never go out with Rod Troughton again. It was unlikely he would ask her, she reflected ruefully. It still grated that Hallam had been right. She *had* been a fool, but she resented him telling her so. Daniel had warned her, too, but oddly enough she didn't resent that.

'Daniel,' she said, curious on one point, 'do you gamble?'

His eyebrows rose. 'Gamble? Well, I have a flutter at the local race-meetings. Nothing spectacular. Why?'

'I meant do you gamble at roulette, or baccarat, two-up?'

A frown appeared between his eyes, a narrow, scrutinising look in them. 'Just where did you go last night?' he asked sharply.

'You know about the casino then?'

'Of course. Who doesn't? But I don't go. I don't even know where it is. Did Rod take you there?' He was beginning to look angry.

Nerys nodded. 'We were having a drink at the club after our meal and a man came round looking for customers.'

Daniel drummed his fingers on the table angrily. 'You shouldn't have gone. You shouldn't have let him take you there. The fool! The place could have been raided. It wouldn't have looked good, you there . . .'

'I didn't think of that until later,' Nerys said soberly. 'I wouldn't go again. I didn't care for it much. It's a bit boring, and everyone is so intense. I just wondered if you . . .'

Daniel shook his head. 'Being caught in an illegal gambling joint is not something I hanker for.' He looked at her straight. 'You'd better not let Hallam know you went there.'

'I'm afraid he knows already. He was there when this man came round looking for customers. So was Barbra Albrecht.'

Daniel shrugged, then smiled grimly. 'Don't be surprised if you get a dressing down this morning!' He added, 'You said Barbra was there. And Klaus?'

'No.' Nerys hesitated, then said, 'I got the impression that she was waiting for Hallam.' She was glad to change the subject.

Daniel shook his head. 'I can't understand why he plays around with her. It just doesn't seem like him.'

'Doesn't it?' Nerys knew she sounded arch but she couldn't help it.

Daniel's look was sharp. 'Hallam likes women, but I would have thought he'd have more sense than to mess about with married ones.'

'Perhaps you don't know him as well as you think you do,' Nerys commented.

'You sound a bit uptight this morning,' Daniel observed, treating her to a searching look. 'Could it be that you're a little jealous?'

Nerys's cheeks flamed. She retorted indignantly, 'No! I'm not the slightest bit interested in Hallam. It's just your devious mind, Daniel, and your stupid wishful thinking!'

She rose abruptly. 'I must dash. See you later.'

But it was all a lie, she thought miserably, as she crossed the lawns to the hospital a short time later. She knew she must fight her feelings for Hallam, but it was a fight she knew she wasn't going to win. Even his anger last night and her resentment of it did nothing to diminish the growing feelings she had for him. She *was* jealous of Barbra. She wanted Hallam to think highly of her, and yet somehow she always managed to make him despise her.

She shuddered with apprehension as she anticipated their first encounter that morning. Would he castigate her as Daniel had predicted? She was, after all, employed by the hospital and he had every right to expect a high standard of personal behaviour from his staff.

She saw him almost as soon as she entered the hospital.

'Good-morning,' he said coldly, his piercing green eyes looking her over as though she was an unpleasant pathology specimen.

'Good-morning,' Nerys replied shakily.

He followed her into the sister's office. She gave a little gasp as he caught her arm and twisted it slightly. He inclined his head to look at the upper part of it. 'You seem to have acquired a nasty bruise,' he commented in a dry tone.

Nerys flinched as he ran gentle fingers over the area. She had not noticed it herself although, now she came to think of it, she had felt a slight pressure pain when she was dressing. She looked over her shoulder and saw the blue and yellow patch in the soft flesh of her upper arm. It had undoubtedly been caused by Rod's rough manhandling. She felt her cheeks begin to burn at the recollection of last night's rescue.

Hallam's eyes were boring into hers, leaving her in no doubt as to what he thought of her. She shook her arm clear, wishing the sleeve of her uniform had been long enough to cover the mark so that he couldn't have seen it. She waited for him to deliver a lecture on it being unwise for a nurse to go to gambling joints, but he said nothing. The silence and his green-eyed gaze became so unbearable that at length she said boldly,

'I realise I shouldn't have gone to that place with Rod, and I have no intention of going again. Or, in fact, anywhere with him.'

There was no sympathy in the ice-hard eyes. 'I should hope not,' he said scathingly. 'But perhaps the experience will teach you to be more careful.' Abruptly he looked away from her and took a step back. 'There was a new admission this morning. Somebody who got the worst of a fight. You'd better take a look at him. Third bed from the door in the men's ward.'

He gave her one of his annihilating looks and silently went out. Nerys stood motionless for a moment, fists clenched, fighting the conflict of hate and love which threatened to overwhelm her. Because suddenly she knew there was no denying it any longer. She loved him. Not the cold, hard man who despised her, but the kind, gentle man she had briefly glimpsed from time to time. The truth came like a sharp pain, then subsided into a dull, gnawing ache for which she knew there would be no cure, not while she remained in Kolbardi.

A few minutes later when she walked into the men's ward to see the new patient, she was outwardly calm and efficient, her personal feelings pushed to one side as her profession demanded. But she knew it was going to be hard to keep them deeper than a hair's breadth beneath the surface.

The patient was a sorry sight. His face and chest were almost completely hidden under dressings, and the bits that weren't were black and blue. His lip was cut and one eye swollen shut. The nurse who was with him grimaced at Nerys.

'Multiple abrasions and concussion. He hit his head on the kerb, so he says, but it's more likely he was kicked. They're always fighting, those miners. Either over money or women.'

'I wonder how the other one is,' remarked Nerys, bending to examine the injuries more closely.

'If he's too bad, we can probably expect him to totter in later,' said the nurse resignedly. She was writing on the patient's chart, which she then handed to Nerys before going off to attend to the needs of someone else.

Nerys remained by the bedside for a few moments. The man was sedated and unaware of her presence. As she looked down at him, she suddenly saw again, vividly, Rod Troughton's raised hand. Had he really intended to hit her? To beat her into submission? In his drunken rage at losing a lot of money, and being thwarted by her, he had lost control. She shuddered involuntarily. If Hallam hadn't come along just then, she might have ended up in a hospital bed, too.

During the next few days she neither saw nor heard anything of Rod Troughton. Not that she was surprised. It was hardly likely that he would bother her. Hallam never mentioned the incident again, and the only reminder of it was his increased coolness towards her. Outwardly he was friendly enough, and she didn't think Daniel noticed anything, but she felt the undercurrent of hostility in many subtle ways. Sometimes it was his tone of voice, at other times the way he looked at her. There were moments when she felt he was about to unbend a little, and then his face would close up tightly and the shutters would come down over the green irises.

Sometimes Nerys wished she had never agreed to take Sister Wimbourne's place. So far there had been no word from Janet as to when she expected to return. Hallam had mentioned a letter from her explaining her mother's condition and intimating that she did expect to be able to return, but she did not know when.

He had said at the time, 'I wouldn't want you to feel under an indefinite obligation, Nerys,' and she had sensed that he would be relieved if she said she wanted to leave. She did want to go, as she told herself many times, but it was something she could not bring herself to do. She knew it was because, somewhere deep down inside, she nurtured a vain hope that was foolish but irresistible. Daniel made it easy for her to pretend there were other reasons.

'Nerys hasn't got any pressing plans, have you, love? You might as well be here as anywhere.' He had added laughingly, 'At least I can keep an eye on you!' This had produced a faintly ironic glance from Hallam, which made Nerys flinch.

Daniel went on, 'In any case, she's settled in so well, hasn't she, Hallam? And it would be a pity to have to get another relief until Janet comes back. Of course, if Janet does have to stay in Perth, then that's another matter.'

Nerys knew she was an idiot. She ought to run now. Quite apart from Hallam, she ought to be making plans for the future. Putting off doing that was all too easy while she had a job at the hospital, which, even though it entailed seeing Hallam often, was better than the vacuum offered by the future.

She was feeling rather depressed one day, not having been out anywhere for a week and the weather having been particularly hot and humid, despite the fact that summer was nearly over, when Sinclair Wilson telephoned. He had said he would, but she had not set much store by his promise. The sound of his breezy voice lifted her spirits considerably. Anything or anyone who could distract her thoughts from Hallam was welcome.

'How's my favourite little English rose today?' he greeted her cheerfully, but did not wait for an answer.

Nerys screwed up her face at the cliché but was so pleased to talk to him she forgave his effusiveness. He went on brightly, 'I see you've been in the news. Quite the little heroine by the sound of it!'

Nerys was embarrassed. She had not forgotten the dash to Ambleside and the aftermath; it kept coming back to haunt her because it was one of the times she had spoiled everything. But she had forgotten the attention they had received briefly afterwards.

'Everybody made far too much fuss about it. They must have been short of news,' she said.

Sinclair laughed. 'You're too modest. I've been telling Mother about you. She's looking forward to meeting you.'

'Oh, is she back?'

'Yes, she came back with me,' he told her. 'So as soon as she's settled down again, you must come out for a weekend. I'm sorry it's been so long since I was last in touch, but I had some business interstate, and then there were the floods . . .'

Nerys was content to accept his excuses, whether they

were genuine or not. No arrangement for her visit was made then, but Sinclair promised to be in touch. She felt sure he would be, and the visit to a sheep station was something to look forward to. In the back of her mind, however, there were a few misgivings. This was inevitable since her experience with Rod Troughton. But Sinclair was a very different person—or was he? Would he expect a reward for inviting her to Yeramba Springs for a weekend? The thought bothered her so much that she eventually made up her mind to say no if he phoned again.

It was a day or two later that Rod Troughton made one last impression on her life. It was only indirectly, however. Daniel breezed in one evening when she was preparing their meal and announced,

'I've got some news that'll rock you, Nerys.'

'What is it?' she demanded, not evening speculating.

'It's about Rod Troughton.'

A rush of apprehension ran through her, although she could not think why. 'What about him?' she asked tremulously. She hoped he hadn't been admitted to hospital. It would be too galling to have to nurse the man.

Daniel sprawled in a chair and flipped open a can of beer she had handed to him from the fridge. 'He's been arrested.'

'Arrested?' It was a shock.

'Yep.'

'What for?' Her first thought was that it must be for being in an illegal gambling joint.

'A whole string of offences, apparently. It appears that the police have been looking for him for quite a while down south. Troughton isn't his real name. He's wanted on a couple of fraud charges and non-payment of maintenance to a wife and kids in Sydney.'

Nerys gasped. 'He told me he wasn't married!'

Daniel laughed. 'You never want to believe anything anyone tells you up here, especially the men. Every other bloke is escaping from something, some petty crime or marital difficulties, debts. It's a good place to lose yourself, the north.'

Nerys looked at him thoughtfully. She was thinking

about Hallam and his reluctance to speak of his former life. Was he one of them? Was he, too, a man with a past he dared not talk about because it was shady? Maybe he had a wife and children? Maybe that was why he had warned her about Rod Troughton. Perhaps someone who was running away from something, recognised someone else doing the same thing.

They were still talking about Rod Troughton when Hallam came in. He'd already heard the news. When he glanced at her with a slight twist to his mouth, an expression far from a smile, Nerys felt her cheeks beginning to burn.

She served up their meal in silence, and throughout it kept stealing sidelong glances at him, pondering on what might have driven him to hide in a town like Kolbardi. Was Hallam Vale even his real name?

At last she could not resist saying, when the subject returned to Rod Troughton briefly, 'Daniel says half the men working up here are running away from something.' She watched Hallam's face, but not a muscle stirred. There was no guilty start, not a flicker of the dark eyelashes, and his green eyes were unwavering. Either he had nothing to hide or he exercised excellent mastery over his emotions.

While they were waiting for the coffee to percolate the telephone rang. Hallam went to answer it, since calls were generally for one or other of the two doctors. This time, however, the call was for Nerys.

Hallam came back and said curtly, 'It's your friend, Sinclair Wilson.' The way he said 'your friend' implied that he didn't think much of her choice of friends.

Nerys went into the hall and picked up the receiver. 'Hello, Sinclair.'

'Nerys, what about this weekend?'

She was only slightly taken aback. 'What about it?'

'Can you come out to Yeramba Springs? If that isn't convenient, what about a mid-week break?'

'I—I don't know.' She had intended to say a flat no, but it was difficult to find a good excuse.

'Oh, come on, Nerys, you must have time off. It's against the law to employ slave labour!'

'We're a bit short-staffed at the moment,' she hedged.

'Listen, I've told Mother you're dying to come,' he pleaded. 'You must be able to make it sometime!'

Nerys felt perhaps she had been a little unfair in her judgment. Why should he be another Rod Troughton? Hallam didn't like him either, but that fact only made her more anxious to prove that this time he was wrong.

'Well, yes, of course . . .' she gave in. 'As a matter of fact, I think I could come next weekend. I'm off from Friday night until Monday morning. I'd have to be back on Sunday.'

'No worries,' he assured her. 'I'll fly over to Kolbardi on Saturday morning early, and have you home for supper on Sunday. Can you get someone to run you out to the airstrip?'

Nerys was astonished. 'You mean, you've got a plane?' She had expected to be driven to Yeramba Springs.

'Didn't I mention it before? It's only a small Cessna. Nifty little job though. Absolutely essential if you want to get about in comfort in these parts. Will that be OK then? Say around 9.30 at Kolbardi airstrip?'

Nerys was overwhelmed. 'Yes, yes, I suppose so. Thank you, Sinclair.'

He answered in a low voice, 'I shall be looking forward to it, my dear.'

A few minutes later she returned to the dining-room and Daniel remarked teasingly, 'Another of your conquests, I suppose!'

Nerys felt obliged to explain.

Daniel nodded approvingly. 'Why not? It'll give you a taste of how the other half lives. The Wilsons are what you might call the aristocrats of station owners. I suppose Sinclair could be considered a good catch, if it was money you were interested in!'

'Daniel, really!' Nerys felt acutely embarrassed, especially with Hallam's cynical gaze on her.

Daniel laughed. 'Well, he *is* rich.'

'Also something of a playboy,' commented Hallam rather sourly.

Nerys terminated the discussion by saying, 'Are you two

going to sit here and have coffee, or go out onto the veranda?'

It was cooler outside, so the two men elected to retire to the veranda and Nerys, refusing any assistance from Daniel, carried the tray out to them. Usually she was the first to excuse herself on these occasions. She always tried to be as unobtrusive as possible, aware that she was an intruder in a bachelor establishment. She felt that there were probably matters the two doctors wanted to discuss without her around. Tonight, however, Daniel excused himself first.

'Must be off, folks,' he said suddenly, glancing at his watch.

Nerys smiled. 'Gayle again?' Her brother had been seeing the attractive book-keeper a lot lately, and she had been in and out of the house quite a bit, although Nerys often wondered if that was more on the off-chance of seeing Hallam than Daniel. Certainly Hallam displayed no more than polite interest in Gayle, which was a relief to Nerys as she was keen to see something develop between the girl and her brother.

When Daniel had left them, Nerys stood up and said she had things to do. It could have been wonderful, she was thinking, sitting there alone with him on the veranda in the cool evening, with the scent of frangipani wafting across the damp lawns where sprinklers were still idly turning. But instead it would only be painful if she lingered. She was not, however, to escape his attention so easily.

Hallam rose too. 'I'll give you a hand with the washing-up.'

Nerys could do no less than accept gracefully. As they despatched the dishes she was reminded of the time they had washed up together at Ambleside, and a wave of longing swept over her. What a strange enigma of a man he was, she thought, half angrily, half despairingly.

Nerys could not help feeling some pleasurable antici-pation when Saturday morning arrived. It was the first, and probably the only time, she reflected wryly as she dressed in a green cotton trouser suit with a green and white striped top under the jacket, that she would be taken on a date in a private aeroplane. She would have to count it as a highlight of her sojourn in Australia.

Daniel drove her to the airstrip a little before nine-thirty. Sinclair's sparkling white and red Cessna was already waiting on the runway, and he was standing talking to two mechanics who were servicing the mining company's plane outside a corrugated iron hangar. There was a bit of a breeze and although it was cooler, the direct sun was hot. Nerys was glad she had tied a scarf around her hair, although she did not expect to be standing in the sun for long.

Sinclair came towards them as Daniel parked. In his characteristically effusive way, he took hold of Nerys's hands, held her at arm's length and said smilingly, 'As I thought—just as beautiful as ever! You look stunning in that outfit, but then you'd look stunning in sackcloth,' he added extravagantly.

Nerys caught an expressive wink from Daniel, who said, only half jokingly, 'Take good care of her, Sinclair. She's rather special to me.'

Sinclair feigned indignation. 'She's rather special to me, too!'

'Daniel's always big-brothering me,' laughed Nerys, 'even though we are twins.'

Daniel squeezed her arm. 'Have a good time. See you Sunday. You'd better let me know what time you're coming in, Sinclair, and I'll pick Nerys up.'

'Shall do,' Sinclair agreed.

It was a short flight to the station, but it was a new and exciting experience for Nerys. She had never been up in a small aircraft before, and from take-off to landing she enjoyed every second.

Seen from the air, the dusty red Pilbara region was even more empty, barren and formidable than it seemed on the ground. Long, straight tracks seemed to vanish into nowhere. Winding creeks, some dry, some partially flowing, patterned parts of the land. In places there remained traces of the recent floods, huge areas of mud that had dried and cracked into a jigsaw pattern. Stark hills broke the monotony of the red plains, as did swathes of spinifex and porcupine grass and other scattered vegetation. Knowing that she was flying over some of the richest iron ore country in the world was exciting, especially knowing that, beneath the stark red and purple hills, some as yet undiscovered mineral could well be hidden.

At the Yeramba Springs airstrip a truck driven by an aboriginal station hand was waiting for them. For a couple of kilometres they bumped over a rough dirt track through almost featureless terrain that looked, to Nerys, totally devoid of animals, until the homestead came into view. She was surprised to find a lush garden and bright green lawns surrounding it.

It was easy to see that no expense was spared here to make life in the outback comfortable. Inside, the impression was reinforced. Cool air-conditioning greeted them as they stepped into the old, high-ceilinged house. It had a great deal of charm, most of which was imparted by the old-fashioned decorative ceilings and antique furniture.

'Come and meet my mother,' Sinclair invited eagerly. Taking Nerys's arm, he guided her to a spacious sitting-room with french windows opening onto a heavily creepered veranda. The room was furnished in muted tones of green and yellow and had a cool, soothing atmosphere.

Nerys, however, found her attention riveted by Sinclair's mother. He had not told her that Mrs Wilson was confined to a wheelchair. White-haired and rather older than Nerys had expected, Mrs Wilson propelled herself across the carpet towards Nerys and her son.

'Sinclair, dear, you're back,' she murmured, with the relief of a mother who has never quite come to terms with the fact that her son pilots his own aeroplane. 'And this is Nerys.'

Sharp blue eyes looked down an aristocratic, aquiline nose, and a beringed hand was extended in welcome. She smiled in a friendly enough way as she greeted the young woman her son had brought home, but in her look there was all the subtle appraisal and slight suspicion of a mother possessive of her only child. A quiver at the corner of her mouth betrayed her apprehension.

'How do you do, my dear?' she said in a cool, clear voice that stated her reservations, although it was politely welcoming.

'Hello, Mrs Wilson,' Nerys said, shaking the slender hand briefly and noticing the painted nails that, together with the jewellery, the faultless hairstyle ever so faintly blue-tinted, spoke of a woman careful of her appearance even in this outlandish place. 'It's very kind of you and Sinclair to invite me to stay,' she added.

Mrs Wilson nodded in acknowledgement, then said, 'I'm sure you would like to see your room and unpack your things. Let Sinclair know if there is anything you want. And then we'll have some coffee.' Her tone was a shade imperious. She was used to ordering servants around, Nerys realised.

Nerys felt slightly lost in the huge bedroom that Sinclair showed her to. It was twice the size of her room at the bungalow in Kolbardi, and like the rest of the house furnished with antiques. As she hung her clothes in the wardrobe, she felt a little uneasy again, almost wishing she had not come. Yet she was glad of the opportunity to visit such a property as Yeramba Springs.

She removed her headscarf and fluffed out her hair before returning to the sitting-room, where she found Sinclair and his mother deep in conversation. The flow of talk ceased as she entered, and Nerys was sure they had been talking about her because just the slightest embarrassment showed in each of their expressions of welcome.

Coffee was served by a young aboriginal girl, who smiled in a friendly way at Nerys while regarding her with open curiosity. Nerys felt that Mrs Wilson adopted a rather patronisingly childish tone with the girl, but she nevertheless spoke kindly. Sinclair, Nerys noticed, was very solicitous of his mother and there seemed to be considerable affection between them. Nerys did not instantly warm towards Mrs Wilson, but she was pleasant and made some effort to make Nerys feel at home. Nerys suspected that Sinclair was more like his father, an intuition later borne out when she happened to see a photograph of the late Mr Wilson.

'How are you enjoying life in Kolbardi?' Mrs Wilson asked.

'I like it very much,' replied Nerys. 'It's very different to what I've been used to, but nursing is nursing wherever you are.'

'Yes, Sinclair mentioned that you were a nurse,' replied Mrs Wilson. 'You are relieving at the hospital while one of their sisters is away, I believe?' The blue eyes registered some interest.

'Yes, that's right.'

'Will she be away long?'

'I really don't know,' Nerys answered, explaining, 'We haven't heard from her lately. Her mother was very ill with a heart complaint.'

Mrs Wilson nodded and seemed to be considering some question in her mind. After a moment she said in an off-hand tone, 'Sinclair says I ought to have a nurse, now I'm getting older.' Her hands were spread helplessly. 'As you can see, I'm not very mobile, and some things are becoming more difficult for me.'

Her son responded a shade tetchily, Nerys thought, although his mother did not appear to notice it. 'Mother would be better off if she lived in Perth all the time. She spends part of the summer down there but she prefers to live here most of the time.'

'I have lived most of my life in the north,' said Mrs Wilson, and her tone revealed a stubborn streak. 'I am not a city person.'

Just from looking at her, Nerys would have thought she was. Appearances can be very deceptive, she thought.

Sinclair, as though reading her thoughts, said, 'Mother could break horses with the skill of the best of the men, but she always looked elegant in a ball gown, too.'

His mother coloured with pleasure at the compliment, and her glance at him was affectionate. He flatters her, Nerys thought, in the same way he flatters all women.

Feeling that it might be expected of her, Nerys changed into a dress for dinner, a prettily patterned, rather demure one that made her look younger, especially with her hair loose and flowing. Sinclair paid her the expected compliments, but his mother merely looked her over as she might inspect a servant she was about to employ—or so it seemed to Nerys.

Dinner was served with semi-formality in a beautifully furnished and decorated dining-room with fine china, crystal glasses and silver cutlery. It was difficult to remember that they were a long way from civilisation in such an atmosphere.

Later, when she was walking in the garden with Sinclair after having, at her request, helped Mrs Wilson to bed, she remarked on it. Sinclair shrugged and said with a smile, as he tucked her arm through his, 'Why rough it if you don't have to? Mother has quite taken to you, Nerys.' There was some satisfaction in the remark, she felt, and a vague suspicion that had been forming in her mind was strengthened.

'She is a very charming person,' Nerys said, feeling she ought to at least reciprocate. 'It's a shame she is paraplegic. How did it happen?' It had been on the tip of her tongue to ask his mother, but she had felt that perhaps such a personal enquiry might be thought impertinent. She had no qualms, however, about asking Sinclair.

'She was thrown from her horse,' he answered. 'It happened about ten years ago, when my father was still alive. It virtually killed him, seeing her like that. She had always been so lively, and still was, even in her late fifties as she was then. She coped much better than he did with her disability and never let it get her down. But this last couple of years things haven't been so good. She's getting older and more fragile. She really does need a nurse on hand constantly. Mrs Dryden, our station manager's wife, is an enormous help, of course. But she is busy and hasn't the time to spare that may be necessary as Mother becomes less able to do things herself.' He smiled in a kind of exasperated affection. 'Mother is very independent. She will fight the idea of needing a nurse for as long as she can.'

'Independence is hard to relinquish,' said Nerys sympathetically.

Sinclair turned to look at her fully. Then, clasping his arms lightly around her, he murmured, 'You're a lovely girl, Nerys.' He kissed her lightly on the lips.

Nerys instinctively turned her head away as he went to kiss her again. He was offended.

'I thought you liked me?' he murmured coaxingly.

'Yes, yes, of course I like you.' Nerys considered him. Tonight he seemed very youthful, very debonair, very sincere. And very romantic. He was just the man to help her forget her feelings for Hallam Vale.

He drew her closer into his arms, saying, 'Then show me how much.'

His mouth was gentle, undemanding, and there was nothing in the kiss she could object to, yet something prevented her from responding to his caress. It wasn't difficult to know what. He wasn't Hallam. But letting Hallam intrude was foolish. She must banish him as she had banished Chris. Only fools dwelt on relationships that had no future. And the best way to forget was to kindle an interest in someone else.

Sinclair was looking reproachfully into her eyes. 'Nerys, darling, surely you could show a little more enthusiasm than that!' He pressed his mouth on hers again with increasing ardour, moving his lips against hers arousingly this time, so that she found herself responding a little more eagerly.

'That's better,' he murmured. 'Much better.'

'Sinclair,' Nerys faltered, then was not sure what she had intended to say. She felt unaccountably mixed up inside.

'Yes?' he murmured against her ear.

She sighed. 'I don't know.'

He ran both hands up through her hair and his fingertips massaged her scalp, making the flesh tingle all the way down her spine. 'You're quite irresistible.'

A small panic gripped her as she remembered Rod Troughton. 'Let's go back,' she urged. 'I'm really very tired.'

'But of course. You shall have an early night and tomorrow, as I promised, we'll take a picnic lunch and we'll ride around the property and visit one or two of our beauty spots, which I'm sure you don't suspect exist.'

On the veranda he kissed her goodnight with restrained passion, making no demands on her and treating her with a deference she could not fault.

In the morning she dressed comfortably in jeans and a cool cotton top, putting out a sunhat to don later over her swept-up hair. At breakfast Sinclair casually asked if she would mind helping his mother rise.

'Since you are here,' he explained, 'and are obviously less inept than either I or Mrs Dryden.'

Nerys was sure now that there was more purpose to her visit than mere friendly hospitality towards a stranger. Sinclair, she suspected, was keen to have his mother accept her as her nurse. But why hadn't he broached the subject with her first, to see whether she would be interested? It was a little puzzling. And a little worrying, too. Nerys wondered what she would say to such an offer if it were to be made. Knowing that Sinclair was attracted to her made her feel uneasy about such an arrangement.

Mrs Wilson had breakfast in bed, and the aboriginal girl, Tammie, was taking the tray out when Nerys went in. Sinclair's mother was, as he had intimated, an independent person, and she required Nerys to help only when she could not manage by herself.

The shower had been adapted to make bathing easy for her and she needed only minimum assistance to cope with this task. However, Nerys could see what Sinclair meant about increasing fragility. Soon the elderly lady was going to need more and more assistance.

She wheeled Mrs Wilson into the sitting-room, fetched her glasses, book of crossword puzzles and magazines, and positioned them all where instructed, including the finely wrought brass bell which was used to summon Tammie, the aboriginal maid.

Tammie's mother, Nerys was told, helped Mrs Dryden in the kitchen. She had been taught by Mrs Wilson herself and was quite a good cook—and Tammie's aunt did the cleaning. All of them had grown up on the station, and according to Mrs Wilson, were not in the least inclined to leave it. She spoke of the people who worked at Yeramba Springs, mostly aboriginals, with sincere affection, and during their conversation Nerys warmed towards the frail little woman considerably.

Quite clearly Mrs Wilson doted on her son, and the only criticism she had of him was that he had not yet produced any grandchildren for her.

'It's high time he had a son to carry on after him,' she said. 'I wouldn't want Yeramba Springs to go out of the family.'

Nerys thought, but did not say, that it was unlikely Sinclair would oblige since he did not seem at all the marrying kind.

When she joined Sinclair after settling his mother comfortably for the day, she received a shock. She had expected that the tour of the property would be on horseback, but she found Sinclair waiting for her with two motor cycles.

'But I've never ridden one!' Nerys exclaimed. 'I thought you meant horses!'

He laughed. 'We only keep a couple of horses now. We found it much easier to muster on two wheels instead of four legs. Bikes are cheaper to keep, too. Come on, it's dead easy! You can have a practice ride around the yard. These are quite light machines, but they're very sturdy.'

A smiling station hand wheeled a trail bike over, and Nerys gingerly grasped the handlebars. Sinclair explained how to start it, stop it, how to handle the gears and the brake, and it did seem quite simple. After all, she could drive a car, so she ought to be able to handle this machine.

'Go on, take it round the yard a couple of times,' he urged.

Nerys nervously swung her leg over the saddle, kicked the starter and opened the throttle. She had no trouble balancing since she had ridden a bicycle as a child, and she quickly proved Sinclair right by circling the yard on her second trip as competently as if she had been riding one for years.

'There's no traffic where we're going,' he said with a grin, 'so you've nothing to worry about. Just watch out for bumps and holes.'

Nerys completed one more practice circuit, watched in mingled amusement and admiration by a crowd of station hands, who had slowly gathered to see her perform. Returning to Sinclair, she said breathlessly, 'All right, I'm ready.'

It proved to be an exhilarating ride, sometimes on rough tracks, sometimes where there were no tracks at all. Occasionally they passed a group of sheep who angled off at their approach. When Sinclair mentioned how many thousand head ran on the station, Nerys was astonished.

'But I've scarcely seen any!' she exclaimed.

'And you've scarcely seen any of the station,' he replied. 'It covers a few hundred square miles.'

They stopped for lunch at a billabong, in the shade of some gnarled old ghost gums, and sheltered by a cleft in a hillside.

'I never would have guessed it was here,' Nerys exclaimed, when they rode up to it. 'What an enchanting spot!' She added soberly, 'It makes you think, though. You could easily die of thirst in this country and never know you were a stone's throw from water.' She shuddered.

They were walking away from the bikes down to the water's edge, and Sinclair slipped his arm around her waist. 'It has happened,' he said. 'But don't worry, you won't get lost with me.' He stopped and turned her face up to his, then kissed her slowly and gently, as undemandingly as before. But he left her in no doubt that he was keeping a tight rein on his feelings.

They spent a lazy couple of hours having lunch and exploring along the edges of the billabong before riding back to the homestead. Sinclair was at his most charming and told Nerys a great deal about the property and family history, but he never once raised the subject of his mother's nurse, and that he had her in mind for the job. It was odd, she thought. If it was in his mind, why didn't he at least sound her out on her inclination, or otherwise, to spend more time in the outback?

'Maybe I just jumped to conclusions,' Nerys said to herself, as she looked down on the now more familiar landscape when Sinclair flew her back to Kolbardi late that afternoon. 'Or maybe,' she added silently, 'Mrs Wilson didn't like me after all!'

Rather dismayingly, Daniel was not waiting for her as he

had promised. Instead, Hallam was standing by the Range Rover when the Cessna landed. Instantly, Nerys felt a violent lurch of her heart. There was just something about the languid way he leaned against the vehicle, the slow, easy way he strode towards the plane, that brought a surge of love swelling up inside her, sheer joy at seeing him, and a faint feeling of regret because she had let Sinclair kiss her. It was with extreme difficulty that she concealed her true feelings. She greeted Hallam very off-handedly as a result.

He was scarcely less indifferent as he said, 'Had a good trip?' and, without waiting for an answer, took her overnight bag from Sinclair and strode back to the Range Rover. Sinclair stared after him for a moment, then let his eyes rest searchingly on Nerys's face. 'Good-looking guy,' he remarked.

'If you're fishing for a compliment, you won't get one from me!' Nerys said lightly.

He laughed and bent to kiss her lips, cupping her face in his hands. 'I'll be in touch. Soon.'

'Thanks for a marvellous weekend,' Nerys said sincerely. And it was true, she had enjoyed herself.

Hallam had little to say on the drive back into Kolbardi, apart from telling her that Daniel had had to go out on a house call to someone who refused to see anyone else. Nerys, mainly to ease the tension she felt, told him about Yeramba Springs, how much she had enjoyed the Cessna flight and how she had ridden a motor cycle for the first time after only a short practice.

'I'm sure you pick up most things very quickly,' he commented, a smile straying briefly across his lips, and that was one of the very few remarks he made. He seemed to be deeply preoccupied and, Nerys felt sure, not really interested in her weekend.

Daniel proved a more enthusiastic audience, which helped to soften the rather let-down feeling Hallam had given her.

'I wish I'd been there,' he laughed. 'I'd love to have seen you careering off across country on a trail bike! Did you do any mustering?'

'No, of course not!'

'Are you sure you didn't fall off?' Her brother looked at her arms and legs for bruises, a teasing grin on his face.

'I nearly did once,' Nerys admitted, recalling the rock she had skidded over. 'But it was great fun.' She added a trifle wistfully, 'I'd still rather ride horses. And it seems strange to use motor bikes to muster sheep, incongruous somehow.'

'That's progress,' said Hallam, emerging from his morose reverie briefly.

During the next few days Sinclair telephoned several times and then came to Kolbardi, staying overnight with friends so that he could take Nerys to dinner at the Kolbardi Club. She had an enjoyable evening, and all the time was waiting for him to broach the subject of her nursing his mother, but not a word was said. She really must have been barking up the wrong tree, she thought, puzzled because Sinclair seemed at pains to tell her how delighted his mother had been to meet her and what a charming girl she had thought she was.

A few days later Sinclair flew in again, and again invited Nerys out to dinner. This gave rise to some comment from Daniel.

'Twice in a week,' he remarked. 'He must be rather keen on you, Neri!' He gave her a searching look, obviously hoping for an admission from her that it was so. He also shot a glance at Hallam, and Nerys knew her brother was disappointed because nothing had come of his matchmaking.

Nerys said nonchalantly, 'Sinclair is a playboy, Daniel!' She caught Hallam's eye, which was very sardonic indeed.

Daniel persisted. 'Even playboys settle down sometime. How would you like to spend the rest of your life on a sheep station, Neri?' he asked bluntly. The idea seemed to dismay him a little.

Nerys had not seriously considered such a possibility. But suddenly she wondered—was a proposal what Sinclair was leading up to? Perhaps it wasn't such a bizarre possibility. She said non-committally, 'Would I have to? Sinclair doesn't spend all his time at Yeramba Springs.'

'But you can bet your life his wife would be expected to,'

put in Hallam in a rather harsh tone. He added with emphasis, 'Looking after his crippled mother.'

Even Daniel looked taken aback. 'Well, of course she is a paraplegic and I know you were saying the other day, Neri, how frail she seemed, but . . .'

Hallam's expression was close to a sneer. 'She needs a nurse, full time soon, I should think. And naturally she's keen to see Sinclair settle down and produce grandchildren. It would be a smart move on Sinclair's part to marry a nurse. He'd be killing two birds with the one stone, so to speak.'

Nerys was angry. 'I think that's a despicable thing to say! You're suggesting that Sinclair is a very calculating and uncaring kind of person.'

'Do you really think Sinclair Wilson would make a faithful husband?' Hallam said. His eyes held hers as he rose to leave the room. He passed her chair and added softly, 'You were wrong about Troughton, remember.'

Daniel raised his eyebrows as the door closed behind the senior doctor. 'He sounds as though he's a bit sore about something.'

'He should mind his own business!' said Nerys angrily.

'Would you marry Sinclair if he asked you?' Daniel asked.

Nerys took a deep breath. She could do a lot worse than marry Sinclair Wilson, she thought defiantly. But he wasn't likely to ask her. Despite what Daniel had said she was sure Sinclair was not the marrying kind. But she said, 'I'd be a fool not to, wouldn't I? Hallam really doesn't know what he's talking about.'

She went off to get ready for her date with Sinclair, but whereas earlier she had quite been looking forward to it, suddenly a depression settled over her and she wished she didn't have to spend the evening with anyone. There was no way she could get out of it now, however.

She dressed with her usual care in a new pale mauve dress she had bought locally, since her blue one had been torn beyond repair that night the zip stuck. In any case, to have worn it again would have reminded her of the unpleasantness she preferred to forget.

She was ready in good time and waiting on the veranda for Sinclair to arrive when Hallam joined her. The first she knew of his presence was a light touch near her shoulder-blades.

'No zip problems tonight,' he murmured, and as she turned, startled, his eyes raked her with a look that was part sensuous, part scornful.

'No,' she replied, more disturbed by his nearness than she wanted to be. Her earlier anger with him, however, began to smoulder.

He looked her over leisurely once more and seemed about to say something, then changed his mind. At the same moment headlights beamed along the street, a car drew up and Sinclair tooted. He got out and strolled towards them.

'Goodnight, Hallam,' Nerys said curtly, and she went to meet Sinclair, knowing that Hallam's eyes were probably still on her.

That there was something different about Sinclair that night, Nerys became aware in the first couple of minutes. He was superficially the same effusive flatterer, but underneath something was simmering, a kind of suppressed excitement. Nerys was intrigued but she did not remark on his mood.

It was not long, though, before she discovered the reason for it. They were in the middle of their meal when he suddenly said, as though unable to hold it back any longer, 'Nerys, I want to ask you something. Something very important.'

Her heart missed a beat. 'Yes, what is it?' Surely he couldn't be going to . . . Now her heart was racing wildly. What was she going to say if he did? But he couldn't be, not Sinclair—and they scarcely knew each other, anyway. Her eyes met his as he reached across the table and held the tips of her fingers lightly.

'Nerys, you may think this is a bit premature—I mean we haven't known each other all that long, although with some people it isn't necessary, don't you agree?' His blue eyes appealed to her wordlessly. Nerys tried to find something to say, but words would not form on her tongue, it was too dry. 'Nerys,' he said earnestly, 'I would very much like to marry you.'

Nerys swallowed hard. She looked into his smiling face and saw that he was completely confident of the answer he wanted. She tried desperately to think. Did she want to marry Sinclair Wilson? Half joking about it with Daniel was one thing. She had not seriously considered that it might be a real possibility.

'Sinclair,' she murmured weakly, 'I wasn't expecting anything like this. I never dreamed . . .'

He squeezed her fingers harder. 'Come now, Nerys, you must have guessed there was something in the wind when I took you to meet my mother.'

'I—I thought you might be going to ask me if I would take on the job of nurse after I finished at Kolbardi,' Nerys faltered.

He laughed softly. 'And have you run out on me in a few months?'

Nerys looked at him speculatively. What would it be like to be married to this man? He was considerate and kind and she was sure he would provide without question everything she wanted. He was rich, good-looking and intelligent. She liked him. But it wasn't love. Did that matter? Twice she had fallen in love and look where that had got her. She might be a great deal happier married to a man like Sinclair Wilson. She might even learn to love him.

Through her thoughts came his voice. 'Nerys, darling, my mother loves you. I've never known her take to anyone as she took to you. She thinks you will make me a perfect wife, and she says she couldn't think of anyone better to look after her. It would be much better to have someone who is family than a string of temporary girls just wanting a taste of the outback, and then getting tired of it. And besides, she's very anxious for me to settle down.' He smiled a little diffidently. 'You know what mothers are, they keep asking when they are going to see their grand-children.'

For a moment his words just seem to wash over Nerys and she was not absorbing them. Then all at once Hallam's recent harsh words began ringing in her ears, drowning out the soft, persuasive tones of Sinclair's voice. Strange sensations began surging through her. Sinclair's face, bland and smiling, suddenly began to blur before her eyes.

'Nerys!' His voice was sharp all at once. 'Aren't you going to say something?'

She half opened her mouth, but nothing came out. All she could think of was that she had come within a hair's breadth of making the biggest mistake of her life. She couldn't marry Sinclair. It would be total disaster if she did. Hallam was right. Sinclair needed a wife and a nurse for his mother. She presented an acceptable combination, but she couldn't marry a man who wanted to run his private life like one of his business deals. He had not said a word about loving her. And she knew she would be a fool if she thought he would give up his other life, the life of a playboy. He would go off enjoying himself, just as Hallam had said, while his wife stayed at home and did her duty as nurse to his mother, nursemaid to his children. There was a painful tightening in her chest as she recognised the truth of it. She felt angry—not with Sinclair for trying to delude her, but with Hallam, for seeing it more clearly than she had herself.

'Sinclair,' she said in a low voice, 'I'm sorry . . .'

His face changed. The smile snapped off and he leaned forward, his fingers gripping hers tightly.

'*Sorry*, Nerys?'

With a supreme effort she spoke her piece. 'Yes, I'm sorry, I didn't realise! Perhaps that was naive of me, but I didn't think you were the marrying kind.'

'You've changed my mind for me, Nerys,' he said, smiling again.

'No,' she said rather harshly, 'I haven't. All I've done is make you think you could solve two problems at once. You don't love me, Sinclair. You imagine it might be rather pleasant being married to me, and knowing your mother was well looked after you would feel so much freer to gallivant about . . .'

'Nerys! That's unkind!'

'But true. You don't do much at Yeramba Springs, do you? I realised that when I was there. Your manager does everything. You prefer to look after your various business

interests down south. Your wife would find herself stuck at
Yeramba Springs without you for most of the time,
wouldn't she? No, it wouldn't work, Sinclair, not for me.'

He looked more shattered than she had ever seen a man
look, and she wondered if she had been too hard on him.
But his reaction wasn't because he loved her. And he was
not distraught just because she had turned him down, she
realised. It was because she had thwarted what he had
considered a very good plan, when he had been confident
she would not.

'I'm very flattered that you asked me to marry you,' she
said, 'but don't you see, I can't? I don't want a playboy for a
husband.'

That did not hurt him as much as it should have done, she
thought. He drew his hand away from hers and ran his
tongue over his lips. He managed a wry sort of smile. 'I
guess I under-estimated you, Nerys.'

'You made a mistake,' she agreed, not liking the way he
had put it.

He shrugged. 'No hard feelings?'

'None.' She mustered a smile. He was still very likeable
in a way. He took defeat resignedly. But looking at him now
she saw how weak he was, how self-centred and shallow.
She knew she had only considered marrying him as a way of
escape.

Later, when he drove her home, she felt just a bit
regretful, again feeling that perhaps she had been too hard
on him, but he had denied none of what she had said.

As she paused before getting out of the car, she said,
'Thanks for everything, Sinclair. I feel a bit badly about it.'

He leaned across and brushed her cheek with his lips.
'Don't be, there's no need.'

And he was right, there wasn't, she reflected as she
walked towards the house and heard his car drive off behind
her. She didn't look back. Sinclair wasn't hurt. He wasn't in
love with her. He would never have changed for her. And
she would have deeply regretted it if she had married him.

CHAPTER NINE

It was inevitable that Daniel would eventually remark on the fact that Sinclair Wilson no longer telephoned or made special trips to Kolbardi to see Nerys.

Nerys shrugged it off. 'I told you, he's just a playboy. I was simply a temporary amusement.'

She almost told her brother about Sinclair's proposal, but somehow it seemed unfair to Sinclair—though why she should feel that she wasn't sure. It was odd really, she had come all the way to Australia to see Daniel, imagining she would confide in him about everything and heal all her wounds by thus cleansing them, but it hadn't worked out that way. She had wanted to talk about Chris but hadn't been able to; she needed to talk about Hallam but that wasn't possible; and even what had happened with Rod and Sinclair she felt a need to be circumspect about.

She looked at Daniel's handsome, smiling face. She was very fond of him, he was her twin, but that didn't give her the right to burden him with her problems. It had been good just being there with him all these weeks, sharing his work. And yet, she thought a trifle wryly, it had only confused her life all the more. That wasn't Daniel's fault, of course, that was Hallam's.

She knew now that going out with Rod Troughton and Sinclair Wilson, pretending to herself that she liked them, fiercely defending them to herself and Hallam, had been her defence against falling in love with him. It hadn't worked. She had told herself that it was because she wanted to forget Chris, but the truth was that she had forgotten Chris the moment she met Hallam Vale. It was to stop herself falling for him that she had tried to fall in love with the other two. She shuddered to think what a mess she could have landed herself in through this self-deception. That Hallam had recognised the dangers before she had herself only made her resent him more.

She would not become involved with a man even just socially, during the rest of her stay in Kolbardi, she decided. It shouldn't be for much longer. Janet's last communication had sounded hopeful that she would be returning shortly. She and Daniel were talking about it one morning while they were having a cup of coffee in the sister's office at the hospital during a quiet period, and Daniel said, 'It'll seem strange here without you, Neri. You've really become a part of the place. Everybody will miss you.'

'Rubbish,' she rejoined, thinking that one person certainly wouldn't. Hallam would be glad when she was gone.

'What will you do?' Daniel was asking, as he had asked before. 'Go back to England, I suppose, for a start?'

She nodded. What else was there to do? 'And you?' she asked. 'How much longer do you think you'll stay in Kolbardi?'

He shrugged. 'I don't know.'

'You must be getting itchy feet by now,' she teased.

He did not meet her eyes, as he said quietly, 'Maybe it's time I thought about settling down.'

Nerys was astonished. 'You? You mean get married?' She eyed him doubtfully. 'I didn't expect to hear you say that for a few years yet, if ever.' She added cautiously, 'Would the change of heart have anything to do with a certain blue-eyed young woman in the mine office?'

He scoffed rather too quickly, 'Don't go jumping to conclusions!'

Nerys laughed. 'I thought so! So you're making progress?'

Daniel shoved his hands deep into his coat pockets and looked gloomy. 'The competition is pretty fierce around here. I think she's more struck on Hallam than me.'

'That'll pass,' Nerys said confidently. 'She won't get any encouragement from him. Not while he's so thick with Barbra.'

Daniel looked grave. 'That's been going on for quite a while, since before you came. She rings him up all the time. I can't help wondering how long it can go on without something blowing up.'

'You mean Klaus finding out?'

'I can't believe he doesn't suspect,' said Daniel. 'But, no, I meant Hallam. He's changed lately. He was never so morose or preoccupied. He was always reserved, even a bit taciturn, but lately . . .' He shook his head worriedly. 'It's tearing him apart.'

There was a sudden tightness around Nerys's heart as there was every time she imagined Hallam and Barbra together at some secret rendezvous in each other's arms. She said, 'There's always a strain involved in that kind of love affair, when people want to be together all the time and can't.'

Daniel looked straight at her. 'I've never been able to fathom what he seems in Barbra Albrecht. She isn't his type at all. And he doesn't normally go for women who run after him.'

'This time it's different, apparently,' Nerys said.

'And it's none of our business,' murmured Daniel, but the worried look was still on his face.

No wonder he's a good doctor, Nerys thought with some pride. He cares about people. She hoped that Gayle Desmond was smart enough to appreciate that.

For a while life was very quiet in Kolbardi. There were no crises, no emergencies, nothing out of the ordinary in the way of medical cases. Half the beds in the hospital became empty and daily routines were unhurried and easily coped with. Everyone was able to take a little more time off to compensate for the days when there was a rush, or long shifts were necessary. Temporary short-staffing could be a real problem in a small hospital, Nerys realised, when you didn't have so many people to share the load.

It was strange, she sometimes felt, that after only a couple of months she felt as though she had lived in Kolbardi for years. Already she knew practically everyone, and everyone seemed to know her. Despite the social problems that she knew existed below the surface, it was a friendly, easy-going sort of place. There was tremendous community spirit amongst the people, even though many of them, like her, would be there only temporarily. The isolation seemed to bind people together in a way that was different to anywhere else.

Nerys went to a few parties and barbecues, swam in the pool and played tennis when she was invited, but she avoided any dates with one person. Daniel or Hallam were usually at the same parties and always, if Hallam was there, Nerys found herself watching him, aching for him, especially when he was with another woman—and especially when that woman was Barbra. Once at somebody's birthday barbecue she glimpsed them strolling away together into the darkness of the garden and her jealousy was a gnawing ache inside her. She would tell herself that she was a fool to love such a man.

At other times she would be reminded why she did. Small, insignificant things would touch her deeply. Like the time she jumped up and shrieked involuntarily as a large, hairy spider ran across the kitchen table. Daniel leapt for the broom, but Hallam said quietly,

'There's no need to kill it. It's quite harmless, but if it's bothering you, I'll put it outside.' He had coaxed the monster onto the end of a rolled up newspaper and transported it at arm's length into the garden. He didn't really like spiders any more than she did, Nerys thought, but the ideal of saving life, not destroying it, had a broader concept in him than in most people.

Equally significant was the way he treated the hospital patients. Despite his air of austerity, his reserved manner, the patients all admired and loved him. He had a knack of making them feel secure and confident. It was his own positive attitude, Nerys knew, that communicated itself to everyone, and his impartiality that made every patient feel as important and well looked after as the next.

Once or twice Nerys helped out during surgery and the mother and baby clinic, and was impressed by the gentle but firm way he dealt with even rather stroppy patients, of whom there were one or two from time to time. He never hurried anyone out and always listened attentively to everything they wanted to say. Once he said to Nerys who had casually remarked on it, 'You never know, what they tell you might be a clue to their condition, or a condition they don't even suspect.'

It didn't help her feelings, being obliged to see him every day, not only in the hospital but at home, too. She could not but help get to know him better in many ways, ways that, in spite of herself, made her love grow. She began to long more and more desperately for the day Janet would return so that she could escape, and yet she dreaded it, too. Hallam was so deeply under her skin it was going to take a long long time to dislodge him.

One morning he took her completely by surprise when she was stacking towels in the steriliser, by coming into the room so quietly she did not hear him enter and making her jump when he said, 'How would you like a trip out to Ambleside?'

Having finished her task, she closed the door and switched the steriliser on. She faced him with slightly anxious eyes. 'Ambleside? The Fortescue's place? There's nothing wrong, is there?'

He was smiling at her, a rare treat for Nerys, so she knew there couldn't be. He shook his head. 'No. Glenys and the baby are fine. They've invited us out to dinner, that's all.' He added diffidently, 'I think they want to say thank you.'

'That's very kind of them,' Nerys said, her heart racing as she thought of driving all that way alone with Hallam. It would be painful, but bliss also. She glanced at his face, wondering if he wanted her to refuse.

'I'd love to see the baby,' she said hesitantly.

His face gave nothing away. 'Good. I'll phone Glenys and tell her. I think we can both be spared this Saturday. It's your day off, anyway.'

Nerys looked forward to the outing with mingled pleasure and apprehension, which turned to real nervousness when the time came to step into the Range Rover on Saturday afternoon. She was wearing a softly clinging turquoise dress which earned her an appreciative look from Hallam, although he did not say anything. However, he seemed less withdrawn than usual.

Nerys, after some indecision, had managed to select a gift for the baby.

'What is it?' Hallam asked as he placed a parcel on the

back seat. 'Mine's a couple of bottles of champagne, of course!'

'I didn't know what to get,' Nerys confessed, 'Babies always seem to have everything! Then I saw a rather attractive mobile of animals in the newsagent's, and I thought it might be amusing. I expect they'll have room to hang it up in the nursey somewhere.'

'I'm sure they'll like it,' Hallam said.

He was at his most affable, Nerys thought, pleased. He was more talkative than usual during the trip out of Ambleside, telling her of several new medical discoveries he had been reading about and, rather to her surprise, asking her opinion.

The homestead came into sight as they debated some of the finer points of modern medical ethics. The sun was already dipping towards the smudge of purple hills on the horizon, and long cool shadows were latticing the red dust. Nerys, stimulated by the lively discussion—it had never, she realised in amazement, degenerated into argument—felt a peculiar kind of elation, a slightly breathless bubbling inside, like champagne that has been shaken up and is ready to froth out of the bottle.

Which was exactly what Hallam's gift bottles would probably do after bumping around in the back, she thought, as she reminded him not to forget them.

Jim and Glenys Fortescue both came out onto the veranda as they approached, evidently having been watching for their arrival. Nerys scarcely recognised Glenys. The last time she had seen her she had been pale and in pain, her fair hair twisted into a bunch, strands of it plastered on her forehead. Today she was a pretty, vivacious girl in her late twenties, her hair swinging on her shoulders, and she was wearing a pale blue cotton dress that flattered her slender figure.

'I'm so glad you could come, Sister,' she said, clasping Nerys's hands. She laughed gaily. 'I only saw you before through a kind of blur, but Jim said later you weren't a bad looker! He was right!'

'And you certainly look a lot prettier and a lot happier than you did that day,' said Nerys, smiling into the welcoming blue eyes. 'How is he?'

'Wonderful! Oh, you can't imagine how grateful Jim and I are to you. We were so afraid.' Her bright face clouded briefly. 'But we were lucky. You came in time.'

'I can't imagine you were exactly thrilled about having a caesarian on the kitchen table,' Nerys said.

Glenys laughed ruefully. 'If only you knew how terrified I was—but not of that, only of losing the baby. I trusted Dr Vale, and frankly, at that point I didn't care what happened so long as something did! But come along in, I expect you're dying for a drink.'

Nerys pressed the small gift into her hands. 'Just something to amuse the baby. What have you called him by the way?'

Glenys was delighted with the gift. 'Oh, you shouldn't have! He's so spoiled already. We called him Hallam James.' She smiled shyly. 'I hope Dr Vale doesn't mind.'

'I'm sure he's delighted.' Nerys guessed that Hallam already knew, since Jim was bound to have told him, but modesty presumably had prevented him from telling her. She added, 'But I think he will mind if you call him Doctor! We're Hallam and Nerys. And I really must thank you both for letting us stay the night and eat your food and use your clean sheets.'

Glenys waved a hand dismissively. 'Good heavens, that was nothing! I'm glad you didn't attempt to drive back in the dark. Anything could have happened and we would have felt responsible. I hope you were comfortable.'

'Yes, very.' Fleetingly Nerys recalled that night and the sudden, overwhelming emotion that had made her so desperate to be in Hallam's arms. She had lost all sense of propriety and had thrown herself at him. She shuddered as she recalled the terrible feeling when he had pushed her away.

'I told Jim to ask you to stay the night tonight,' Glenys was saying, 'but apparently Dr Va . . . Hallam insisted you must go back. At least it won't be so bad driving at night now there are no floods to contend with.'

'We're both on duty tomorrow. But, thanks anyway,' Nerys said.

Glenys nodded understandingly and ushered Nerys into the nursery. Presently they all went out to the front veranda where Jim brought them drinks and some dainty savouries that Glenys had made. Nerys, relaxing in a cane rocker, could not dispel from her mind the picture of Hallam holding his namesake in his arms, almost as though the child were his own. He would make a wonderful family man, she thought wistfully.

Later they went back inside to have dinner, an excellent meal as everyone told a modestly blushing Glenys. Glenys refused to let Nerys help with the washing-up, insisting that she and Jim would do it later, so back to the veranda they all went again to have coffee.

Glenys, without embarrassment, breast-fed the baby, a look of utter contentment on her face as, for a time, she only listened to the conversation swirling around her. Nerys, glancing once at Hallam while Jim was speaking, saw him looking at the two of them, mother and child, then back to Jim, and she could have sworn there was envy in his gaze.

At ten o'clock Hallam apologised and said they must be going.

'I mustn't be responsible for Nerys falling asleep at work tomorrow,' he said. 'Thank you for a delicious meal, Glenys, and a delightful evening.'

'It was our pleasure entirely,' said Glenys. 'I've enjoyed it so much.'

'Try and come into Kolbardi with Jim sometime soon,' suggested Hallam, 'so we can give you and the baby a proper check-up, although I don't think he's going to give you too many problems.'

Jim shook hands with them both, and the goodbyes stretched out into a few more minutes. When they were finally driving away, Nerys sighed happily.

'I did enjoy this evening,' she said sincerely. 'What really great people they are.'

'Two of the best,' agreed Hallam, then chuckled. 'Or perhaps I should say three!'

'Wasn't that nice of them to call the baby after you?' Nerys commented.

'Charming, but embarrassing.'

'There's no need to be so modest,' she replied. 'They have every reason to be grateful to you.'

'And you,' he insisted, with a glance across at her that she could not fully interpret.

Nerys was suddenly filled with a rush of emotion and it made her unable to speak for some time. She stared ahead through the long beam of the headlights piercing the solid darkness and thought she wouldn't mind if they just went on forever like this, getting nowhere, just together in a vacuum.

They did not resume the discussion they had been having on the journey out. Hallam seemed to prefer silence. There was a companionship in the darkness that Nerys was afraid to shatter with mere words. She remembered the time they had come on the mercy dash to save Glenys's baby. It had been like this that day. And that day in Port Hedland when Hallam had rescued the pelican. But in between . . . She sighed. In between there had been nothing. How could there be? There was Barbra.

Just when she fell asleep, Nerys had no idea, but the humming of the engine, the silence between them, the food she had eaten and the wine she had drunk all combined to make her drowsy and eventually she dropped off. She awakened to find that the Range Rover had stopped. Headlights no longer pierced the darkness ahead, and only the dashboard lights glowed. She looked up, startled, into Hallam's face, which was very close to hers.

'What's wrong?' she asked, a little bemused. 'Have we broken down?'

'Nothing's wrong,' he murmured soothingly, smoothing her hair from her face with a tender touch. 'You fell asleep, that's all.' He was smiling at her with a gentleness she had not seen before in those penetrating green eyes.

'But why have we stopped? Not because I fell asleep?'

'No.' His voice was low and husky. 'Because I am unable to drive and kiss you at the same time.'

Before she had time to register the improbability of this astonishing statement, she was gathered into his arms and his lips were slowly melting into hers, at first with a gentle, rousing pressure that gradually hardened and became more demanding and exciting to her senses. Suddenly the fact that it was Hallam making love to her was no longer unbelievable. She was totally lost in his arms, eagerly clinging to him as if her life depended on it, and responding to his ardour with all the pent-up feeling that these past weeks had been denied. The fact that they were in the middle of nowhere, miles from Kolbardi, and she was totally at his mercy, did not even occur to her She didn't want to fight the man she loved.

The touch of his hands on her body as he purposefully pushed the shoulders of her dress aside, then gently freed her breasts for eager contact with his mouth, sent spirals of fire leaping through her and a welling up of such love and desire as she had never known before.

'Nerys . . .' his mouth caressed her neck and shoulders. His fingers raked through her hair, and when his lips met hers again, there was an urgency in their union that made Nerys feel breathless and a little afraid.

And then all at once he pulled back, cupped her face in his hands and looked into it for a long moment. He laid his lips fleetingly on hers, and then roughly tugged her dress back onto her shoulders.

He sat back in his seat and gripped the steering-wheel. 'Sorry, that wasn't intended to be on the programme.' He did not look at her.

Numbly, Nerys stared at him. 'Hallam, it's all right, I . . . I didn't mind.'

He did look at her now, a twisted smile on his lips. 'No, I could tell you didn't.' There was a touch of scorn in his tone. It seared her to the bone. She could not speak. What would be the use of telling him she loved him? The shadows seemed to close around her suffocatingly.

He re-started the engine and they continued on through the night. Nerys did not fall asleep again, but sat hunched in her corner, staring out into the blackness, feeling inside a misery as empty and impenetrable as the black night outside.

It was long after midnight when they reached Kolbardi. They must have stopped out in the desert for quite some time, Nerys realised. She walked into the house alone. Hallam went up to the hospital, saying goodnight as he went. Nerys looked back on the evening miserably. It had been wonderful . . . until she had fallen asleep.

A few days later Janet Wimbourne returned. Her mother had insisted on it. She had been fitted with a pacemaker and was now enjoying better health than she had for years.

Nerys was all prepared to leave, but didn't get a chance, for within a couple of days a sudden 'flu epidemic hit the town. It was a new, very virulent virus brought in, Hallam said, by somebody who had flown in from Europe. Within days every bed in the hospital was occupied with cases of pneumonia, pleurisy and a variety of respiratory complications which seemed to be the hallmark of this particular virus. Nerys felt obliged to stay on to help cope with the situation, and was busier than she had ever been.

Neither she nor Hallam caught the virus, but some of the staff did including, inexplicably, Daniel, who had scarcely ever had a day's illness in his life. For a couple of days he was in bed at the house, but instead of getting better, he grew steadily worse. After seeing him one morning, Hallam decided to move him up to the hospital.

'He's not responding as well as he should to antibiotics,' he told Nerys, his face creased with a concern deeper than he was communicating.

Daniel's illness shocked Nerys. She had always regarded her brother as indestructible, and now suddenly she was faced with his vulnerability. Panic seized her.

'He isn't going to die, is he?' she breathed anxiously. Hallam had never looked so grave.

Hallam looked openly into her face. 'Not if I can help it,' he said grimly, and laid a hand gently and reassuringly on her shoulder, a gesture which caused such a wave of emotion to surge through her that she involuntarily leaned against him, then quickly drew away.

The next few days turned into a nightmare for Nerys. She completely forgot her emotional problems in her anxiety over Daniel. Looking down at his white face she almost could not believe it was happening. Daniel had always been so healthy, so strong, so dependable. It was incredible that he should succumb like this. But he seemed to have developed every possible complication and was by far the worst case in the ward.

And in some curious way, her anxiety for Daniel deepened Nerys's feelings for Hallam. She saw more clearly than before Hallam's strong personal regard for her brother, and knew that his anxiety was almost as desperate as her own. That Hallam was a man who cared deeply about people, she had known before, but seeing it demonstrated where her brother was concerned, served to underline it. They did not talk much about Daniel, but often at home, sitting at the table trying to eat the meals Jean had cooked, both would suddenly look up together, their eyes would meet, and there would be a brief moment of unspoken understanding. But Nerys was under no illusion that it meant more than compassion on his part.

It was during this time, too, that she came to know Gayle Desmond better. From the first day of Daniel's illness, Gayle had come to visit him, heedless of the possibility that she might catch the virus herself. When he became really ill, Gayle was at his side whenever she could manage it. She came in every morning before she went to work and appeared again during the lunch-hour and in the evenings. For someone as ill as Daniel, visiting hours were elastic, and no one ever refused her permission to see him.

One evening, very late, Nerys entered his room quietly, not realising Gayle was still there, and found the girl weeping. She went to her and put a comforting arm around her, even though her own eyes were filled with tears.

'Don't,' she begged in a whisper. 'He wouldn't want you to cry. He liked people to be happy and . . .' Her voice broke with emotion.

Gayle clung to her. 'I know, but I've been so unfair to him! Oh, Nerys, what if he doesn't recover?'

'He will, he's got to,' Nerys said fiercely, with more conviction in her words than deep down she really felt.

'He's a wonderful doctor and a wonderful person,' Gayle said, 'and I don't deserve . . . Oh, Nerys, this has made me realise just how much I love him.' She burst into tears and

Nerys, looking at the comatose form of her brother, wished he could hear her.

Gayle was saying between sobs, 'I knew he was keen on me, right from the first, but I didn't want to get hurt. I've been hurt before. I knew he wasn't the kind to want to settle down—but I'd go with him anywhere now. I was afraid of falling in love with him because he'd soon be gone from Kolbardi, so I strung him along, flirting with other men and enjoying making him jealous. Oh, I was a fool, and now I might never know whether he loved me!'

Nerys gripped her shoulders. 'He loves you, Gayle, I'm certain of it. And if you truly love him, tell him! Tell him every moment you're here. It may get through. It may make all the difference. He'll want to live if he knows there's something important to live for.'

Gayle's desperate brown eyes reached out to her, cloudy with uncertainty. Nerys insisted, 'You must, Gayle, you must tell him. I love him too, and I don't want him to die.'

Gayle nodded and brushed her tears determinedly away. A new composure came over her and her shoulders straightened. 'I'll tell him,' she whispered. Silently Nerys left the room.

Hallam came along the passage and, seeing Nerys leaning wearily against the wall, stopped. 'What's the matter? You look all in.'

'Nothing. Everything . . . I don't know.' Suddenly she felt weak, unable to stand upright without support. Hallam caught her as she swayed and she leaned thankfully against him, his arms holding her securely. It was a momentary bliss she had no right to indulge, but she was too weary to deny it to herself.

'How's Dan?' he asked quietly.

She looked up into his face and placed a hand on his arm. 'Don't go in right now, Hallam. He's just the same and Gayle's in there, telling him she loves him . . .'

'He's conscious?' he exclaimed, startled.

'No, not yet, but you know how it is with delirium, consciousness comes and goes. I thought if she kept telling him, it might penetrate and he might, well, rally.'

He nodded. 'Is it true?'

'I believe so. I think she's realised it during this past few days. She just didn't want to commit herself before. She was hurt once . . .'

His eyes held hers, a searching look in the flecked green irises. 'Strange,' he remarked, 'how a crisis can change the way people feel about each other.'

His nearness was unbearable. Nerys was afraid she would blurt out how much deeper it had made her feelings for him, and she turned out of his arms, saying, 'I'd better go. I've got some reports to write up and the drugs cupboard to check. We're running low on a few things.'

'I'll be along later,' he said, smiling suddenly. 'A cup of coffee wouldn't go amiss.'

And later, as they sat in a quiet, companionable silence drinking coffee, Nerys could not help shutting everything else out for those few precious minutes, pretending that they were two people in a developing relationship that sometime soon would leap from this state of mutual understanding into a declaration of love. For a few precious minutes there was no one but the two of them, no Barbra, no former clashes, no underlying hostility, no barrier between them.

The next day supplies of vaccine arrived and Hallam held up one of the vials with a wry expression. 'A bit too late,' he said. 'Just about everybody's had the virus now. But I suppose we'd better offer inoculation to all those who haven't, just in case. It could flare up again, I suppose.'

'And next year there'll doubtless be another new strain of influenza,' Nerys said, 'that this vaccine will be powerless against.'

'It's a maddening business,' agreed Hallam. 'By the time the laboratories produce the vaccine for a new virus, the epidemic is practically over. I suppose it will be effective for any other outbreak of the same strain elsewhere. It was our bad luck we were a breeding ground. I hope we've contained it here and it's exhausted itself.'

'It's exhausted everyone else in the process!' said Nerys with a weary smile. She added, 'What did you think of Dan today, Hallam?'

His face was inscrutable. He said cautiously, 'You

thought you noticed a slight improvement, too?'

She nodded. 'There's a slight change in his breathing and his pulse was steadier, I thought. I—I was afraid to put too much faith in it. It's time I looked in on him again,' she said and, leaving his office, walked briskly along the corridor to Daniel's room. The urge to check on him constantly was something she often had to curtail. She had other duties, other patients, and there was a nurse with him constantly except when Gayle was there.

The small intensive care ward where Daniel lay was at the far end of the corridor. As she walked towards it, a figure came flying towards her. It was Gayle. A swift panic seized Nerys. Her chest and stomach tightened and she quickened her step.

'Gayle?'

Gayle fell into her arms. 'Nerys, he's awake! He knew me! Oh, Nerys, he smiled!'

For a split second Nerys clung to the girl, a feeling so overwhelming flooding through her she thought she would burst. Then she came to her senses. 'Why didn't you ring?'

Gayle gaped at her. 'I didn't think . . .'

'Go straight back to him,' Nerys said. 'I'll come. I must get Hallam.'

She turned and flew back to Hallam's office, bursting in without knocking. 'Hallam, come quickly, it's Daniel!'

He leapt up, his face grim.

'No!' she cried, realising he thought it was bad news. 'He's regaining consciousness. Gayle just came flying down the passage.'

Already he had hold of her arm and they were dashing through the door and back to the intensive care ward. An ecstatic Gayle, tears streaming down her face, was holding Daniel's hand and he was looking at her, smiling thinly. As Nerys and Hallam entered the room he turned his head slightly, looked at them with a somewhat glassy stare and said in a whisper, 'Hi!'

'Oh, thank God,' Nerys murmured, and took hold of his other hand. She felt him squeeze it weakly.

Never in her life, she thought, had there been such a moment of relief and joy as when she knew Daniel was over the crisis. Only Gayle, she realised afterwards, could have felt it more strongly.

Daniel improved rapidly and by the end of another week it was almost impossible to keep him in bed. Only when he tried, against orders, to get up and discovered just how weak he still was, did he stop insisting that he was well.

Things were now back to normal at the hospital. The worst cases were better and going home, and Nerys caught up on her sleep as did everyone else. The epidemic was over but there was still a trickle of patients with complications coming in. As the virus had hit the nursing staff as well as the rest of the town, Nerys continued to help out. Janet Wimbourne, who had returned to Kolbardi just as the epidemic was starting, was one of the unfortunate ones to get the influenza badly, so Nerys agreed to carry on doing her job until she was completely fit. She had decided to stay on for a few more weeks in any case, to look after Daniel and to be at his wedding. This was to take place in about a month, which time, Hallam insisted, it would take Daniel to recover fully.

'You can't go off on your honeymoon a weak-kneed wreck!' he joked. 'Gayle deserves better than that!'

'And besides, she's got to give them some notice at the office,' Nerys put in. 'Don't be so impatient, Daniel.'

He grinned. 'I suppose I'm a bit afraid of losing her.'

'You'll never do that,' Nerys assured him, and was confident that it was true.

Daniel was moved back to the bungalow, where he spent most of his time either lounging on the veranda or, when it was too hot there, reading indoors. Nerys knew that the stronger he grew the more bored he would become, and she saw signs every day of his increasing restlessness. Gayle visited often and sometimes Nerys would hear the earnest murmur of their voices from the veranda or living-room. They suddenly had so much to talk about.

What some of it was about she discovered one day when Daniel said, 'Gayle and I are going to leave Kolbardi, Neri.'

She was hardly surprised. 'Oh? And where do you plan to go?'

He smiled. 'Back to England. Gayle's never been overseas, and I want to do some more study.' He studied her for a moment. 'You'll be going back too, of course, after the wedding, so we might as well all go together.'

'I'm not playing gooseberry on your honeymoon!' Nerys laughed.

'You bet you're not! But we could fly back together, and,' he paused, then said a little self-consciously, 'I'd like to see you settled—somewhere you'll be happy.' He reached for her hand. 'I haven't thanked you for looking after me, Neri. I know I was lucky to have you and Hallam.' It wasn't like Daniel to be emotional and Nerys was touched. He added seriously, 'Dashing off around the world like I have, I've rather neglected you, haven't I?'

Nerys laughed. 'Rubbish! I don't want to be molly-coddled.'

'No, but you had no one to turn to when things went wrong, so you came out here. And I wasn't the least bit of help, was I?'

'Oh, coming here was a foolish impulse, but I don't regret it,' Nerys said, 'I've had a tremendous experience. I certainly never expected the things that have happened to happen.'

'Well, I still think it would be a good idea if we all went back together,' Daniel insisted. 'Gayle thinks it's a good idea too. You can take her shopping in London.'

'All right, if you insist,' agreed Nerys. The thought of going home with Daniel and his bride was a comfort. She might feel a little less bleak, perhaps, than if she were travelling and trying to pick up the pieces of her life alone. But on the debit side, her brother's new found happiness would be a painful reminder of her own failure to find it.

A day or two later Nerys, on her day off, went to visit Janet. Hallam had said she was well enough to return to work, but he had suggested she take a couple more days off to be sure.

'I feel such a fraud,' Janet moaned, 'leaving you to carry on for all those weeks, then coming back and collapsing with a bug when I was most needed!'

'Hardly your fault,' said Nerys. 'Just about everybody caught it. I don't know why I didn't.'

'It was some bug!' said Janet, with a grimace. 'I've never felt so rotten in my life. I honestly thought I was going to die, and I didn't care much if I did. Poor Daniel, he really got a double dose, didn't he? You must have been frantic.'

'I was,' murmured Nerys, a chill breaking over her as she recalled the long days of Daniel's illness.

'Hallam came to see me yesterday,' Janet said. 'He insisted I have a couple more days off. Apparently a few people have tried to get about too soon and it's knocked them out again with twice the force. Nasty.'

'Yes, don't take chances,' Nerys advised, 'and don't worry about me. I don't mind carrying on. I've enjoyed working here, it's been quite an experience.'

Janet laughed. 'Yes, it must have been. I confess I was a bit envious when I saw that story in the papers about you and Hallam. I've been here five years and not one solitary moment of glory! You're here five minutes and you're news.' She gave Nerys a careful look. 'More than one person around here has even hinted at a romance. You haven't fallen for Hallam, have you?'

Nerys struggled to control her colour, 'No, of course not.'

Janet's smile was not totally convinced. 'I wouldn't blame you. He's a very attractive man. Most of the girls I know have had a crush on him at some time or other. But he's a strange guy, very deep, never says much about himself, and now I think I know why.'

Nerys could not help her curiosity. 'Oh?'

'It's strange what a small world this is,' Janet said slowly. 'While I was in Perth I ran into a nursing sister at the hospital where my mother was, a girl I did my training with. Naturally we chatted about Kolbardi and I happened to mention Hallam. It turned out that she knew him in Sydney, and she told me something very illuminating.'

Nerys was alert. She did not want to show too great an interest but she was desperate to know what Janet had found out. 'Did she?' she murmured.

'Don't tell him I told you,' said Janet, 'and I'm only telling you because you'll be leaving Kolbardi anyway. I shan't mention it to anyone else, it's too gossipy up here, but it really shook me.'

'How do you mean?'

'Well, I know some people come to places like Kolbardi to escape from things, life they can't cope with, crime, all sorts of weird things, but I never thought Hallam was one of those.'

'Is he?' Nerys felt all her muscles tensing.

'In a way. I don't know how much truth there is in what Sally told me, but she said he used to be a red-hot surgeon. In Sydney. But he quit.'

'Why?'

Janet's face was a study of mingled disbelief and horror. 'He operated on his brother—and his brother died.'

'No!' Nerys let out a gasp. 'How awful!'

Janet went on, 'As I said, I don't know how much truth there is in the story, but Sally said there was a rumour that he was in love with his sister-in-law. You can imagine how the gossip ran. Did he let his brother die because he wanted his wife?'

'Oh, no,' said Nerys at once, shaking her head vigorously, 'Hallam isn't that kind of man.' She stopped. Did she really know him well enough to say so?

Janet shrugged. 'Well, I wouldn't have thought so either, but you never know, do you? I mean, who would have thought Rod Troughton was a crook and had a wife and family in Sydney. Did you?'

Someone had already told Janet all about that, apparently. Nerys sadly shook her head. Janet was right of course. You never knew. Could she be right about Hallam? A great wave of revulsion welled up inside her. She would not believe it, it couldn't be true. Hallam wouldn't do a thing like that . . .

And yet he had run away, given up a brilliant career by the sound of it, to bury himself in a mining town, the kind of place men with a past run away to. 'Quite a few of the fellows up here probably have something to hide,' Daniel had said.

'But he doesn't seem to have married her.'

'No,' Janet agreed. 'It looks as though she must have

rejected him after all. Perhaps she couldn't live with it, knowing—or just suspecting—what he'd done.'

'It's horrible,' said Nerys, feeling all churned up inside.

'And may not be true, so keep it to yourself,' Janet said. She added quietly, 'I wouldn't have said anything even to you, because I don't like gossip. But,' she smiled sympathetically, 'I think, in spite of what you say, you have fallen for him.' She shook her head. 'It's just as well you can go soon, Nerys. You'd only get hurt.'

Yes, it was just as well she would soon be far away from here, Nerys thought as she walked into the bungalow after her visit to Janet. Daniel was not there. Gayle had taken him out for the day, for a nice quiet picnic, she had said. And for some real privacy, Nerys had thought with a smile to herself.

It was cool and quiet in the house. Nerys walked through the rooms feeling numbed. There were signs of Hallam everywhere—his medical magazines, bits of photographic equipment, photographs he had taken, the odd item of clothing, his books, records . . . all his personal things. She had never been in his room, but now she dared to push open the door and look in. It was neat and tidy, a very spartan bachelor's room, but it exuded his presence as though he were there in person. In a sudden tumultuous wave of emotion, she flung herself across the room on to his bed, and wept.

Only seconds later the shrill jangling of the telephone made her leap up guiltily, hurriedly smooth the bedspread where her body had crumpled it, and run to answer it.

'Nerys! I hoped you'd be there!' It was Hallam, and her heart leapt and sank at the same time. Whatever would he think of her if he knew what she had just done? Then she registered the urgency in his voice.

'Hallam, what is it?'

'Emergency. There's been an accident—an explosion— at the mine. I'm calling from there. I've already alerted the hospital and the ambulance is on its way.'

Nerys asked quickly, 'How many hurt?'

'Four, one critically.' There was the briefest of pauses before he said, 'It's Klaus.' And then, 'He may need an emergency operation. You'd better contact the Flying Doctor service.'

Nerys did not know whether he had heard her say, 'I'll go straight up to the hospital.' The connection was cut and she crashed the receiver down and paused only long enough to wonder what Hallam was doing out at the mine.

CHAPTER TEN

THERE WAS an atmosphere of intense anxiety at the hospital while they waited for the ambulance to return with the injured men. Time seemed to move very slowly, whereas in reality it was a very short period indeed before the four victims of the explosion were being carried into the casualty room. Nerys was instantly aware of the grave condition of Klaus Albrecht. In a few terse words Hallam explained what had happened.

He did not say why he had gone to the mine, but he had been there, with Klaus, when a detonation had failed to fire. Klaus and the other three had gone to investigate but, despite their precautious, the charge had suddenly blown spontaneously. Fortunately it had gone off before they reached it, or else, as Hallam grimly and succinctly put it, 'We would still be searching for the pieces.'

All four had serious injuries, but only Klaus was critical. A splinter of flying metal had pierced his temple near the right eye. There was a fifty-fifty chance, Hallam told Nerys, that he would die. And even if he did not, he could lose the sight in his eye or suffer irreparable brain damage, or both.

'Has someone told Barbra?' Nerys asked bleakly.

Hallam nodded. 'Someone from the mine will have gone to tell her. The flying doctor was contacted?' he checked.

'Yes. They'll be here as quickly as they can.'

Shortly afterwards, Barbra Albrecht arrived at the hospital. She was distraught and weeping and, looking at her, Nerys suddenly found herself wondering if the emotion was genuine. Did Barbra really care, or was this just reaction to shock, a show that she knew would be expected of her? Nerys caught an unreadable exchange of looks between her and Hallam and she felt a little sick.

When the flying doctor arrived there was an immediate consultation. Nerys expected that Klaus would be transferred immediately to the air ambulance and flown to

Port Hedland, so she was taken aback when one of the two medicos who had come, said, 'I agree, Dr Vale, there is a grave risk in moving him again. Can you operate here?'

The other doctor agreed. Hallam said quietly, 'If his wife consents.'

As he said this, a chill gripped Nerys's heart. Klaus Albrecht's life hung in the balance. Hallam had in no way tried to persuade the other two doctors that he should operate, but he had emphasised the risks involved in moving the man further. Janet's recent disclosures were vividly imprinted on Nerys's mind, large and horrifyingly. Could it possibly be true that Hallam had let his own brother die because he wanted his wife? Could history repeat itself, and could Hallam let Klaus die because he was in love with Barbra?

A wave of nausea washed over her, followed by anguish and a violent desire to put the horrible notion away and forget it. She must be mad even to think it. And yet it was implanted too deeply to be brushed aside.

'I'll talk to her,' Hallam said, and hurried away.

On a sudden impulse Nerys ran after him. 'Hallam!' She called him back sharply as he was rushing along the corridor.

He turned around, agitated. 'What?' he rapped out.

She came up to him and faced him squarely, although she was trembling. 'Hallam, I know about your brother.'

His face became a mask of incredulity and anger. 'What the hell's that got to do with anything? What are you bringing that up for at a moment like this?'

'For a very good reason.' She knew her face was white with strain.

'What reason, for God's sake? What's got into you, Nerys?'

'You know perfectly well,' she answered, amazed at the calm tone she was adopting despite the churning of her stomach.

'I do not. And I haven't time for this sort of thing now!'

He started to walk away from her. Stubbornly, she went after him. 'Hallam, if Klaus dies . . .'

He did not flinch. 'There is every likelihood Klaus *will* die if you don't get out of my way!' he said angrily.

'You want him to die, don't you?'

There was a flash of understanding in his eyes. He grasped her shoulders and shook her violently. 'What the hell are you on about?'

'It would be so easy,' she said, 'so easy to let him die. It would be the same story all over again.' Suddenly bitter, she added harshly, 'You're the kind of man who always wants what someone else has got, aren't you? Someone else's wife!'

He let go of her, visibly shaken. 'You're hysterical,' he said, but there was a flicker of apprehension in his eyes.

'You wanted your sister-in-law,' she accused, 'but she rejected you in the end, didn't she? Are you sure Barbra won't do the same, Hallam? And remember, if Klaus dies, I know.'

'How dare you!' His hand rose threateningly, and the gesture stopped her in mid-sentence.

She averted her face, sure he was going to slap her, but he lowered his hand and said in a quiet, but highly charged voice, 'I am not usually a violent man, but . . .' His control gave way and he shouted, 'Get out! Get out of this hospital at once!'

Terrified of him now, she wheeled round, but he reached out and pulled her back roughly.

'No, get along to the theatre! You're the one with the most experience. And watch every move I make. See whether I deserve your accusations, your . . . unmasking. Go on, hurry up! Unless *you* want to be responsible for his death.'

As he spoke Barbra appeared, very distressed, looking for someone to give her news. She ran towards them, and as Nerys backed away she saw the woman fall into Hallam's arms. He held her close. Nerys retreated quickly, trembling all over but glad she had had the temerity to speak to him. Hallam would do everything in his power to save Klaus now, she was sure of it. He would not dare do otherwise.

There was a moment, as she stood in the small operating, theatre, when she almost panicked and lost her nerve. It was ten thousand times worse than that day at St Margaret's when she had looked at Chris, knowing he could never be hers, and the knowledge had made her tremble so violently she had run from the theatre, her nerve deserting her.

Today there was even more reason for losing her nerve. The conflict inside her was unbearable. She loved this man and yet believed he could—no, not murder, she would never call it that! She felt the trembling begin, but she steeled herself. She must not run away this time. She had to stay. She had to see for herself.

There was complete silence in the small, white-walled room, the tension that always attended a delicate operation and was not quite overridden by the activity. Time seemed to stand still for Nerys and she never knew exactly how long the operation took, only that it had been accomplished in a surprisingly short time. All her concentration was on Hallam's gloved fingers and the instruments he was wielding. There was a faint sound as the fine splinter of metal dropped into the waiting kidney dish, followed by an audible expulsion of breath from everyone present. One slip, one millimetre's error, and Klaus, if he did not die, might have become blind, or a vegetable. Nerys caught Hallam's eyes above his mask once, and they were as cold and hard as the splinter of steel.

It was hours after the operation before she saw him again. Klaus was still unconscious when she had come off duty and Hallam, in a chilly tone, had told her that until he regained consciousness there must remain a question mark over whether he had sustained any lasting brain damage or impairment to his sight.

Nerys was sitting disconsolately in the kitchen of the bungalow, trying not to think, when Hallam came quietly in. It was dark and she was sitting in the gloom, not having bothered to turn on any lights. Daniel had not returned and she assumed he had gone back to Gayle's place, or out with her for a meal. Hallam came in so quietly she was not aware of him until he switched on the light. His eyes were as coldly green as emeralds.

'Has he come round yet?' she whispered quaveringly.

He shook his head. 'Not yet. Barbra's with him still.'

Nerys moistened her lips and pushed the teapot across the table towards him. 'There's some tea left.'

She got up to leave but he stayed her, pushing her back into her chair roughly, and perching on the edge of the table beside her.

'Not yet. There are a few things I need to straighten out. I'd like to know, for a start, who told you about my brother.'

She shrugged. 'People talk.' She didn't want to give Janet away.

His eyes narrowed. 'They gossip. They spread lies.' His tone was bitter.

'If it isn't true, why did you run away?' she demanded.

He considered her for a long moment. 'Because, after Ronald died, I lost my nerve.'

'You what?'

'I lost my nerve! Haven't you ever felt you were losing yours?' His fist came down hard on the table-top. 'My brother died on the operating-table. It was my fault. Imagine how you would feel if Dan had died while you were nursing him. I failed where I should have succeeded. Louise—my sister-in-law—didn't want him to have the operation, but it was a case of taking the risk or dying within a year. Ronald wanted to take the risk. The decision was his; the right to make it his alone. He said he'd rather die taking a chance on living than die soon anyway. And he insisted that I perform the operation, even though it was unethical. He refused to let anyone else operate—he said he had complete faith in me.' Hallam concentrated on his hands as they rested on the table. 'Unfortunately, faith wasn't enough. Louise blamed me for his death and encouraged all the inevitable, ugly rumours that sprang up. I was a fool to have gone through with it—I know that now.'

Nerys listened numbly, unable to believe or disbelieve. She drew a deep breath. 'You were in love with her,' she accused in a quiet, tense voice. 'You wanted to marry her.'

'Louise? I certainly did not. She was neurotic, always imagining that Ronald was having affairs. She plagued me with her troubles.'

'I don't believe you,' Nerys said wearily. 'You'll be

telling me next that Barbra is only crying on your shoulder . . .'

He ran agitated fingers through his hair. 'God help me, she is!' He looked at her. 'You wouldn't believe me if I told you the truth about Barbra, would you?'

I want to believe him, she thought, but I mustn't! I'll never get him out of my system unless I can despise him. I mustn't be tempted into believing.

His eyes narrowed and he moved away from her, skirting the table to stand on the other side of the room. He looked back at her briefly, a strange look, almost of hurt. He did not speak and Nerys got up and left him there. From her room she heard the front door bang and knew he had left the house.

She sat on her bed, her head in her hands, numbed by the emotions that swirled around inside her. It was all too much, and yet there was more to endure. She was going to have to stay for the wedding. She couldn't let Daniel down, even if her instinct was to run. Just as she had kept her nerve in the operating-theatre a brief time ago, she must keep it until the end. Otherwise the humiliation she would feel, the guilt and shame, would remain with her for the rest of her days.

She took a shower, spending longer than usual letting the needle-jets of water bombard her skin, first boiling hot, then cold, like a punishment. She had dressed again in skirt and sleeveless top, as it was too early to go to bed, and was combing her hair when there was a call from the front door.

'Nerys?' the caller was hesitant. 'Are you there?'

To Nerys's astonishment, it was Barbra Albrecht. By the time she had called out, 'Come in!' the woman had pushed open the screen door, which was seldom locked, and was half-way down the passage.

'Barbra?' Nerys looked at her strained, almost haggard face. 'You're the last person I expected.'

'I'm sure I am.' Barbra's unpainted mouth turned down in a rueful smile. 'But I want to talk to you about Klaus.' She paused, then said, 'Do you suppose we could have a cup of tea?'

'Of course. I'll put the kettle on. Come into the kitchen,

we can talk there. But Hallam can give you more explicit information about Klaus's condition than I can. Isn't he up there now?' she added.

'Yes, but it isn't Klaus's condition I want to talk to you about, Nerys,' said Barbra, her voice so soft it was almost inaudible, 'it's about Klaus and me.'

'I don't understand,' Nerys frowned, puzzled.

'I'm hoping you will.' Barbra smiled a wan, weary smile.

As she laid out the two cups and saucers and emptied the teapot ready to make a fresh brew, Nerys was struck by how different the woman was today. The brash, self-consciously sexy Barbra was softer, less brittle, a quite different person. Nerys surveyed her narrowly as she spooned tea into the pot while Barbra stared vacantly at her own clasped hands on the table-top.

Had Barbra, even for a moment, wished her husband would die? Nerys shuddered. How would she have felt in Barbra's place, loving someone desperately? Supposing, for instance, the patient on the table that time at St Margaret's had been Chris's wife and she had known he didn't love her. Wouldn't she have entertained, in spite of herself, a treacherous hope? Nerys shuddered again. There but for the grace of God, she thought with sudden overwhelming compassion, not so much for Barbra as for Hallam.

Barbra did not speak until Nerys had poured out the tea and pushed the biscuit tin and sugar-bowl across to her. She stirred a spoonful of sugar into her tea and nibbled at a ginger-nut. Nerys waited impatiently for her to speak. At last Barbra began, slowly and painfully.

'There's been a misunderstanding,' she said, 'and it's all my fault. If I hadn't been so silly and vain and—well, you can decide for yourself, and whatever you think of me, I deserve it.'

'Barbra, what are you trying to say?' Nerys asked gently, leaning towards her. Barbra evidently needed to confide in someone, but choosing Nerys as her confidante was surely rather odd.

Barbra's tongue moistened her lips nervously. 'Hallam was afraid people would talk. He said even Klaus might get the wrong idea.' She drew a deep breath. 'But I *wanted* Klaus to think, to know, that other men found me attractive. I wanted him to be jealous! I wanted him to think I was having an affair with Hallam.'

Nerys began to understand, although she still could not see why Barbra was confessing to her.

Barbra twisted a strand of her uncombed hair around a finger. 'I'm afraid I used Hallam. I was despicable. I thought only of myself. I flirted with him because my marriage was on the rocks. Klaus was always working. He had no time for me, hardly knew I existed. We rarely made love and when he wanted to, perversely I didn't. But Hallam didn't want me either. He didn't meddle with married women, he said. I was affronted and vowed to change his mind. I used every rotten trick I knew. I even threatened to tell Klaus we were having an affair, when we were not, if he refused to see me. And I,' she bent her head in shame, 'I even threatened to commit suicide if he didn't make love to me.'

She looked up at Nerys. 'Perhaps you can't understand how desperate a person can become when she believes no one loves her. Oh, it's all very well having a casual affair, but it isn't lasting. Men who have affairs with married women only make use of them.'

'But you were in love with Hallam,' Nerys said.

Barbra nodded, then shook her head. 'I don't know. I was crazy! And he was the only person who had ever refused me. Imagine!' she laughed without humour. 'It was almost worse than Klaus's rejection. It was an insult. I wanted him to give in, you see, so that *I* could reject *him*. I was crazy, Nerys, I hardly understand it myself.'

'And now?' Nerys asked.

Barbra looked at her earnestly. 'Can you understand that it was all because I really loved Klaus, not because I didn't? Do you know how hateful it is to love someone you believe doesn't love you?'

'Yes,' replied Nerys with simple honesty.

Barbra's eyes flickered. 'I thought so. You're in love with Hallam, aren't you?' When Nerys did not admit or deny it, she went on. 'Hallam went up to the mine today for a private talk with Klaus. About me. He was afraid I might be heading for a breakdown and he was worried about the threat I'd made. He knew I was probably bluffing, but he couldn't take the risk, so he told Klaus everything. They were still talking about it when the accident happened. Klaus had told Hallam that he loved me, but he was sure I didn't love him. He wasn't as blind as I thought. And he was deeply hurt. He told Hallam he didn't know where we'd gone wrong. He said he lived for his work because there wasn't much else to live for.'

'And Hallam told you all this?' Nerys asked.

'Oh, yes. In fact, it seems Klaus and I have been deceiving each other practically since the day we got married.' She sighed deeply. 'It's all been such a waste.'

Nerys reached out and covered Barbra's shaking hands with a hardly steadier one. 'I'm sure you can start again,' she said reassuringly.

Barbra nodded. 'I hope so. I feel terrible now, but a little while ago, Klaus recovered consciousness. He spoke my name and when he saw me there he smiled.'

There was an emotional pause while Nerys registered the fact that Klaus was almost certainly going to be all right, and Barbra pulled herself together and gulped down her cold tea.

'So you see, Nerys, there was never anything between Hallam and me. I know you think there was, and I thought I ought to put the record straight,' Barbra said.

Nerys said softly, 'Hallam asked you to tell me?'

Barbra blushed slightly. 'Well, yes, he did, and I do hope it helps to straighten things out between you.'

Nerys said quickly, 'There's nothing romantic between us. It was something else. I rather badly misjudged him and he was justifiably angry about it. Thank you, Barbra, for coming. I'm glad, even though it means I owe him an apology. That won't be easy.'

Barbra looked puzzled. 'I must confess I thought there was something going on between you. That first night I saw you at our party, I knew I had a rival. That made me even madder at him. Oh, I've been such a fool! If you want to get it over with, he's probably still in his office.' She smiled.

'I'm going back to sit with Klaus. They don't seem to mind.'

Did she have the nerve, Nerys wondered, when Barbra had gone, to go and apologise to Hallam now? She shuddered as she recalled the way she had berated him before the operation on Klaus, the unforgiveable accusation she had made. And when he had explained later she had bluntly refused to believe him. He had been forced to ask Barbra to tell her one truth, hoping no doubt that she would then believe his story about his brother. She must have hurt him very deeply, she thought, in shame. But why had she been so determined to disbelieve him? Because she wanted a reason to despise him? Was she like Barbra, frustrated because he didn't want her?

She knew she had to go and make peace with him. Her conscience would never let her rest, otherwise.

He answered her knock with a curt, 'Come in!'

She entered the room and slowly closed the door behind her. Her heart was fluttering nervously. He did not get up from his desk but sat impassively looking at her, his eyes steely, his mouth a tight line.

She remained near the door and said in a small, hesitant voice, 'I've come to apologise. I'm sorry. Barbra explained everything. I ought not to have said those dreadful things to you. It was unforgiveable.' Her voice faltered and died away.

'But understandable,' he said quietly. 'Sit down, Nerys.' There was no rancour in his tone.

She shook her head. 'I just came to apologise.'

He stood up now, reaching her before she could open the door and escape. His hands dropped firmly onto her shoulders and turned her away from the door. His eyes bored into hers with a searching gaze. 'Did you really think I was the kind of man who would let someone die in order to gain something for myself?' The deep wound she had caused showed in his face.

'No,' she answered, 'but I couldn't be sure of my own judgment, could I? I hadn't proved myself a very good judge of men.'

'No, that's true. You were very foolish over Rod Troughton. And Sinclair Wilson, too.' There was a curious lift to his mouth. 'What *did* happen with him?'

Nerys decided she might as well be honest with him. 'He asked me to marry him, but I realised he only wanted a nurse for his mother, just as you said.'

'And if it hadn't been like that?' he asked. 'Would you have said yes?'

She shook her head. 'I wasn't in love with him,' she admitted softly, not daring to meet his gaze.

He tilted her chin and made her look at him. 'There was someone else, wasn't there? Before you came here. Someone you were in love with?'

She nodded reluctantly. 'Yes, at least I *thought* I was in love with him. I wasn't, but he was married, anyway.'

His hands moved caressingly across her shoulders and slowly up her neck, his fingers probing into her hair, then sliding forwards to hold her face in his palms, his thumbs lightly stroking her temples.

'Nerys, why did you feel so strongly that you must stop me from doing what you feared I might be tempted to do?'

She looked startled. 'It seemed it could be history repeating itself. I couldn't let you do that to Klaus.'

'Was that the whole of it?'

She lowered her lids so that she would not have to look at him. 'No. I don't know—I only know I didn't want you to be like that! Oh, I don't know, Hallam, I'm all confused! Perhaps I thought if I believed it, then I would be able to despise you, and that would stop me from . . . loving you.' The words were said. She didn't dare open her eyes. She just stood there trembling at his continuing touch.

'Nothing,' he said gently, 'can stop two people who love each other from loving. I've been trying to stop loving you almost since the first time I saw you, and without success. It was only today that I began to think you might feel the same.'

'Hallam!' Her brown eyes were wide with incredulity and sparkling with unshed tears.

He kissed her lips tenderly and the warmth of his flesh on hers made her quiver with a natural response. There was no passion in the kiss at first, only tentative discovery, but their closeness, as his arms gradually gathered her closer and closer, awakened the suppressed desire each had been nurturing. Small tongues of fire leapt through Nerys's veins, sweeping onwards towards an inevitable conflagration.

When he raised his mouth from hers, the fire receded but smouldered, waiting for the next breath of passion to fan the flames.

'You believe what Barbra told you,' he murmured, 'but do you believe what I told you about my brother?'

'Yes, yes, of course I do.' She looked up at him, unafraid of showing her love now. 'But, why, if you fell in love with me, did you treat me as though you disliked me? You were positively hostile at times.'

He chuckled softly. 'My love, can't you see? It wasn't hostility, it was self-defence. I was afraid to fall in love. There was a shadow in my past that I thought could never be erased. If I didn't confess to it, the woman I loved might find out, as you did. And if I told her, I would always wonder if she really believed me and trusted me, or if the shadow would haunt us. I preferred not to take that risk.'

'You still prefer not to?' Nerys asked hesitantly.

He held her close. 'No. When you've been through the fire twice, you learn some things.' He paused and said, 'I had to fall in love to learn some of them.'

'You mean you were never in love before?' she said wonderingly.

He laughed at her dubious tone. 'Believe me, no!'

'You must have met plenty of women,' Nerys said, still doubtful.

'I did. Plenty of women who were beautiful, or wanted to marry a successful surgeon, or wanted to use me. When Louise put out ugly rumours about me I found how very few real friends I had, and how ready people were to believe that where there is smoke there must be fire. So I quit in disgust. I vowed I would never let a woman use me, I would use them. But Barbra managed to use me. Maybe I'm just a sucker after all.' His mouth twisted in a self-deprecating smile.

'You're too compassionate,' Nerys said. She added softly, 'I didn't use you, did I?'

He chuckled. 'No. Far from it. You disdained me, preferred other men, even shallow creatures like Troughton and Wilson. It's no wonder I fell in love with you. You wanted nothing from me. You were arrogant, proud and independent.'

'No—no, I'm not like that,' Nerys said quickly, wanting to dispel this wrong view of her. 'I run away from things.'

'I don't believe that.'

'It's true.' Falteringly, she told him about Chris and the dreadful day she had lost her nerve. It was a relief to do so after so long, to bring out the bitter recriminations against herself, to relive the humiliation that she had relived so many times in her head.

'My poor, dear, girl. But there was no need to feel ashamed. Losing your nerve happens to everyone sometime, and you've proved you have plenty of nerve in spite of it. I know you have. I've seen you in action. Why, if there had been any time your nerve should have been tested, it would have been that time at Ambleside, or when I operated on Klaus,' he soothed her.

'I nearly did,' she confessed. 'Both times. Not because I was frightened of the operations but because of you.'

They looked into each other's eyes and the barriers were all down at last. Nerys did not doubt that he loved her as she loved him, but there were questions she had to ask. She couldn't help herself.

'You know, you were quite hostile towards me right from the moment we met, in that roadside restaurant when I sat at your table.'

He chuckled. 'And hit me right in the solar plexus with your softness, your sensuality and your air of wistfulness. It was a shock to find out later that you could be imperious and arrogant.'

'I'm not usually like that,' Nerys assured him, shamefacedly. 'I was angry with you for being contemptuous of my car—and me!'

'I wasn't. Well, of your car, yes! But with you I was smitten. Even though I knew I probably wouldn't see you again, I was angry with myself for letting a chit of a girl in a road-house pierce my defences. I knew, you see, that it wasn't the usual physical thing. That given the opportunity there could be so much more. I didn't want to acknowledge that I was vulnerable. I consoled myself that there wasn't going to be any opportunity, and then what happens? I find out you're Dan's sister! I was appalled. How was I going to resist you? Dan had been hell-bent on match-making long before you arrived. He said he suspected you'd had a broken love affair and needed to be distracted. He hoped I would distract you! I tried not to let my feelings become involved because I didn't think I could ever escape the past.'

'You weren't hostile towards me that day in Port Hedland when you took me sight-seeing,' she reminded him.

He smiled lovingly at her. 'No, I was weak that day. I almost began to believe—with you beguiling me so innocently—that perhaps the past didn't matter after all. I almost gave in to my true feelings. You were so much the kind of woman I knew I could love.'

They looked at each other for a long moment, unspoken understanding between them. Then Hallam said, 'Barbra guessed right from the start that I was deeply attracted to you. A woman's intuition, I suppose. It was what made her turn nastier than I had ever thought she would. I thought she would just tire of my non-cooperation, but instead she threatened to tell Klaus we were having an affair, and much later she even threatened to commit suicide. That was the last straw.'

Nerys rested her head against his chest and listened to the rhythm of his heartbeat. It was very comforting. 'Hallam, when Rod brought me home that night, were you there by chance or had you been waiting for us?' she asked.

He stroked her cheek lovingly. 'I had a feeling. I was worried about you, and I was right.'

'I was pretty stupid,' Nerys said. 'I kept telling myself I liked him, same as I kept telling myself I liked Sinclair. I thought I was trying to forget Chris, but really I had already forgotten him and I was trying to stop loving you.'

He caressed her hair back from her forehead as he tilted her head up and kissed her lips. 'Are you quite sure now that you have no doubts?'

She said softly, 'You said when you've been through the

fire twice . . . well, I know what you mean. No, Hallam, no doubts.' She paused. 'I would still love you, even if the gossip had been true. I realised that today.'

He looked down into her eyes, long and searchingly, and she knew he couldn't help but see the truth there. Suddenly he smiled and gave her an urgent hug. 'Do you suppose we could persuade Daniel and Gayle to let us make it a double wedding?'

Nerys laid her head thankfully against him again. 'Hallam! Yes, that's a wonderful idea. Oh, yes, let's do that.'

His fingers caressed the nape of her neck, 'And what then, my love? Where shall we start our new life?'

Nerys raised her head. 'You mean you want to go away from here?'

'We both ran away. We have to go back. Perhaps we'll have more strength to face up to things together. I'll go wherever you want to,' he said seriously.

'I'll go wherever you want to,' she said emphatically.

He laughed. 'Impasse! We're not even engaged and we can't agree on a simple thing!'

'It isn't all that simple . . .'

'True,' he agreed.

'And it isn't something we should decide in a hurry,' Nerys said. 'So why don't we stay in Kolbardi for a while longer? We can't go at once, anyway. The hospital would be left without a doctor at all when Daniel goes. We've got all the time in the world to make up our minds.'

'You're right,' Hallam said. 'We'll go when we're good and ready.'

They smiled happily at each other. Then Hallam bent his head and merged his mouth with hers, pressing her body against his with increasing fervour until, breathless, she broke away.

'Hallam, we shouldn't be doing this here!' she gasped.

He grinned impishly. 'You're so right! So let's go somewhere else, shall we? I think the night nurses can manage perfectly well on their own, don't you? Come on, back to the house!'

THE END

# Doctor Nurse Romances

Amongst the intense emotional pressures of modern medical life, doctors and nurses often find romance. Read about their lives and loves in the other three Doctor Nurse titles available this month.

THE PROFESSOR'S DAUGHTER
by Leonie Craig

When surgeon Oliver Steele arrives at St Clement's everyone is captivated by his surgical skill and his thoughtfulness for staff and patients alike. Everyone except Sister Sara West, whose encounters with him in her Men's Surgical ward lead her to believe that he's not only Steele by name, but steel by nature, too…

NURSE HELENA'S ROMANCE
by Rhona Trezise

Haven't you got a young man yet? That's all Nurse Helena Chamberlain hears from her matchmaking Aunt Norah. Helena daren't admit that she is hopelessly in love with inaccessible surgeon Miles Tracy, for just one hint, and Aunt Norah would interfere. And that would be a disaster…Or would it?

A SURGEON'S LIFE
by Elizabeth Harrison

Leo was recognised to be the most outstanding surgeon at the Central London Hospital. But he was hardly a conventional romantic figure. So who would have guessed that his affair with his frail young secretary Judith — who was threatened by a disabling illness — would turn out to be the greatest love story the hospital have ever known?

Mills & Boon
the rose of romance

Mills & Boon

4 Doctor Nurse Romances
FREE

Coping with the daily tragedies and ordeals of a busy hospital, and sharing the satisfaction of a difficult job well done, people find themselves unexpectedly drawn together. Mills & Boon Doctor Nurse Romances capture perfectly the excitement, the intrigue and the emotions of modern medicine, that so often lead to overwhelming and blissful love. By becoming a regular reader of Mills & Boon Doctor Nurse Romances you can enjoy EIGHT superb new titles every two months plus a whole range of special benefits: your very own personal membership card, a free newsletter packed with recipes, competitions, bargain book offers, plus big cash savings.

AND an Introductory FREE GIFT for YOU.
Turn over the page for details.

Fill in and send this coupon back today
and we'll send you

4 Introductory
Doctor Nurse Romances yours to keep
FREE

At the same time we will reserve a
subscription to Mills & Boon
Doctor Nurse Romances for you. Every
two months you will receive the latest
8 new titles, delivered direct to your door.
You don't pay extra for delivery. Postage and
packing is always completely Free.
There is no obligation or commitment –
you receive books only for
as long as you want to.

It's easy! Fill in the coupon below and return it to
**MILLS & BOON READER SERVICE, FREEPOST, P.O. BOX 236,
CROYDON, SURREY CR9 9EL.**

Please note: **READERS IN SOUTH AFRICA write to
Mills & Boon Ltd., Postbag X3010,
Randburg 2125, S. Africa.**

- -

FREE BOOKS CERTIFICATE

**To: Mills & Boon Reader Service, FREEPOST, P.O. Box 236,
Croydon, Surrey CR9 9EL.**

Please send me, free and without obligation, four Dr. Nurse Romances, and reserve a
Reader Service Subscription for me. If I decide to subscribe I shall receive, following my free
parcel of books, eight new Dr. Nurse Romances every two months for £8.00, post and
packing free. If I decide not to subscribe, I shall write to you within 10 days. The free books
are mine to keep in any case. I understand that I may cancel my subscription at any time
simply by writing to you. I am over 18 years of age.

Please write in BLOCK CAPITALS.

Name _____

Address _____

_____

_____ Postcode _____

SEND NO MONEY — TAKE NO RISKS

*Remember, postcodes speed delivery. Offer applies in UK only and is not valid to
present subscribers. Mills & Boon reserve the right to exercise discretion
in granting membership. If price changes are necessary you will be noti-
fied. Offer expires 31st December 1984.*

8DN

EP1

Death understates

Chief Inspector Odhiambo, *en route* back to Kenya, feels somewhat out of place in Washington, DC, where his wife Cari moves easily between international deals and the Georgetown arty crowd. He is thrust back centre stage when his father-in-law is suspected of the murder of an international banker and promptly disappears.

Cari and James Odhiambo probe the secrets of a powerful international bank and the shadowy men who run it, but find themselves reminded of an old unsolved murder in Kenya.

The pace quickens both in Washington, where another body brings the killer closer to Cari, and in Nigeria where sex-bomb economist Romaine Caradonna stumbles on a massive conspiracy and puts herself at risk.

As he doggedly moves around scenic Washington, Odhiambo's every move is watched by diplomats and killers, and more bodies impede his search for the truth until he faces death himself in an untended rain forest within sight of the White House.

As Odhiambo in this third mystery continues his odyssey, with death as his constant companion, Dennis Casley exhibits again his sure touch with exotic locations and fast-moving plots.

Also by Dennis Casley

Death underfoot (1993)
Death undertow (1994)